PROJECT TITAN:
REVOLT

RIAN ADARA

Book Cover by @wegotyoucoveredbookdesign

Developmental Editing by Suzi Lazear

Copyediting by Traci MacKannan

Formatting by Rian Adara

First Edition May, 2026.

ISBN: 978-1-971541-00-6

For anyone feeling angry, use it.

ALSO BY RIAN ADARA_

<u>Dystopian Thriller</u>

Project Titan: Defect

<u>Erotic Horror</u>

A Thing Divine

The Inn of Beautiful Remains

AUTHOR'S NOTE_

Lottie is a complicated character. Hell, all of my characters are complicated. They're not meant to be one thing or another. They are not good or bad. They are human beings trying to course correct. Weakness and complacency got them in the mess they find themselves. Action and sacrifice will get them out.

Maybe.

Redemption is not promised. No one is owed forgiveness. But people must act in spite of that. They must do what is right for them and their neighbors with no promise of accolades or pats on the back. Trust is earned, not handed out like a participation trophy. Sometimes, people do things they can never come back from.

Revolt is about cleaning up the mess people have made. Doing the hard work to fix what inaction and poor decisions have done. It's not pretty. It's not easy. Endings aren't always happy with people embracing former enemies. It's also not a promise for the future, that this is the only hurdle that must be jumped. Hurdles will exist into the end of time, and if we don't keep jumping them, the threat of reversion will more than nip at our heels.

I hope this story entertains above all else. It's full of action and it's a thriller, after all. And don't forget those spicy bits. But I hope it makes you think too, at least a little. I hope it makes you feel complicated feelings. Some may be a tough pill to swallow, but it builds character to choke them down. This story contains child death (not detailed), mass death, war, feelings of isolation and despair, public execution by hanging, public execution by firearms, medical mutilation, and suicide. Read with care.

1

Blood-red rays of sunlight slick the sky as I wait in an alley next to the main University building. I've spent most of my life here. I know all its secret corners and hidden stairwells. I also know it's covered top to bottom in closed-circuit security now monitored by Compound intelligence, of all people. University always had its own on-site security, but since my death, the general has been reaching his tentacles further and further out. More cameras in Harvest in an attempt to catch the rebels. More street patrols, making my little visits even riskier. It's all part of his game. It forces us to adapt and respond in kind.

The nearby metal door squeals open. I flinch, cursing the noise despite there being no one around to hear it. At least I hope there's no one around. There shouldn't be, but that doesn't mean there isn't. The door hangs open for a moment before a blond head with a pixie cut peers around its edge. Bright blue eyes scan skyward before landing in the shadows once again.

The petite person slides all the way through the door before closing it gently behind them, careful not to make a sound. The clothes the University worker wears are as asexual as they come. Loose trousers, a boxy shirt that hides their shape, and an ill-fitting blazer to cover even more. I watch each move they make. Quiet. Calculated. Nervous as fuck. They can't see me yet and won't until I move out of the shadows. If I even do.

This person is supposed to be the sibling of someone in Harvest. One of Evan's closest allies. I've been told repeatedly I can trust them, but they look shaky to me. Anxious. The kind of twitchy that gets a person followed for acting out of the ordinary. That means I'll be staying in the shadows for this drop.

There's a hole in the cement foundation of the building just around the corner from where they stand. That's where they've been told to deposit the drop. Armand said it's too close to the University building. We'd have to go too deep into protected territory to retrieve it. I told Armand to stick to politicking and leave the subterfuge to those who have some idea how to do it.

It's less of a risk for us to get into University than it is for this nervous, anxious individual to make it down to Harvest and be inconspicuous in the process. They would have immediately raised suspicion with The Compound and the Hounds—the security district whose job it is to look out for suspicious behavior and the people ironically behind the coup—and there goes that. Armand bristled when I told him that, but he knew I was right. That doesn't mean he wasn't rankled by being called out. At least there was no one around to witness it, and I didn't have to deal with his yelling as a result.

I have a deep connection to Armand. It's this nostalgic gut reaction that doesn't let me write him off completely. He's my boss. *Was* my boss. I was his right hand, making sure he stayed in power. But I'm in this position because of him. I'm playing dead because of him. Because the image of him remaining on top was more important than doing the right thing. Now, we're waist deep in shit trying to get ourselves out of it when we could have only been ankle deep.

As the mayor, the leader of Seven Hills, he could have taken General Courts out and stopped the coup from happening. I probably would have been the one to do it. Except appearances mean everything to the mayor, and the general is far too high profile of a hit despite Armand being the object of the general's ire. So, Armand chose the game that must be played, which is this bullshit. Which means the rest of us putting our necks on the line while he barely has a hair out of place. Needless to say, there are more than a handful of rebels, myself included, who are less than impressed with this deal.

I appreciate this person's verve. This is no easy task they're doing. If they get caught, they'll end up on one of the general's tables as a Hound pulls information out of them one shallow cut at a time. I just wish they would have worked on their stone face a little more before going through with it. Beggars can't be choosers, I guess. They were willing to do this with little cajoling, or so I'm told.

They turn the corner and crouch behind the wall, out of sight of the door. They pull a black case from within their jacket and make quick work of sliding it into the secret space they were told to place it. It fits nicely, like they were told it would.

Just as they're pulling their hand away and standing as they brush dust from their fingers, the metal door slams open, making both of us jump. I push deeper into the shadows and crouch behind a nearby dumpster. I'm in the dark, but my face is white. It'll only take a little bit of eye adjustment to see me if I were to remain standing. Here, I can't be seen, but I can still see the person who came barreling into the alley.

"What are you doing?" the man asks with a frown.

Dirt and grime splatters his lab coat, and the scrubs underneath are also soiled from who knows what. The general, as Jericho informed us, caught another Defect the other day. Maybe this is someone experimenting on them. Or maybe he's playing around with enhanced dirt to increase our yields. It's hard to tell from here.

I blink on my lie detector and let my internal computer do its work. Doctor Marcus Imentus, head of medical research and development. Various works include refinement of the procreation program, biological resources development, and biological security enhancements. Yeah. Definitely not working with dirt. I do my best to keep innocent folks out of my sites. Judging by this guy's file, and what department he works in, he's far from innocent. Granted, that would also mean this Harvest-adjacent contact isn't as clean-nosed as they appear. Most of us aren't. Some are just more knowledgeable of that fact. I stuff the snap judgements down and hope this guy gets back to work so I can get the fuck out of here.

"Just getting some air," the person says.

Ash Divolo, my brain computer tells me. Research and development student. Doctoral candidate. Biological and anatomical enhancements focus.

Of course. Still, what bill they were sold and the reality they walked into could be two different things. Hence the help they're providing. The thing is, me giving people the benefit of the doubt tends to backfire. I really wish these fools would hurry the fuck up.

"Because the temperature-controlled room was too stuffy for you?" Marcus asks, his hand smacking into the door as if to hammer his point home.

Ash's throat bobs, and their shoulders pull back as they stand straighter. "Because my eyes were crossing, and I needed to step away. I've been at my desk for hours without a break. I had to clear my head."

They bring their hand to the side of their head and tuck non-existent hair behind their ear. An old habit, probably. Which tells me this haircut of theirs is new.

"Well, if it's clear, I have samples for you to review. If it's not too stressful for you." The sneer pulls up his lip as he eyes Ash in the most derogatory way.

Rich coming from the waifish man still clinging to the last shreds of his hair. He disappears through the door, leaving Ash clenching their fists at the empty space the good doctor just occupied. They look at the hole where they left their drop, then over their shoulder. Their eyes glance around the dingy, dirty space, but right now I'm hard to see. Whatever their ultimate reason for helping us, I have a feeling that asshole has something to do with it.

The setting sun slashes bloody gouges across the sky as the darkness stabs its way in. Thick, viscous shadows sit in its wake, covering me as good as can be without it being full night. Their eyes glance right over me, not seeing me or not acknowledging I'm there, it's hard to tell. Likely the former. After a moment, they pull themself together and follow the doctor back into the building. The door squeals as it shuts, and an anxious quiet settles over the alley.

Ten minutes pass before I move. Twilight has set in. The best time for blending if it isn't dark, when everything is a smudged shade of blue-gray. I never made my hits at twilight for this reason. Too damned hard to see my targets.

There is no being inconspicuous as I step out from behind the dumpster and crouch to pull the black case out of the side of a building. It's why the dead drop is in out-of-the-way places like this. The fewer eyes that can see me, the better.

The box shifts as I tuck it into my crossbody bag. Little glass vials of The Compound's truth serum—the serum that got me killed to begin wit—clink together as they settle against my chest. The serum gave me my uncommon side effects that turned my brain into a lie-detecting computer, gave me super strength and increased my healing capabilities by a million. It turned me into even more of a liability with General Courts because it makes me that much more uncontrollable. It's our best bet to stand a fighting chance in a toe-to-toe war with The Compound and the general.

These drops give us enough doses for a hundred people at a time, and we're not short of volunteers. Everyone wants to be a Defect and save the day. Except out of the nearly five hundred Harvest and Service people we've administered the serum to, only twenty have the Defect side effects. It's better than the small handful we had before, but it's still not nearly enough. Not if we're up against the evolution of the serum the general is trying to concoct.

The general has Project Titan locked down tight. Gabriel, my former ex and the general's right hand, is the only one with access to the program files. It's been weeks since we've been in contact. It's too risky for Bennie or Jericho to try and get it from him. There are too many eyes in The Compound for that, and they don't have the relationship or the clearance to do that and not draw unwanted attention. So, we're working blind. All we can do is set up these drops and hope for the best.

I stand, scan my surroundings, and make my way back to the

sewer entrance a block over. No one can spot me. Not even those conspiring with us from the inside. It's too dangerous. The fewer people on the Upper Hills who know I'm alive, the better. Plausible deniability.

There's an innocuous sewer grate waiting for me. I lift it without so much as a squeak. I hang by one hand down the hole as I drag the grating back over me with the other, slotting it into place while hopping from hand to hand. My strength is completely in, and hanging by my fingertips is like a walk down the street.

My feet strike the tunnel's damp ground with an echoing clap. I move out of the way of the grating just to be on the safe side before I turn my pen light on and follow the discrete insignia dotting the walls that will lead me where I need to go.

Both Gabriel and Jericho were adamant I can't do these runs. The risk I'm taking is too high. I, in turn, told them I'd lose my mind if I couldn't stop staring at screens all day. I'm not built to sit as a desk. I'm built to maneuver. To hunt. To fight. That's what I need to be doing. It's how I remain useful to the cause when my primary function—sitting at the top of the heap with access to all of their secret plans—got destroyed. Plus, it also keeps me away from Evan, even if it's just for a little while. I can never seem to prove myself to him, and his treatment of me as a result leaves something to be desired.

I have nothing but time as I navigate my way through the dark tunnels. Time and the drip-dripping of water to keep me company. It's when I'm alone like this that I spiral. The could-haves, should-haves, and would-haves haunting me from just outside the safety of the light.

The worst of it, though, is knowing I helped set this ball in motion. Not being assigned to The Compound to help initiate the general's plan to kill everyone in Harvest. No. That was the last step. The first was Armand bringing me on in the first place all those years ago. Someone to do his dirty work. A pretty face who no one would suspect and everyone would eventually grow to fear through rumors alone. I helped a power-hungry man get more powerful. When someone else saw that power and wanted it for themselves, they decided to take it.

Seeing Armand at the Sisters' safe house was certainly a shock when I was brought to their doorstep weeks ago. His was the last face I would have expected on the downtown side of the arrangement. He'd backed himself into a corner. Flew too close to the sun and burned off his wings. All the hits Armand ordered over the years, many personal friends to powerful people like General Courts, fomented resentment. He was growing too powerful. Too power-hungry. Someone had to put him in his place. Stop the killings.

Stop me.

Put someone in power who gave a shit about the city, not just themselves.

The irony.

I will eat my boot if the general cares about anyone other than himself. He's good at convincing people he does, though. I'll give him that. I snort into the darkness at the thought and shake my head. The damp chill of the sewers slithers under my tactical gear, and I shiver. The gear is old and not nearly as weather-resistant as the most recent tech. Tech that's carefully accounted for and difficult to filch. I take what I can get now. So do the rest of the rebels.

Right now, that's a score of truth serum and another round of potential Defects we can create.

The insignia leads me to a grimy ladder and a manhole cover that I push out of my way with ease as I climb to street level. I quietly seat it in its hole before I walk away and back to the safe house.

My skin doesn't itch for Pixels the way it used to. Jericho suspects that's the side effect healing me of the physical addiction I wasn't supposed to have in the first place, the drug having been touted among its takers as not being addictive like the harsher drugs of the world Before. The ghost of it still lingers in my mind, though. The need for the high. How a touch feels like divinity when I'm on it. How sounds were probing pleasures. I miss it. I don't *need* it. I don't crave it like I used to. But the nostalgia of it makes me long for a hit.

What I wouldn't give for a hit.

Or a visit to The Pit.

That is definitely out of the question.

News of my death ricocheted around Seven Hills like a gunshot. Me popping up in my favorite fuck club would not go unnoticed nor not talked about. People in The Pit are discrete, but not that discrete. My cover would be blown immediately.

My days are filled with dead drops and doldrums. I interact with Miryam—the Sister who welcomed me to the safe house in the first place—the handful of folks operating out of the safe house's war room, Evan, and two of his most trusted associates. My friends, the people I care about most, I see the least. Jericho—my co-worker-turned-lover from intelligence when I was first assigned to The Compound—I see the most often, which is once a week if I'm lucky. Bennie—Jericho's childhood friend and now mine, also a high-level Hound working to destroy everything from within—I see less than that. Gabriel I've only seen once since he helped squirrel me out of The Compound after helping to fake my death. He's in too deep to get away like Jericho can, and the effort needs him right where he is.

Gabriel is as good as having the general himself on our side. Although his messages have been growing erratic and infrequent. Inventory of the current farming equipment should be winding down by now. They'll be moving new equipment into the fields and implementing them ASAP. Hopefully that's all it is. Transition from one major task to another.

I'm not allowed out to help with administration of the truth serum. I'm not allowed to help train those who do develop the side effects. I'm not allowed to interact with anyone other than those on my go-to list for my own safety. More importantly, the safety and security of the rebellion.

I'm not stupid. The people I do see are afraid. Afraid I'm going to act rash. Do something stupid. Make a show. Act on a whim.

The only thing I'm about to do is fuck myself to death because I have nothing better to do with my time most days. My wrist is starting to hurt.

I walk through the front door of the safe house, unafraid of who might see me because this street is unpopulated. Darkness and stale air wrap around me like an uncomfortable blanket as I wind my way through the hallways and the empty rooms to the basement and the secret passage waiting there. I could have come in through the back, through the tunnel that would have taken me right to the war room. I need to breathe fresh air every once in a while, and I have permission from Miryam to use the front door. Hooray. The help has privileges.

The wall beeps and pops open after I press my finger to the lock's secret place. It happens again when I enter the war room. I hand off the package to a Sister. She nods her thanks and rushes out of the room, leaving me standing in the middle of a technological bustle with nothing to do.

The door swings open and a few heads, mine included, turn to see who walks back in. I expect it to be Miryam, but it's Evan, dirt smeared on his face. I pull out my handheld—the network wired into a backdoor server that keeps me off the city's network and off its grid—and check the time. The day is over. He would be done in the fields for now.

Evan breathes hard as he searches the room, eyes scanning each face until his gaze lands on me. He lifts his chin in acknowledgement and quirks his lip.

"I got a job for you."

"You're talking to me like I've blown things up before," I tell Evan. My breath shudders as I follow him out of the war room.

The leader of the rebels, Evan was and still is a worker in the fields. Like everyone else, he has to maintain his cover. When he's not working, he's here making sure all the cogs in the rebel machine run smoothly. Also to make sure I haven't fucked anything up. I'm not sure what he thinks I'm going to do, but he doesn't trust me. He hasn't been shy about that.

He leads me through a warren of underground spaces that I log into my memory. Should I ever need them later, I'll be able to call them up with little more than a thought. That particular Defect skill has done me, and the rebels, well as I've traversed the sewers of Seven Hills. It removes redundancy and bad memories, if nothing else.

"Shooting, blowing things up, what's the difference?" Evan says with a hint of humor in his voice.

"Quite a lot, actually."

He peeks over his shoulder and smiles in my direction before turning back around and leading me onward. His hair has gotten grayer over these last few weeks. The lines around his eyes are more pronounced. The clock is ticking. We only had ten months, a year max when this all started. Now we're creeping toward six months before the general releases the biotoxin that'll kill everyone in Harvest. The amount of work we have left to do feels insurmountable, but the wheels haven't stopped turning. Especially for the Defects. The more we change, the less sleep we need. It comes with the territory of super-healing capabilities. We don't need to shut down for a whole night to restore. Unnerving is what it is.

We reach a door, and as Evan places a hand on the knob, he turns to me. "We're turning things up a notch." He looks toward the ceiling, thinks for a moment, and looks back at me. "A lot of notches, actually."

He opens the door. At first I don't comprehend what I'm seeing. Digital display panels, wires, and circuit boards blend together in a miasma of stuff I know next to nothing about. Then I see the blocks of moldable explosives. The half-open cylinders filled with nails and broken glass. Someone sits in the corner tapping away at a computer, their screen flashing images faster than I can clock them.

"A fuck of a lot of notches," I mutter, as I gaze around the room in awe and a hint of fear.

The air in the workspace is charged. Literally. It feels like one wrong move—a too-powerful sneeze—and this all goes up in a fiery blaze of whatever the opposite of glory is. It would spare the general the effort of putting on a show of a mass contagion.

"Final assembly is done elsewhere when the unit is ready to be delivered. It spares us from having to worry about being vaporized," Evan says with a shrug, seemingly immune to the very real possibility of that happening.

I guess when he's staring down death, a dollop of dark humor is necessary. I certainly can't hold that against him. What I can hold against him is what he wants me to do in relation to these explosive devices.

"We need you to plant them when they're ready. Just one at a time in a location we tell you."

Evan's voice is calm, almost serene. Such an odd tone against what he's asking me to do.

"We haven't mapped the tunnels around The Compound or Olympia yet. Too dangerous for us. But for you . . . "

My gaze flicks to him as I try to reign in my emotions. "I don't know the tunnels under those districts either, you know." I tap the side of my head, trying to keep my annoyance in check. "I have to actually be there for it to log. It doesn't just fly into my head like a dream."

Evan was one of the first rebels we injected with the truth serum. To say he was pissed when the side effects didn't materialize was an understatement. Now, there's an edge to him, a bitterness that he holds against Defects for drawing the short straw in this war. Because that's what it is. We're more durable. Better able to take bullets or explosions. Never mind the limits of our abilities have never been tested. It seems like Evan is more than willing to make me a guinea pig. With a hint of glee at that.

"I'll give you the time, date, and drop site. All you have to do is place it," he says, gliding right past what I just said. "You can start mapping those tunnels while you're at it. Two birds, one stone," he says with a smirk.

I blink slowly, intentionally. Trying to absorb what he's telling me. But my head still doesn't compute. So, I ask, "Where's the first one going?"

I hope it's somewhere near enough to make an impact with minimal, or no, loss of life. We want to draw attention to where we demand it. Not have the Hounds rain down on us as retaliation.

Evan looks at his fingers and picks at a cuticle. "A waste receptacle on the corner of Crystal and Sunset. This Saturday. Early morning for an early evening detonation."

As each letter sinks into my gray matter, Evan makes a concerted effort to not look at me. His gaze drills into his fingers as the din in the explosive room grows to an ear-piercing ring.

"You want me to dead drop an explosive device outside the Colosseum so it'll go off on a Saturday evening? Are you eating the mushrooms you find in the field?" My voice grows in pitch the further into my sentence I get. Each word climbing the staircase higher to indignation. Heads look up, hands paused over their tinkering, to stare at me. I only have rage-filled eyes for Evan.

My lie detector snaps on. Blaring blue. He's not fucking with me. He's as convinced this bomb drop is something as right as our whole fight.

His head slowly rises, simmering eyes glaring at me. "You'll do what's needed of you. You signed on for this." He huffs a laugh. "Fuck, you died for this once already. Are you all in or not?"

I shake my head and put my hand up as if to physically stop him from what he's telling me. "You can't just attack people. You will get zero sympathy for that. In fact, people will applaud that biotoxin getting released if it means it stops a bunch of terrorists from killing people. You'll be doing the general's job for him." My head continues to shake. "No. I didn't sign on for this."

I pull my gaze away from Evan's face just as his expression shifts into something rage-filled. I need to pull my head together. Send a signal to Jericho. Get him to stop this because I hold zero sway with Evan. Before I can get more than a couple feet away, fingers wrap around my arm and squeeze before I'm yanked back and thrown into the wall.

My back bounces against the grimy stone. The wind rushes out of my lungs. Before I can recover, Evan moves his hand to my neck and smashes me into the wall again. Rage pulls his mouth into a snarl. Pain shoots through me, but the feeling is temporary. My Defect ability to recover kicks in immediately, and whatever dregs of pain were triggered are quelled.

It takes everything in me not to throw Evan down the corridor. I know I could. He knows I could. He also knows smashing him to pieces against a wall won't help my case any. Evan holds far more weight with the rebels than I do. Considering I've overstayed my welcome already by getting dropped on their doorstep after we faked my death, they won't hesitate to figure out a way to get rid of me.

"They don't give a shit about us!" he yells, his breath hot and spittle flecking my face. "Not one single shit. As long as they have the tech to replace us, our existence means nothing to them. We're just returning the favor. Fuck you for expecting me to care about them when they'd so readily snuff us out of existence in order to keep eating lavish meals."

I want to lash out, to rage back at him. Tell him how stupid he is. How short-sighted. I don't disagree with anything he says. Olympia, the wealthiest district in the city, along with The Compound and University, are more than willing to throw the people of Harvest on the fire to warm themselves, and they'll do it without a second thought. The general will be applauded for taking the bold, hard step to do what's necessary to ensure survival of the city. Never mind that it'll be at the cost of thousands of lives.

The notion of bringing the fight to them, those people so comfortable high up on their hill, is tempting, I will admit. Make them afraid on their own streets. In their own neighborhoods. In their own homes.

That's it. Maybe I can meet Evan halfway. We can use terror to our favor without turning us into mass murderers.

"I know, Evan. I do." I gently place my hand on his wrist as his fingers wrap tighter around my throat. I swallow hard, but don't try to pull him away. "Can I propose an alternative with a more surgical approach?"

His grip tightens a little more, the light in his eyes manic as he grits his teeth. I let out an involuntary choke before he eases his hold on my throat. He doesn't answer my question. As the silence grows thicker between us, I take that as my cue to proceed.

"We target The Compound and anyone on Armand's shit list." I quickly reevaluate what I just said and shrug. "Which is one and the same, but he has names. The general and his lackeys are the ones doing this. We target them and theirs. By targeting them, we rattle Olympia. If their security force can't keep themselves straight, how are they going to keep the folks they're meant to protect safe? Evan —*please*—we need to be smart about this. Tactical. I am good for something, and it's this. We need to make people uncomfortable. We need to make them *afraid*. If you want people to die, it needs to be the right ones."

I'm desperate to get him to understand what I'm saying. There is a way to do this that will have the desired effect without blowing random people to bits. Evan isn't a stupid man. He's just neck-deep in the middle of a conspiracy to kill him and everyone he loves. I can't blame him for doing everything he can to survive. What I can do is try to guide him down a smarter path.

We don't have the luxury of taking things slowly. Trickling information out there. Trying to subvert the general with non-violent means. Every tick of a clock is a boom of thunder, getting us closer to zero hour. We have to move, but we have to be smart about it.

Evan's grip lessens. A blooming pain roars to the surface only to be snuffed out in seconds by my rapid healing. A little sneer still lingers on his lip as he pushes into my collarbone to stand. He's a full head taller than me and looks down his nose at my face, his dark gaze assessing me. What feels like hours but is only a handful of moments later, his hand slides away from my throat. My shoulders relax a fraction. I don't think Evan would do anything to actively hurt me, or go out of his way to sabotage me. But I am a means to an end for him, and to lose me would not be much consolation for him.

"Let me guess. You need permission from your boss." Evan sneers.

I try not to let his words rankle me. "You know I don't report to him—"

Evan snorts. "Sure you don't. Even dead you're such a good little bitch for him."

I inhale deeply through my nose, trying my damndest to not put my fist through Evan's skull. "He is not the leader of this operation—"

Evan snorts again. "Did you tell him that?"

I scoff and shake my head. Not at Evan, but at the reality of his words. Armand thinks he's on top of this whole operation, that the rebels work on his orders. He is grossly mistaken. No matter how much I've tried to correct that line of thinking, it doesn't seem to stick.

"Every time I meet with him. I will need a list from him, yes. He does need to give me that. But for The Compound," I shake my head, "we have plenty of sources for that."

"What about University folks?"

I shake my head. "Only if it's someone Armand can verify as part of the coup. Otherwise, it's guesswork. We don't have enough people in University like we do in The Compound to accurately suss out that information. Not yet, anyway."

"And you think this'll work?" he asks, an eyebrow raised.

"I think it'll help," I tell him. "A lot more than randomly blowing things up. We need to be smart about it. We take out our adversaries and rattle Olympia. They won't listen to anything we say. They don't even view people in the Lower Hills as human. We don't have time for getting them to see reason."

Evan turns toward the bomb room, the subtle sounds of tinkering filling the space between us while the people inside continue to work. "What if this gets The Compound to come after us faster?"

"Then there will be fewer of them to do it, and we'll be prepared. All balls keep rolling, Evan. Nothing else stops. We only have six months tops anyway. That's not a lot of time, and I don't put it past the general to get bored and drop the biotoxin when it suits him. We need to be ready."

Go-date is fast approaching. We don't have the number of Defects we'd like to have, and what little effort we have in The Compound internally isn't enough to slow the mission down. We've had a couple little hiccups, but nothing substantial. The arms and food that keep trickling in have been just that. We need to turn it up, hard and fast, if we want any hope of keeping the people of Harvest alive.

Evan motions with his head for me to follow him. We walk past the bomb room, down another hall, and to a low-lit office not unlike the fake one I was brought to when I first met him face to uncovered face. Only here, there are no stacks of menus and blank papers made to look like something was going on. Instead, there's a monitor on the desk and on the wall along with a couple of file folders next to the keyboard. He motions to a chair. I take a seat as he walks behind the desk and sits.

"You're thinking what now?" He wakes up his computer and hovers his fingers over the keyboard.

"Teams would work best. Multi-pronged approach to hit as many places as we can. Cover as much ground as we can. The higher up The Compound folks, the harder they'll be to hit." Which means the likes of Jaxon and Kai won't make the list, at least not initially. "Signal Jericho to get you some names. He'll know who works where and when they'll be most vulnerable. I'll get a list from Armand, and we can reconvene after that. I won't have a ton of time to set up reconnaissance, but Jericho can fill in those gaps with as much intel as he can. Then we strike. I can hit, your explosives team can hit." I tap the side of my head. "Think about *how* you want these hits to happen, because the act itself sends a message, not just the body."

Evan smirks as his fingers fly across the keyboard. Taking notes, I assume.

"I can try to reach Gabriel. I'm sure he can give us information—"

"Another note to pass from him. Fucking great," Evan spits.

It takes everything in me not to lash out. Gabriel is our main source of information, more than Armand even. What he has provided has been invaluable, especially with what's going on with Project Titan. But Gabriel's skill is in muscle and maneuvering. He can keep the general's eyes away from the sneaky things Jericho and Bennie are doing. Then my friends go in and do the grunt work to upend things. Gabriel is the white collar worker of the operation, and Evan has a hard time seeing past that. I give him the benefit of the doubt with it. I understand where he's coming from. That doesn't mean I don't hate his words any less.

I swallow what I really want to say and replace it with, "He does what he can, where he can, and paves the way for us to come in behind him and do what we need to do. We all play our parts where we can play them. Wouldn't you agree?"

It's a subtle reminder of what we just talked about. Not everything is about blowing shit up and killing people. It can't be. I understand Evan's frustrations that we're not making as big of a splash as he wants. I do. This is more delicate than he's giving it credit for. If we're not careful, thousands of people are going to end up dead for no fucking reason.

I didn't go and get myself killed for that to happen.

He clears his throat and arches his eyebrow. "I'll put some teams together based on skills. You get that info from your boss. We'll meet up again tomorrow to see what we come up with. See if it's better than what I had in mind."

Evan continues typing, his gaze drilling into his screen, no longer glancing my way between sentences. I take that as my dismissal and see myself out of the small office, anger simmering. My empathy for Evan and his situation is dwindling, especially as he spits in the face of plans that could actually work better than what he came up with. My inability to get through to him, and his constant needling at my situation, wears on me. It's a miracle he listened to me as long as he just did.

My next step is to meet with Armand, update him on where we stand, and get a list of people to target. This is about as useful as I can make myself right now, and I hate it. The fact that I have the mayor's ear, and that he's on our side, or as on someone's side as he can be, is monumental. Evan likes to minimize that as much as possible. As if Armand's contributions have been nothing, when they've been just as valuable as any intel Jericho and Bennie have been able to provide, or what Gabriel has given us.

Somehow, I seem to keep finding myself defending Armand, even if it is only to myself. The more I have to meet with him, and on his terms—never mine—wears on me. I'm the one exposed every time we meet. Sure, it's always good information, but it comes at a far greater cost to me than it ever does to him. I grow weary of him the same way I grow weary of Evan. I feel used on both sides, yet that nagging voice at the back of my head seeking validation and accolades keeps sniffing it out.

I open the door to my room and close it behind me. It's a suite compared to the rest of the safe house. It has its own bathroom and space enough for a bench at the end of the bed and a chair in the corner by the dirty window looking over a crumbling brick building.

I remind myself that at least I'm not actually dead. I still have a purpose, even if that means being used like a puppet by people with seemingly good intentions. We all have our parts to play. It's just that mine is getting a little old. I swallow my feelings and set to work on compiling what Evan and I just talked about so I can present it to Armand. He needs to be convinced that what I want to do—what *we* want to do—will benefit him, not just the rebels. That's the important part. A part that scratches a bigger gouge in my mind after every visit I have with him. Every time I see him, I have to remind him that helping the rebels and the people of Harvest not die at the hands of a psychotic general is good for him too. A reminder that's growing thinner each time I say it.

3

I HATE THIS.

No matter how many times I complain about our setup, Armand talks it down. He can't possibly keep coming down to the Harvest safe house because so much time away will be noticed. The handful of times he did do it were enough. I'm more mobile, he says. More flexible. With my Defect side effects, I can recall schedules he can't in order to move around the city unseen. And my favorite: what else could I possibly be doing?

Fomenting a revolution, Armand. That's what I'm doing. Of course, he sees none of that. He chooses to not recognize it because, according to him, he is the most important piece of this seditious puzzle. Without him, none of this works.

If Evan thought I was a lot to deal with, he better be glad he's not the one managing Armand.

I pull a manual key out of my pocket and slide it into the lock. With an old-fashioned click, the door unlocks, and I slide in using the least amount of space as possible to get my body through.

It's University headquarters during morning rush. Armand might as well set up a parade every time I come up for how exposed this makes me. He doesn't see it that way, of course. He sees more people as more anonymity. I see it as more eyes on me. More eyes that can potentially spot me. At the very least, this door is situated in an alley off of a less-traveled road. Less traveled, not empty. I still have to be careful crawling out of the sewers like a rat and squeaking my way to the entry door.

Like I said. I hate this.

The only thing I have going for me is that no one is looking for me. Dead people don't run. So I'm not expected. What a hell of a shock that would be.

It's a dark, unused hallway off of Armand's near-private elevator bank. In this hallway is a room I'm to enter. Empty and unused, it contains a dusty table I make sure to not touch and a handful of equally dusty chairs that my ass can't sit in if I don't want to leave a mark. The saving grace is that the floors in the whole building, the building people have access to, anyway, are at least vacuumed once a month. So, if I want to sit anywhere, it'll be on my ass on the floor.

I pull out my handheld and connect to Armand's private server—a connection he assured me is outside of Compound access—and send him a message through the secure link that I'm here. Then I wait.

It can be a fuck of a wait.

Another reason I hate this. I just sit here, sometimes for hours, waiting for Armand to get his ass down here. I don't expect him to come when called, but this is a regular meeting at a regular time. The least he can fucking do is make it look like he's going to take his morning shit at the same time. No one will question gastrointestinal regularity.

But no. My message has been sent, and now I wait. Because I am nothing compared to Armand. The rebels are nothing. All of this is nothing without him.

I sigh into the empty room, the noise dampened by the closed door and small space. I don't dare turn on a light because god forbid someone happens down this hallway and sees it on. I'm pretty secure down here, but not completely secure. Which makes me, for all intents and purposes, a sitting duck. A duck sitting and fuming the longer I have to wait for someone who still sees himself as my boss.

A vision we don't see eye to eye on.

When he was in Miryam's safe house, when I arrived after my initial tussle with death, I was shocked. Then ecstatic. He was on our side. He wanted to stop the senseless murder of thousands as much as we did! Except that's merely a bonus side effect of his ultimate goal: save himself. Armand's involvement with the rebels is less about saving *them*, and more about saving *him*. In hindsight, my vision is perfect. In the moment, the realization was the slow pull of a caul from my eyes. Armand's first, and only, goal is to stop the general from overthrowing him. That just so happens to also stop the genocide. If people die along the way, oh well.

Because of this mindset, the decisions he makes, the control he tries to exert, centers on him, not the rebels. It's created a clash between the leaders with me taking it up the ass from both sides. Unfortunately for Armand, my patience with him is wearing thinner faster than it is with Evan. Not to mention I align more with Evan's goals now than I do with Armand's.

I should have seen all of this, of course. Armand's behavior is not revelatory or out of character. It's as in character as it can get. I'm just the one who has changed, the one looking at everything with different eyes. He will see me as the good little bitch who will do his bidding and is unwilling to accept that I no longer act on command.

Evan and I have had tension from the beginning, for valid reasons. My growing tension with Armand hits different. It's sharper. Cuts deeper. I've grown up and realized my parents, or in this case my parental figure, is just human, and he kind of sucks. I was just in his good graces long enough to not see it. Or not be willing to see it. Or not able to see it through the Pixel haze.

Footsteps tap down the hallway. I scuttle into my appropriate corner, out of reach of any light from the hallway. Just in case it's someone other than Armand, when the door opens I'll still be shrouded in darkness and can take action should I need to.

The knob clicks and the door slowly swings open. I hold my breath in the shadows and watch the silhouette enter the room. I know, without a light being turned on, that it's Armand. The ambient light from the hallway brushes across his face, turning his olive skin a sickly gray. He steps into the room and closes the door behind him without a word, shutting out the little light the hallway offered.

I pull my pen light out of my pocket and click it on, blazing light into the small room. I wince against the brightness before the speckles in my eyes settle, and I get a look at the nonplussed face of my former boss.

Armand crosses his arms over his chest, the fabric of his suit rustling. "I don't have the luxury of time today, Lottie. So let's make this quick."

Never mind that he just made me wait an hour. It could have been a lot worse, and has been. But his lack of caring about my time or its value is certainly grating on me.

"We've decided to take a different approach," I start before launching into the high level details of our new plan to target Compound folks and amp up the destruction of property.

The less Armand knows, the better. I refrain from giving him specifics, ignoring the fact that I still have to work a lot of them out. I'm not asking for his buy-in. It's what we're doing. Him knowing what's happening allows him to act appropriately and not be taken by surprise as we move through the city. Unfortunately, he doesn't see it that way.

His head shakes, casting shadows across his face as he moves it. "That's too messy. I can't have the city in shambles. That'll only give General Courts more ammunition to come after me."

I take a steadying breath as I gather my thoughts, making sure to not say the first thing that comes to mind. "The attack is on The Compound. They are the security force. Our goal is to rattle and dismantle them. You are not in charge of how they operate. The general is. So, if it looks like the general can't keep his affairs in order, so much so that the security force of the city is crumbling and it's seeping into Olympia, it's the general who will look incompetent, not you. It'll give you fuel with which to go after the general."

Armand's inability to think beyond the end of his own nose infuriates me. Decades of surrounding himself with yes-men and sycophants has softened his brain to mush.

He sniffs and straightens his back. "Are you sure those rebels can actually pull that off? I can't have them messing this up."

Evan would have put his fist through Armand's face. My muscles itch with the need to do it myself, but I clench my fingers into a fist before stuffing my free hand into my pocket.

"Armand," I clear my throat, "they are as invested in this as you are. The last thing they want to do is mess this up for themselves. It's their lives on the line."

"It's *my* life, Lottie. *Mine* is on the line," he says, jabbing his finger into his chest as if to nail the point home. "Everything crumbles if I'm found out. Everything crumbles if the general gets anymore fuel to throw on my pyre. I can't allow that to happen."

The Pixels were great at helping me snuff out the intrusive thoughts that often tap-danced their way through my head. Sobriety is not good for me in moments like this. Silly me thinking Armand was ever on the side of saving the people of this city. No. He saw an opportunity and he took it. The cost is everyone else's to pay.

I put my hand out, placating. Hoping I can move him in the right direction. "You trust me, right?" I bob my head. "Yes?"

When Armand gives me a worryingly grudging nod, I carry on. "Then trust me to make sure this is done to your standards. I know what you want. I know what needs to be done to have minimal negative impact on you. Trust me to do that."

After a beat too long, he says, "Fine. They can't look like your hits. It'll draw too much attention."

On that I don't disagree. We're getting somewhere. "So, you're okay with destruction of property?"

"Keep it in control. No bystanders. That'll draw the wrong attention." He scrubs his hand across his face and sighs. "How much closer are they to fixing this whole debacle?"

Because it's on the rebels to fix the broken system Armand created. Of course it is. "It would move faster if you could utilize contacts within University to help us. Surely there's people inside you trust as much as me."

He shakes his head, an erratic movement that makes the light reflecting off his face strobe. "No. No one. It's too risky. You're the only one I trust, Lottie. The only one I've ever trusted like this."

Probably because I'm the only one he has this level of blackmail over. I'm a murderer dozens of times over. A drug addict. A sex fiend. He made it so he was the only one who would ever come to my rescue. I was a contagion to everyone else. Untouchable. A disease. He isolated me. Fed my addiction. Kept me in his orbit. It's only now that I'm really seeing it, and the enormity of my predicament makes my head swim.

Except now I'm dead. What the fuck do I care about perceptions or status or repercussions? I'm living in a hovel in Harvest, a ghost with a gun. For how alone Armand is, he still has his finger on the trigger. He may not be able to trust anyone but me, but the strings all end with him.

This moment feels more precarious than it should. Armand has isolated himself, and he's made me his last ditch effort to save *him*. That has been my job for nearly twenty years. I just never realized how alone he made himself, not just me. That also means if Armand thinks for a second that I'm out from under his thumb, he'll do something drastic. He's all about his own survival. Despite me being the only person he can trust, I'm afraid as soon as I stop being useful to him, he'll find someone else to latch onto if it means he gets to keep breathing. I have to play this carefully.

"Okay. Give me a list of names, and we'll get this done." His gaze snaps to me, and I hold up a hand. "As you need it done. Don't worry."

No. I'll worry enough for the both of us as I walk the tight rope strung between Armand and the rebels.

"We all have the same goal," I continue. "Stop the general."

Not save Harvest. That is not Armand's goal.

"Defeat the general. He must be eliminated. I can't have him nor any of his lackeys hanging around when this is all over. It's too many loose ends," he says.

Do I know how Armand hates loose ends.

He spits out a short list of targets. As soon as he says their names, their information pulls up in my internal computer, and I file it all away. It's ironic that I have to keep the people on either side of me from being too trigger happy. Both Evan and Armand are growing far too twitchy, and that's good for no one.

"Get it done, Lottie. I don't want this dragging on longer than it needs to."

Armand runs his hands through his hair, turns, and exits the room, letting the door close quietly behind him. No goodbye. No job well done. I am a servant to him to do as I'm told and nothing else. The door clicks shut. I stand in the empty, dark room, breathing deeply. My hands shake at my sides as I listen to the rattle of my breath.

It's all going to break. I can feel it. The glass is already fractured, the cracks a network of spiderwebs sprawling across it as the tension grows. I just hope we can end all this before it does.

EVAN GETS THE CONDENSED VERSION OF MY conversation with Armand. He doesn't need to know the details of how Armand's brain operates. It'll only piss him off more. Besides, he's not dumb. He knows damn well the likes of Armand only see him as something to be used. He's smarter than I am in that regard. It took me twenty years to figure that out.

We don't waste time. I use my brain files to get cursory information on each of our targets, and Evan sends word through the channels to Jericho to get us the rest. High level schedule information is a good start, but if we want to minimize innocent impact, we need more.

"Vehicles would be the best," Evan says. I send him the information I typed into our database. "Fuck up some property and the person inside it, but we can rig it to dampen the tertiary impact. Easier to target."

I look at him from the desk, my eyebrow arched. "How about that? Are you warming up to my plan?"

Evan snorts, but the corners of his lips curl a fraction. "Don't get ahead of yourself. If this doesn't hit the way we need it to, I'm taking my gloves off."

"It'll hit," I tell him with more conviction than I feel.

I think it will.

I'm pretty sure it will.

The list of people Armand gave me are higher-level individuals in University and The Compound. It'll certainly rattle the richer people, put them more on edge as the dirty fighting gets brought to their doorstep. In terms of disrupting the general's plan, I'm not sure how effective it'll be.

"I'm adding some people to the list," Evan says.

A message pops up on my handheld, telling me he just sent me something. When I open it, the names are mostly unfamiliar to me. The couple that are, are people I met on the mission team. Just as I'm about to open my mouth to ask why them, Evan beats me to it.

"These are people more directly involved with the mission roll-out, although they might not know it."

It would explain why I don't know most of them. That would also mean they're not aware of what they're being made to do.

"Evan," I point at the screen, "I can confirm a couple of these people as being on the team itself, but if they weren't in that room, they have no idea what's happening. I promise." My gaze finds his over the screens. "Most of the team didn't have the full picture, let alone anyone working to remove machinery from the fields, for example. We can't go after them."

His gaze hardens. Whatever moment we just had freezes.

"I have it on good authority that they're more involved than you know. You're going to have to trust me on this. We're moving forward." His tone is as icy as his stare, and I shudder under its chill.

I'm about to remind him we need to stick to the list Armand gave us, remind him of the approved plan, but I stop myself. This isn't Armand's mission. It's ours. We don't work on Armand's approval, no matter what he thinks. As soon as people not on his list start dying, he's going to have something to say about it. I'll deal with him should I even need to cross that bridge. I'm tired of defending him. It's such a knee-jerk reaction at this point, I don't even think of it as I'm doing it. I'm not his good little bitch anymore. The dog barking on command. The leash is off, and there's no way Armand can catch me.

"Can we at least move them to the bottom of the list?" Evan's shoulders stiffen, and I hold up my hand. "I know you hate it, Evan, but we have to play the game here, at least a little. Start with Armand's list. Get him comfortable that we're doing what he wants. While he's distracted with that, do what you need to do."

"We don't answer to him, Lottie. Or did you forget that?" he snipes.

"You're right. We don't. But he's getting shifty, and a shifty Armand is a dangerous Armand. If he thinks for a second that things are going to go sideways *for him*, he will pull the plug. I don't even know what that would look like other than all of our heads on a chopping block."

Evan frowns. "Where is he going to go? To the guy who's trying to overthrow him?" He motions to the door with his hand, his face twisting as his anger rises.

"Never underestimate someone staring death in the face. If he thinks it'll save his ass, he just might. Put nothing past him. So do me this one thing, please? Play the game just a little bit. You still get to blow shit up, take people out, and make the impact you want. Just in a different order. Please?"

Jericho is better at talking sense into Evan. Hell, he's better at talking sense into everyone. But he's not here. He's images on a screen more often than he's flesh and blood. I am a shit replacement for Jericho's calming presence. Not to mention he has the lifelines down here. Evan, and everyone else, trust him and Bennie so much more than they trust me.

He rolls his eyes as he looks away from me and back to his screen. "Fine. You better not be wasting my time or diverting me from anything. Or you're fucking dead."

I hide my own eye roll at his words. Just when I think I'm building trust with him, it shatters like the finest layer of glass. I am getting so incredibly tired of this. Evan is exhausting. His jibes are exhausting. Him keeping me at arm's length but holding me to higher standards than anyone else is exhausting. Maybe this time, as we roll out the kill list, he'll warm to me a little more.

My lips remain tightly closed as I swallow everything I want to say. Just as I remind Evan we have to play the game with Armand, I have to play the game with him. As much as I don't want to, as much as I want to leave the woman I was behind, I have to seek his validation. His approval. I am the child who can never be enough in their parents' eyes. It reminds me far too much of my early years with Armand and how desperate I was for the slivers of good reward he gave me. I fucking hate that feeling, and I hate Evan for making me feel it.

THE BORROWED rifle lays across my lap, filched from the rebel stockpile for this mission alone, ready as a backup should we need it. If everything goes to plan, it'll stay cold. The lowest hanging fruit with the most predictable routine is a Hound flitting on the outskirts of the mission. A sycophant willing to do whatever he needs to do to get on the general's good side. Whatever he's doing, it's not working, because he remains firmly on the outside, close enough to just brush, but never grasp.

Every Thursday night he and a small group of his friends hit up The Gauntlet for after-work libations. My mouth waters for the crisp quench of a white wine, and I swallow the desire. I think if I were to drink now, my body would burn through the alcohol's effects faster than I can consume the drinks. What's the point in drinking if it doesn't get me at least relaxed? I don't like the taste of the stuff *that* much.

I shake the thought away as I wait. According to Jericho, this guy moves like clockwork. Facial recognition picked him up on cameras on the same day, at the same time, day after day. Down to minutes. I guess we have that going for us. The military arm of the city is uber-regimented. Who would have thought? All Jericho had to do was trace the man's image through the appropriate databases.

Time to play.

I have roughly ten more minutes before the target stumbles out of The Gauntlet and makes his way back to his apartment three-quarters of a mile away. The bomb is planted in the shadow of a curb that he'll step off of right when the rebel presses the go button.

There is no joy in taking a life. At least not for me. I can't speak for Evan, who appeared a little too gleeful for my liking as I was leaving. It's easier to revel in the destruction when someone isn't directly involved in it. Which Evan is not. I would say that's why the general is so callous with the mission, but I doubt it. Too few people even qualify as human to General Courts. That's an empty bucket if that's the starting point.

Music thunders from The Gauntlet as the door opens and the target marches out. The music snuffs as the door slowly closes behind him, and he makes his way down the street. I lift my mirror and wiggle it in the direction of the rooftop ahead of his path, letting the next person on the leg know that the target is en route. The rest of them will communicate via their handhelds over encrypted transmissions.

The target only has to get to the halfway point between the club and his home. At the rate he's walking, we have ten minutes tops. I settle into the shadows with a clear line of sight to my signal rooftop and wait. It's an interminably long time before the boom rattles through the night, yet once it sounds, it feels too quick. Like ten minutes couldn't possibly have passed yet. However, within thirty seconds of the bomb going off, I get the signal from the rooftop that we're clear. Target eliminated. Another thirty seconds after that, a smaller boom, farther away, rumbles like thunder under an otherwise cloudless sky. The bomb we planted at a store in Olympia selling artisan something or other has gone off. No casualties at that one. Or at least there shouldn't be. One property, one human.

That's my signal to get gone. I sling the rifle over my shoulder and make my way to the street, and then to the nearest manhole cover. I feel like a rat scuttling through the city's sewers all the time. It would have been nice just to sit under the open sky for a little while longer. But if I'm north of Harvest, I have to be as invisible as possible, and this is how I do that.

Unfortunately.

Sirens pierce the night before I uncover the sewer opening, and I'm underground before they roar any closer. There will be damage to nearby buildings, but it should only be superficial. At least that's what Evan assured me. We'll see in the morning when the news breaks.

I feel like there should be more inside of me. More feeling. More guilt. More anything. All I feel is numb. After so many years of killing on command, one more isn't going to move me. Especially when it's someone so willingly associated with the mission. I can't blame people for brown-nosing their bosses to get ahead. But when people get whiffs of what their superiors are really like, what they're really doing, and they still want to be a part of it, all bets are off.

We have to eliminate the general's support structure. We have to make the people on Olympia nervous. Uncomfortable. A feeling they're certainly not familiar with. We do that with this two-pronged approach. Disrupt life in Olympia while simultaneously removing their security structure. The weaker we can get the both of them, the better.

At least it's what I tell myself as I meander my way south in the dark underground. My nose itches for a Pixel hit, and I try to brush the feeling away.

5

NORMAL PEOPLE WOULD BE ASLEEP THIS TIME OF NIGHT, but the Hounds are on a raid of a Harvest building, still trying to root out rebels after we took out one of their own and a precious shop in Olympia. We did it right. Only the Compound member died. The rest was property. It got their attention. Much to The Compound's chagrin, we keep appearing to be a couple steps ahead of them every time they try to catch us. The general isn't stupid. He knows information is getting out. He just doesn't know how. Hopefully, it stays that way. At least long enough for us to take him out at the knees.

I would have loved to have stayed up on that roof and gazed at the sky after I was done. A few unencumbered minutes to myself, allowing me access to the wider world I once belonged to. But because I pried where I was expressly told not to go, giving myself backdoor access to the general's computer to try and find information on Project Titan, we had to fake my death in order to save my ass. Now, in order to stay dead and off of people's radar, I need to actually stay off people's radar. I always thought I existed in the shadows when I did hits for Armand. For the most part, I worked alone. Researched alone. Reconnoitered alone. Did the job alone. All by Armand's design, I now know. I was at least able to exist when I wasn't doing those things. I could turn the shadows on and off at will. I don't have that luxury now, and I hate it.

I luxuriate in every breath of freedom, even if it smells like urine and the sky is blocked by rundown buildings. I never realized how much I was taking for granted until it was taken away from me. What brings me joy now, instead of fucking and getting high at will, is watching a Hound raid fail. It's a morbid curiosity, but it's easy enough to watch those fuckers down here where overhead surveillance is limited.

Hopefully I'm not too late.

I pop up into yet another alley, this one just around the corner from the safe house. The scattered CCTV layout of Harvest is already tattooed in my computer brain, so it's all too easy for me to get to where I need to go with relative ease.

When I get to the derelict four story structure, Compound MRAPs—bulky vehicles used to transport the Hounds—hum while parked at curbs along the street. A few Hounds pulling patrol hang back around the vehicles while others scout nearby buildings as the breach team moves throughout the structure itself. I don't know what bullshit Bennie fed through the lines, but this failure of a raid is going to land squarely on Jaxon's shoulders yet again. I so wish I was able to see him humbled. I don't miss his presence, but I certainly miss the faces he makes when the general makes him eat shit.

I tuck myself into an alcove of a nearby building just outside of surveillance range of the Hounds. The handful of soldiers loitering outside the building pulse with a low thrum of energy, a build-up of unspent adrenaline and anxiety that they realize with each passing minute they won't get to take out here. Raids don't usually warrant massive amounts of people. A couple dozen at most. Four MRAPs if they're being generous with space. There are five scattered around the perimeter of the building. A little bigger tonight. A show of force against the attack we just committed. Understandable. Useless, but understandable.

The big boom must have already happened because I don't see anyone hanging around the doors. Muffled shouts and some heavier-than-normal stomps echo across the street as they clear the building. Once the breach team went through, the rest would follow, clearing each floor as they went, leaving team members behind as they moved through just in case someone squeaked by. The escapee would get snagged by people stationed on the lower floors. There's no one who needs to escape, though. Nothing to find.

A smile curls my lips as I listen to the shouts grow more frustrated. Minutes tick by. Nothing of note continues to happen. My smirk disappears when the passenger door of a MRAP opens and a form slides out that I haven't seen in weeks.

Clad in heavier cold weather gear, Gabriel's broad shoulders are like a beacon. I'd know them anywhere. At this moment, I want nothing more than to run to him and wrap my arms around his body. Instead, I exercise Herculean effort to keep my feet rooted. He flicks through something on his handheld, and then turns his head. His lips move, but he stares into the distance. There must be a comm in his ear.

I blink my lie detector on. The red pulse is a blinding warmth before it settles into a dull throb of anger. He doesn't agree with the raid. I didn't need the red aura around him to know that. Not now. With how angry it is, I can't help but wonder how intense that disagreement has gotten.

Soon enough, people file out of the building, shoulders slumped and weapons lowered. All this work, in the middle of the night, with nothing to show for it. I knew how this would pan out. I imagine Gabriel did too. He's doing a good job of hiding that knowledge under irritated impatience as his hands wave. His voice echoes across the street, but the words are indecipherable at this distance. I want to settle into the notes of his voice. Have them wrap around me like a security blanket. Instead, I take a step deeper into the shadows, afraid my eagerness will give me away.

A resounding "fuck" bolts around the empty, or seemingly empty, buildings as Jaxon stomps his way through the tide of people, plowing through shoulders and throwing his gun onto the ground. *Bad form, son.* If I were his commander, I would give him a ration of shit for that, then make him clean his own and everyone else's firearms for a week. All Gabriel does is stare at him, hard and long. Even from here, I can tell his gaze is intense and pulsing with all the anger he knows the general will carry. He plays his cards well, I'll give him that.

A clang from behind me rattles my nerves. I audibly gasp before slapping my hand over my mouth. It's not my shock that draws attention. Whatever rat made that noise had the shittiest timing as a half-dozen heads turn in my direction. I take another step deeper into the alley.

Gabriel's eyes blaze as he turns his head back to the team and points. His voice echoes around the street. My heart thunders so loud I can't make out what he says.

When he faces me again, he's expressionless. His gaze finds mine in the dark. I don't know how, but he's looking right at me. My heart thunders for a whole new set of reasons. Boots stomp against the blacktop as he makes his way to me. I press even further into the dark until my back hits a brick wall. It truly is the darkest night where I stand. The buildings looming overhead block out whatever ambient light the sky offers, and the nearest streetlight is too far to reach.

A broad form fills the entryway, black clad and blocking what little light was trying to reach me. I wait a moment for others to join him, but he remains alone. A pen light clicks on. The beam scans nearby trash cans, litter, old clothes, and eventually my boots.

As his light trails up my legs, my torso, and stops at my neck, I can't help but smile as Gabriel's shadowed face smiles back. He motions to a nearby trash can. I kick it over, making sure it clatters loudly. He holds up his finger, then steps back to the street and nods to the Hounds.

"Get back to HQ. I'm going to pursue this," he yells to them, his voice booming over the low rumble of the MRAPs.

I assume someone asks if he wants help or backup, because he responds with a shake of his head and says, "I got it. It's probably nothing. But I want to see if I can bring the general some good news for once."

Ouch. Gabriel is deadly with that dagger. He never had any love for Jaxon, and now it seems he no longer has to pretend. Another failed mission thanks to his subordinate. A man who is supposed to verify all the information that comes in and just fucked up yet again. Jaxon is going to be wading through some shit, and everyone knows it.

As Gabriel turns back to me and walks deeper into the alley, the MRAPs rumble by one after another. If anyone were to look in our direction, they'd see Gabriel's back at most as his pen light points toward a brick wall. When the last vehicle disappears up the street, Gabriel's shoulders sag as if all his tension fizzles away. The smile he gives me is warm and broad, cutting around his chiseled features.

When his eyes sparkle, I know I'm in trouble. I snap on my lie detector out of habit. Bold blue. With a blink the color disappears, and it's just Gabriel and me with all the possibilities between us.

A smirk pulls up the corner of his mouth as he steps out of my way, allowing the entrance to the alley to open up. I don't know what he's planning, but desperation fills me. I want every inch of him. I want to crawl into his bed and stay there, luxuriating in the feel of him. But I'll take what I can get, whatever that ends up being.

"I'll give you a five second head start," he says, his voice gravelly. "Run."

A laugh erupts out of my mouth as Gabriel watches me hungrily. I skip past him, my muscles ready for the jolt. "Catch me if you can," I say with another laugh and run out of the alley, Gabriel's stomping boots on my heels.

6

My Defect capabilities may not have given me super speed, but my muscle endurance is top notch. Imagine my surprise when I look over my shoulder to find Gabriel keeping pace with me. To anyone else, it'd look like a Hound chasing a suspect. No one would be able to get a read on my face as I run, assuming there would even be anyone around who could identify me to begin with. To undiscerning eyes, it's just predator and prey.

I know better. A laugh clogs my throat as I guide Gabriel through dark roads, knowing where not to go to keep us out of CCTV eyes. I'm not sure if Gabriel could have beaten me in a race when I was human Lottie. I know he can't beat me now. Still, something worrisome settles in my gut as I peek over my shoulder again and find him keeping the same pace. Not slowing down. Not catching up. As if he's purposely holding the same distance. The illusion of the chase.

The smirk sitting on his face tells me he's enjoying this. It's not like I'm not. But the side effects allow near-instant recovery. Despite how hard I'm running, I'm not breathing hard. Not even close to being out of breath.

Neither is Gabriel.

No flush to his cheeks. No open-mouthed panting. It's like he's not even running at all.

That can't be good.

A stone drops into my stomach, the worry growing. I don't have time to dwell on it as I guide him to a safe area in Service, the same run-down warehouse Jericho and Bennie took me when I was first developing my strength. It's out of the way and off any surveillance. We'll both be safe here.

Loose hair sticks to my face as I slow and tromp down the alley leading toward the broken door of the derelict space. The squeal of metal slices through the quiet night, but I don't afford it a flinch. Not out here. This is considered a dead section of Seven Hills, within city limits by definition only. Even if there was anyone around to hear it, they wouldn't say anything.

Moonlight slices through the ripped-open ceiling as I enter the vast space, nothing but my footsteps and Gabriel coming up behind me to greet us. Bird wings fluttering in the shadows make my heart jump, but it settles immediately. The last time I was afraid, Gabriel's gun was pressed to my forehead. No. It's not me I'm afraid for. It's everyone else. It's the rebels and this mission. If the wrong people find out I'm still alive, the general will raze Harvest to the ground and not think twice about it. Game over.

I turn, my worry kept in check as I take in Gabriel's shadowed visage. His face is soft yet hungry, eyes gleaming and gleeful as he approaches. I want to ask him why he's not out of breath. Why it looks like he didn't just run dozens of blocks with me to get here, but one arm slides around my waist and the other cradles my head as he gently lowers his lips to mine.

All thought, all worry, dissolves under Gabriel's kiss, and it's all I can do to stay standing.

The sweetness of it lasts for a mere second before Gabriel's hands wander and tug at my pants. My bare hands slide under his shirt, the heat of him pressing into me as I melt into him. His lips leave mine as he trails fiery kisses down my chin, my neck, nipping at the flesh as he goes along. The sharp sting of teeth pulses pleasure to my pussy, and a moan escapes my throat.

"It's been too long," he mutters into my neck, as his hand slides into my pants.

He palms my cunt before plunging one finger, then two, deep into my core.

"Don't be such a stranger," I mutter back and gasp with each wave of his fingers inside me.

I make short work of his pants, freeing him of their confines as I take his solid cock in my hand.

"I'm a stranger even to myself nowadays," he whispers as he tugs my pants to my ankles and spins me to face the wall. "You're the only familiar thing I've seen since you left."

My head spins as he talks, his words nonsensical. But the pleasure mounting inside me warbles my thoughts. Gabriel's panting, his touch, his heat spins everything together in a smudge that I can't comprehend.

Before I can get another word out, he rams into me, knocking a shocked cry from my lips. The thickness of him is a welcome distraction, a comfort I've been missing for far too long. His hands wander up my stomach and cup my breasts as he thrusts into me, my hands splayed on the wall for leverage.

Through the building orgasm—the press of his thighs against my bare ass sending images running through my head—Gabriel's words haunt me. The slide of him in and out of my body provides the distraction I need to help the building pleasure along. It mounts, then releases. Seconds later Gabriel finishes, then rests his head on the back of mine, leaning into me as I feel him empty into my body.

The cold he leaves behind when he steps away sends his words rushing back in unimpeded by cock and touch. I hide my wince as I pull my pants back up, mess and all, unable to do much about that at the moment. There's enough light in this frigid warehouse for me to see the hunch of his shoulders and the clench of his jaw as he pulls himself together. His hands shake as he zips himself up. Fear claws its way out from the pit of my stomach.

"What is it?" I ask without preamble.

Time is not a luxury for us. There isn't enough of it to play games. He only has so much time he can spend "chasing after someone" before he has to get creative with his excuses.

A chuckle erupts from his mouth, curling the corners of his lips, but his eyes remain cold and hard when he turns his gaze on me. His mouth twitches a couple times, itching to form words, but he just shakes his head, steps up to me, and wraps his arms around my body.

"Please. Just let me enjoy this for a few more minutes before I have to go back," he whispers into the side of my head.

A chill, bone-deep and ice cold, slices through my body. My fear crawls even higher.

The heat of him presses into me, cuts out the marrow-cold chill of winter. Yet ice still slithers its way in. Through the cuffs of my sleeves. Down the collar of my shirt. Straight into my heart.

"You're scaring me," I mutter into his chest. His arms flex, pushing me deeper into him.

"I know." The rumbling of his voice vibrates through my body. "But what's going on with me doesn't matter. Not right now. Just let me feel you. That's all I want to do. Feel you."

I'll be the first to admit I don't know a whole lot about Gabriel. Not the man I reacquainted with as a fully formed adult. I was convinced I had to keep him at arm's length until the day I woke up dead, and I haven't seen him since. Sure, we talked like any other couple. We got to know each other in ways different to what we did when we were kids. It was only a few months before everything went tits up. Not nearly enough time. What I do know about him—how much he holds back, how much he buries, how much burden he takes on himself—there is something buried deep in him right now. Of all times, now is not the time to keep anything from each other.

"It does matter," I tell him, as I push myself away. His arms remain resting on my sides. For the moment, I'm grateful for the contact. "You're not hiding it very well. Not from me."

I blink, and my lie detector pops up. Sure enough, he's red ringed with purple closest to his body. I don't need that internal mechanism to tell me that. It just verifies what I already know. I blink again, and it disappears, leaving Gabriel in the darkness of the warehouse.

He smirks and stuffs his hands in his jacket pockets, leaving cold emptiness on my body where he just was.

"You're too perceptive for your own fucking good," he mutters, a laugh in his voice.

"You already got the truth serum, Gabriel. It can't be that. Please tell me it's not Project Titan. That that sick fuck isn't forcing experimental tech on the Hounds." My teeth clench with every word as the idea forms into a knot in my throat.

Project Titan is an experimental shit show that even Armand didn't know about. The general had been hunting Defects almost as soon as they started popping up. The Hounds knew that. What only Gabriel and the general knew, and soon enough me, was that General Courts was taking the Defects they captured and tortured and handing them over to his own private payroll in University to experiment on. His goal was to harness the side effects of the truth serum that spawned all this—the side effects he knew about, anyway—and create his own super soldiers with it.

Not terrifying at all.

Just a few short weeks ago the latest tests were duds. That batch was still eating its way through test subjects, giving them some abilities before it dissolved them from the veins out. He couldn't possibly have advanced much beyond that in the time I've been gone. Yet, I'm not stupid. It doesn't take much to read between the lines.

Gabriel has gotten something, and I don't think it's doing good things to him.

"That sick fuck has more backers than you know. People who are fed up being Armand's targets. Money means everything, Lottie. You've got to know that," Gabriel says, his voice edged in sadness. "He's bankrolling more people in University to work on Project Titan. And they're willing. They don't like Armand either."

I huff out a "fuck" and roll my eyes at the impossibility of Armand. Guilt crawls its way under my skin. I try to shake it off as much as I can. I helped put him in this position. He wouldn't have ended up with the wolves at his door if it wasn't for me. Well, maybe not me personally. If not me, then someone else. I just happened to be the dumbass kid who didn't know any better. Resentment swirls under that guilt. I am where I am because of Armand's greed. My life has been cleaning up his messes. Even now. He wasn't wrong, though. There really wasn't anyone he could trust in University. Gabriel just confirmed that.

One problem at a time.

"Did you have a choice?" I whisper, yet my voice carries in the empty warehouse.

I desperately want to fall back into his arms and never leave. There's a comfort there that I can't get anywhere else. Jericho and Bennie know me even better than Gabriel does. They held my secrets for so much longer. But there's a familiarity with Gabriel I can't escape. A nostalgic comfort that I find myself seeking more often than not.

"Not if we want to see this through to the end," Gabriel responds just before he audibly swallows.

"What does that mean?" I spit back, as I knot my arms over my chest. An attempt to stifle my fear of his answer. "Is it being administered to everyone?"

Gabriel shakes his head and steps forward, but doesn't put his arms out, doesn't take me in them. "It means he trusts me absolutely. I know everything, Lottie. There isn't a single fucking thing Courts keeps from me now."

Tears well in my eyes, and I snort. "Yeah. Because he gave you an expiration date, didn't he?"

"It's next generation. It might not have," he says so earnestly I almost believe him.

Almost.

I huff an indignant grunt and run my fingers through my hair, ready to rip the strands from my scalp. When I spin back around, he's looking at me with a sad smile, his eyes watery but no tears to shed.

"I was never getting out of this alive, Lots." Gabriel snorts and shakes his head.

His childhood nickname for me nearly buckles my knees. Not

long ago it sent a shudder through me, an unwanted reminder of what we once had and what we'll never have again. Something impossible to have again. Now, though, it's a term of endearment. A resignation.

"Ever since that day in Armand's office, I knew Courts would be the death of me one way or another. Thing is, I'm going to drag him down too," he says with a smirk.

Fractures and fissures open up inside me. I'm falling apart upright. It takes everything in me to keep it together.

Gabriel's shoulders relax more, and I take a step closer to him as he speaks. "I'm tired of being his fucking lapdog. It's what I thought I wanted." He laughs, this sardonic thing, and motions to me. "Threw you out to get it. In the end, it wasn't worth it. So, I'm going to burn it all to the fucking ground."

I scoff. "And you do that by lighting yourself on fire, do you? Tell me. What the fuck have you really done?"

He closes the gap between us and takes my face in his hands. He tilts my chin so I can meet his gaze and runs his thumb along my jaw.

"I have to get back. They'll get suspicious if I'm away too long. Everyone is more suspicious lately. It's hard not to be when the mayor's right hand turned out to be a Defect. No one's safe. Just the way I like it."

The last words are a whisper as he leans down and plants a tender kiss on my forehead. I close my eyes against the feeling, revel in the intimate touch free of sexual tension and need. Just him and me and the world that exists within us. For just a moment, all my strength, all my will to push forward, shrivels with his touch. I want nothing more than to be protected by him. Kept safe by him. To not have to be so fucking strong all the fucking time. I'm so incredibly tired, and I want to sleep.

As the cold air slithers between his mouth and my forehead, I know rest is far off. Unreachable. I don't have a choice. Gabriel doesn't have a choice. None of us do.

"This isn't the last time I'm seeing you," I demand. I will brook no argument on that if I have to break into his flat myself.

Gabriel shakes his head, a smile on his face. "Of course not."

A blankness settles behind his eyes as he smiles. Gabriel's mask. I'd know it anywhere. There's a subtleness to it. To those who don't know him, or are afraid to look, they wouldn't see the details. I do. I don't need to flick on my lie detector to know the truth, but I do it anyway. The blaring red aura pulsing around him is all the confirmation I need.

He doesn't push it. He wouldn't have a leg to stand on anyway. Not at this point.

"I'll see you soon then," I say to the vacant space between us, adding to Gabriel's charade.

When he smiles, it reaches his eyes for once, as he shakes his head. "You will."

Without another touch, another kiss, or fake, placating words, Gabriel turns and quietly walks out of the warehouse. I stand stock still for a minute, or an eternity. It's hard to tell. The city appears frozen, the moon stuck in the sky as the cold settles heavy on my shoulders. Or perhaps that's just the weight of the world.

I don't have supersonic hearing, but the night is too quiet for anyone to be nearby. When I know it's been long enough, that Gabriel is far from here by now, I let the suffocating wave of emotions roar up from within. A gasping, choking sob erupts out of my mouth as my eyes blur with tears and my knees buckle. It's a conflagration of feelings ripping through me, burning everything in their path.

Everything I've stifled for the last twenty years. Everything that's been bubbling to the surface within the last year. Everything from these very moments, rushes out of me in stomach-twisting sobs. I cry and heave until my throat is raw and my face is swollen. Until my shirt is soaked in a waterfall of tears. I cry until my stomach aches, the pain of it twisting out even more tears.

If I let it go on any longer, I'll be crushed by it. By the thought of what's happening to Gabriel. Of what may happen to innocent people if I don't pick myself the fuck up right now. Of everything I've lost.

By the time the tears stop, I'm curled in the fetal position on top of cold, dark cement, wallowing in a crumbling warehouse that more than perfectly reflects my crumbling life. When I catch my breath, hiccup for the final time, and wipe the last dregs of tears from my cheeks, I sit up. My muscles ache for the briefest moment before my Defect capabilities take over. The swelling in my eyes reduces. The soreness in my throat disappears. The ache in my stomach unfurls. All that's left is a running nose and an exhausted headache that begs for sleep so it can rest too.

This will not be the last time I see Gabriel. I don't care what he believes. I won't believe it. I can't believe it. He hasn't gotten this far just to lie down in the middle of the street and let the end happen.

Shaky legs pull me to standing and I take a full, deep breath. Cold slices into my lungs. It's the sharpness I need to push the funk away. That's enough for now. I've had my moment. Now it's time to get it the fuck together.

I have a job to do.

Only Gabriel's lingering demise will be hanging at the back of my head while I do it.

7

EVAN'S EXPLOSIVES TECHNICIANS ARE WAY TOO TWITCHY. He wouldn't listen to me about it, though. I asked Jericho to talk to him. Maybe the same words coming out of a different mouth would hold more weight. Not so much.

What I know is he placed the explosives he was supposed to place in the right spot. I know that because I'm looking at it through a scope I removed from a rifle. Images flicker across my eye unbidden. Flashes of faces in my crosshairs, blood spray and brain matter arcing through my viewfinder. For once, it's not occupied by anything living. What I'm seeing is only in my head.

Instead, I'm staring at the dock space near Exodus, the club Bennie took me to when I first got to The Compound. It's the middle of the day. No one is around. The point is there's enough structure to make an impact. It's what I convinced Evan our next move should be. He had his taste of blood with the Compound man. Those need to be spread out. We want people on edge, not scared out of their wits and willing to do something stupid.

Exodus is a bane of Olympia's existence, but one the younger crowd, and The Compound, loves to frequent. This hit is meant to divide Olympia. Blowing it up, the older folks of Olympia will thank us. Everyone else will get riled up. When The Compound brass don't make a more immediate move with this hit, feathers will be ruffled.

In theory.

It wasn't the easiest sell to Evan, but he's humoring me, as he reminded me multiple times before I left. We're starting small, hitting Olympia's conveniences, its niceties. Taking away their luxuries one by one until there's nothing left but to look reality in the face.

I wanted to be on a rooftop, but on the down slope of the hill, it's too exposed. The last thing I want is someone to spot me who shouldn't. Instead, I'm yet again stuffed in a nearby alley, watching from around a corner. I'm growing incredibly tired of alleys.

The time on my handheld tells me I have three minutes left before the boom. Seconds tick by interminably slowly, the moment dragging as if in a dream. It's in lulls like this that the intrusive thoughts move in. How something is happening to Gabriel. How Armand keeps trying to make all of this about himself. How desperately alone and disconnected I feel.

Thirty seconds.

I glance around my alley one more time. Check nearby windows. This is more of a weekend or weeknight area of The Compound. Deserted.

Until a woman and her small child come tottering hand in hand into the picture. She points at the water and the remnants of the bridge in the bay as my mind stutters.

Ten seconds.

There is no rational thought. No second guessing. I run out from my hiding place and scream, "Hey!"

I yell it again and wave my hands, but the woman only looks up. Her toddler bends over to pick at something on the ground as the structure gets wrapped in a fireball and the sound waves of the blast blow me back. My flinch is automatic and the explosion is stunning. I'm lifted off my feet and flown backward. I crash into the sidewalk, the curb smashing into my ribs, yanking the air from my lungs.

The heat of it is like walking in front of a roaring furnace. Fire, crackling and pulsing as if it were alive, plumes from the wreck. My ears ring, a high-pitched screech that makes my head swim. When I set myself on my elbows, my whole body throbbing, the woman and her child are gone. The dock, the club, and some nearby unused pillars are engulfed in flames. Wood splinters coat the street, mixed with chunks of dock and stone flooring from the club.

Smoke clogs the air, blotting out the sky as it pours over the wreckage. The smell of scorched debris fills my nose, reminding me of a dream I had months ago, at the first onset of the truth serum mutations.

A dream of a burning club.

Except in my dream it was filled with people and it was night. Not broad daylight. We purposely didn't attack when the club was full. That wasn't the message we wanted to send. Yet. No one was supposed to get hurt this time.

No one was supposed to die.

Especially not a child.

Pain pierces my side. I gasp as I try to sit, then stand on wobbly legs. A fierce bolt of pain tears through my nerves. I gasp again as my side throbs. Likely broken ribs that are already healing. I doubt my Defect side effects would be able to heal an explosion. A scattering of body parts. A complete snuff of life like I just witnessed.

It's not until movement in the corner of my eye brings my spiraling brain back to earth that I realize I'm exposed. I've wobbled back to the middle of the street—in the open—and people have started making their way to the scene. A scream echoes around the buildings, and thudding footfalls stomp down the street as more people swarm the wreckage.

I should dash to the edge of the docks. I don't know if anyone saw the mother and child other than me. They could be down there. Perhaps they're only hurt, waiting for rescue. Or perhaps I'm being delusional. Sirens increase the tension to bursting. I flinch at the noise, the sound grounding me even further, snapping sense back into my head.

Panic and fear rise inside of me. Feelings I'm not used to. The thicker the crowd grows, the more my anxiety spikes. I've been sequestered from the greater world for weeks out of an abundance of caution. Now, I've just thrown that into the wind. In reality, no one is going to know who I am just by looking at me. Not here. What I don't need is getting picked up by medical. I need to get gone before I draw the eyes of any good samaritans.

With a step backward, then another, I swallow my guilt. The woman and her child are dead, and it's only a matter of time before their bodies are found. Evan won't mourn the accidental loss of life the explosion caused. More power to the movement if anything, he'll say. This is what he wanted all along. Except this is going to ruffle all the wrong feathers. What will fuck things up even more is me being discovered. I have to go.

When I turn back to my alley and the sewer entrance therein, my gaze scans the growing crowd. A mass of hair and bodies and faces all looking away from me. Except one.

As my boots glue themselves to the street, I stand stock still and stare at the face staring at me. The black-rimmed eyes. The snarl on her lips. The pink hair.

Kai.

Oh shit.

Of all the people to catch sight of me, of fucking course it has to be *her*.

My first instinct is to dash into the alley and disappear down the sewer, but I don't want Kai to follow me down there. It's too risky. Within a nanosecond, my brain course-corrects. I dash down the street, away from the chaos of the explosion and the death it caused, and up the hill toward Olympia.

I put all my effort into being as light as I possibly can. Running on my toes. Pumping my arms to move me faster. All I have to do is keep moving, and I'll outpace Kai sooner rather than later.

I'm nearly to the top of a hill before I look over my shoulder, expecting to see her lagging up the steep incline. Instead, she keeps pace. The determined look on her face is all I need to keep moving. Turn after turn I weave my way through the wealthy streets of the richest district of Seven Hills. Mansions behind tall gates, pristine lawns, shiny cars, all the ornamentation of the wealthy, including ample CCTV, which I dodge as best I can. A stark difference to Harvest and Service.

It's only when I take yet another turn, pounding footsteps matching mine, that I remember Olympia isn't mapped. Not underground, anyway. Even if I were to drop into a sewer, I'd lose Kai and myself. I'd eventually have to pop back up onto the street to get my bearings. Or, if I'm bored, try and map wherever the hell I end up. It's too much right now.

I stick to the surface and the vague idea of the area I already have. Each street I run through I clock, adding it to the stores in my mental computer. It's something that I'm sure will be useful later. The underground would be better, but I'll take what I can get. Make a positive out of a fuck of a negative. The deaths of bystanders, and a kid to boot, is not the kind of attention we need. This is going to be bad. Doubly bad now that Kai has seen me.

When I look over my shoulder for the umpteenth time and find Kai nowhere in sight, I turn yet another corner and collapse against a wall. Deep breaths help to steady my brain, even if my body doesn't need it. The question is whether anyone will believe her. A whole room full of people saw me get a bullet to the head. Odds are in my favor anyone she tells will chalk it up to the chaos at the bombing site, smoke, whatever else it could be.

After a solid ten minutes and no one rushing by the alley opening, or running down it toward me, I make my way out. My steps are careful, deliberate as I get closer to the street. Slowly, I slide my head beyond the corner of the wall, only to have the street view blacked out by a fist flying at my face.

It's as if the wall lunged at me itself. Pain bursts in my head, temporarily stunning me. I reel back. It's only for a second, but it's long enough as another fist flies and lands on my cheek. Blood pours from my nose, and my face throbs. I gather myself enough to step out of the way of a third swing only to find rage twisting Kai's features.

There is no weaponry I can see, which would explain why she

keeps lunging. Swinging. Kicking. I dodge and bat her away, the question settling heavier and heavier on my shoulders as I watch her move.

Kai isn't tired.

Not even close.

Panic and fear build in me all over again. This rage monster is too efficient. Too fit. She lashes out. I grab her arm and hurl her over my back, slamming her onto the sidewalk. She kicks at my hand, nailing my fingers with a stinging blow before she kicks into my knee and drops me to the ground.

Faster than I can take in a breath, Kai is on top of me. Her hair is disheveled, tears trailing down her cheeks as fury fills her eyes.

"I should have fucking known," she hisses through her teeth, as she wraps her fingers around my neck and slams my head into the ground.

The hit sends my vision swirling. She shoves me again, the crack of my skull into the cement is loud even in my ringing ears.

"A bullet to the head wasn't enough, you fucking cunt," she spits.

She doesn't give me a chance to respond as she squeezes and cuts off my air. I swing my arms into hers. They barely budge. Instead, she squeezes harder and my vision blares white.

The strength, the speed, the recovery. It has to be what Gabriel is on. The general must have administered something from Protect Titan. It's the only explanation.

Black speckles my vision. As Kai leans into her choke with rage-filled eyes only for me, I try one more move with what's left of my fading strength. I sweep my arms under and through hers while bucking my hips to knock her forward. The pressure leaves my throat as she braces herself against the ground, leaving me to get in one good gasp of air before I trap her arm and leg, swipe them out from under her, and crawl on top of her.

She reaches out an arm that I quickly grab and drop into an arm bar before snapping. Her screech echoes throughout the alley. For a moment, I'm afraid someone will come running. Then I remember no one is going to pay attention to a scream like that with the explosion aftermath to deal with at the dock.

Tears fill her eyes, but her fierce anger still burns into me despite the pain I know she's experiencing. My fist slams into her face over and over again, blood exploding out of her nose and splattering my face. I flinch at the spray, but keep hitting. Kai's one good arm fists the sleeve of my jacket while I lift her by the lapels and smash her into the pavement, making sure to slam her head into the concrete.

As I land blow after blow, afraid if I stop she'll just shake her wounds off and keep coming, her fist releases my sleeve and her arm drops to the ground. When the fight leaves her completely, my sore fist stops punching and I sit back on her torso, my breaths heaving as I watch her. Rattling gasps bubble blood on her lips as her eyes roll and find me. Kai is alive, but barely. Her lip shudders, but no sound comes out, and I smirk at her effort.

There are so many things I want to say to her, but I think my fists spoke enough. Just as I'm about to get up, I catch it. A bruise along her eye quickly stitching itself back together. The slice in the skin closes, the angry blood pooling under her skin dissolves before my eyes, and my panic spikes.

Something is very, very wrong here.

If I leave her, all signs point to Kai healing, gathering herself, and reporting back to General Courts what happened. I need to stay as out of the picture as I possibly can. It was one thing if Kai reported back she saw me in the smoke of the wreck. She would have been laughed at, and that would have been the end of it. She's certainly not going to let it go that I kicked her ass so thoroughly, especially now that she clearly has some variant of the Defect effects in her.

Fuckity fuck fuck *fuck*.

This day just went from shit to catastrophic.

As Kai's split lip heals before my eyes, I make a decision. One that likely will bite me in the ass, but my options are fucked. Without another word, I grab Kai's head and yank her chin around. The resounding crack bounces off the cement alley and her body goes limp. Her neck twists at an inhuman angle, her eyes wide and unseeing. The healing on her face has stopped, and her chest remains still.

To stop a Defect, the body has to stay more damaged than it can heal. When I was in confinement at Compound headquarters, they pumped something into me that kept me hurt more than my body could heal. Death is the ultimate infliction to a Defect. There is no coming back from it. Stopping the heart is the healing mechanism kill switch.

My current problem now is I have a dead Kai on my hands. Her absence will be noticed, and leaving her here with all my biometric data on her corpse is not the tell I want to give to the general. Thankfully, a hundred and thirty pound woman is nothing against my Defect strength. Kai's deadweight falls over my shoulders easily. Blood spray speckles the pavement, but there's nothing I can do about that right now except clock the location and come back later with some bleach. It'll take anyone much longer to trace Kai to this hole between a couple of buildings.

With her threat mitigated, I hobble to the nearest manhole cover, my own bruising slowly knitting itself back to whole, and drop her corpse into the sewer. I follow with tentative steps and close the cover behind me. When I turn on my pen light, the sickly glow lights up Kai's dead features, her arms draped over her body at odd angles, and the blood crusted on her skin.

I wish I could say I feel some way about Kai's death. Beyond the inconvenience she's caused me, and what this could mean for the rebels, I don't give a shit. I never wished for Kai's death until she gleefully had a hand in killing me. Glad I could return the favor.

Leaving her here would be too risky, so I throw her over my shoulder and aim the light down the tunnel only to gasp into the dark. The beam lands on the hooded head of a Sister. Faceless, motionless. The dingy gray frock of their order hangs limply over her body. I open my mouth to ask what she's doing down here only to remember my time under the Harvest building running from the Hounds. When Evan was leading my and Jericho's escape after a visit, I saw a Sister in the bowels of the building with us, just like I see one now.

Sure enough, as I get closer, her edges fade and her body blurs, like my eyes are watering. After a few steps, I walk right through the image, a dead Kai over my shoulder. When I turn, there's nothing there. The Sister was just a figment of my imagination. If only I knew what that meant.

I shake my head as I make my way back to the safe house and mull over how the fuck I'm going to explain this.

8

"OF ALL THE PEOPLE YOU COULD HAVE KILLED, IT HAD TO be this bitch?" Evan screeches as he motions to the Kai-shaped lump on the dirty basement floor.

"I didn't seek her out to kill her, Evan," I remind him, my pinched fingers motioning for emphasis. "She saw me. I ran. I thought that was the end of it. I would have happily taken that as the end of it."

Miryam sighs and presses her fingers to her forehead. "Have you notified Jericho?"

"Evan signaled to him. We're waiting for his response. I don't know how long it'll take Kai's absence to be noticed at headquarters," I tell her, my mouth tight.

In reality, we probably have twenty-four hours max before someone gets suspicious. The mission has been rolling for months. Everyone has their parts to play and their assignments to complete. We had daily briefings when I was there. No way Kai will be able to go weeks with no one missing her, let alone days. We're lucky if we get hours.

"Let's assume someone knew her general whereabouts at the time of the explosion. Whether from her handheld—fuck!"

I lunge for her corpse and pat her mangled form down, only for my body to turn to ice when my hand hits the unforgiving metal of Kai's handheld. My shaking hand pulls it out of her pocket, the interface on, messages nesting on the screen. Handhelds, when they're accessing Seven Hills's servers, are trackable. My colossal fucking error could have led the Hounds right to the one place we consider safe.

"Give me that," Evan hisses as he glares daggers at me. He turns and hands it to someone nearby. "Disable it and wipe it. Signal Jericho again to get him to wipe this bitch's logs so her breadcrumbs don't lead right to us."

When he turns back around, his gaze is fire, ready to light me up. "Why the fuck didn't you ditch her handheld where you killed her?"

My heart is a bass line of panic in my chest. I thought killing Kai was bad. Nope. Leading our enemy right to us is it. And I did just that, assuming Jericho can't wipe Kai's trail in time.

I clench my jaw and return Evan's glare with the same blaze. "My expertise is in killing people, Evan. Not disposal. That was a whole different team. Forgive me for fucking panicking. I did the best I could in the moment. I don't know why you think I should be robot perfect, but I'm not. I'm human like everyone else, whether you want to admit it or not."

Evan invades my space, his form towering over me as he sticks his finger in my face. "But it wasn't fucking good enough. Now look at what you did. You couldn't even handle some privileged asshole running after you." He snorts and looks me up and down. "You're turning out to not be worth the trouble."

As he turns his back on me, rage builds in my bones, in my blood, ready to burst from my skin. I get it. I fucked up. Big time. Evan has never given me the benefit of the doubt. Ever. And I'm fucking tired of it.

"She's a fucking Defect, Evan!" I yell at his back, my hand motioning to the body at my feet. "She wasn't before, but now she is. She wasn't even winded when she chased me. I punched her and watched the bruise start to heal on her face. The general is giving them something. Something *like* the truth serum, and he's changing them to be like me. I couldn't not kill her, and I definitely couldn't leave her body up there."

A muscle in Evan's jaw twitches as he glances at the body, still an unmoving, unhealed lump of bones and flesh staring blankly into the world. His nostrils flare as he grinds his teeth, his chin moving back and forth ever so slightly.

"You said Project Titan wasn't close to creating soldiers. That the test subjects were still dying." He points at Kai's body. "That serum didn't kill her. You did."

I swallow hard. "They were. But that information was a couple weeks old by the time I got to it. Obviously they had a breakthrough between then and now."

My encounter with Gabriel bubbles to the surface, the need to explain thick on my tongue. But there's nothing to explain. Our conversation was nothing but innuendos and half-sentences. Something is happening to Gabriel, likely due to an expedited batch of Project Titan bullshit. The general is cold, but I have a hard time believing he'd inject something he knew to be deadly into his closest ally. Then into top members of his innermost team.

I glance at Kai's corpse again. It's begging me to find its secrets. Figure out why the hell she could physically match me. Why Gabriel is now a physical match. Why he feels like he's losing himself.

I could have been wrong in what I saw. Maybe I wasn't looking at the most recent information. Doubtful. I didn't see anything dated further along than what I found. I also know, or rather have a feeling, that information was missing. Something hadn't been logged yet. Maybe that's the piece that can bridge everything together. There had been a development between what I'd seen and what was uploaded after it. General Courts decided to jump right into it, starting at the top.

A damp cold slithers under my clothes. I clamp my arms tight around me to force it away. Gabriel is the top. Kai, and subsequently Jaxon, under him. It would make the most sense to start with the Hounds involved with the mission and work out from there. Which means if the general hasn't gotten to them yet, Jericho and Bennie will be tagged soon enough. Who the fuck knows what kind of interaction the real side effects will have with the manufactured ones?

"They're not supposed to have that kind of leg up on us. They already have enough. Your last gasp for making yourself useful, figure out what the fuck is going on with this," Evan motions to Kai's body, a sneer on his face, "and clean it up. Whatever you were doing before, you're done. Prove to me you're not a complete liability for us."

I've never felt so small than under Evan's gaze, buried under his words. Armand was harsh, but there was encouragement laced through his criticisms. There was scolding, then a healing hand. Punishment, immediately followed by relief. He trained me well, his good little bitch. I used to chase his accolades and his praise, despite how much Pixels I consumed and how many people I fucked. My job shredded me, but I did it all for him.

Obviously, that's my problem.

I feel the pull to chase Evan's praise, find it buried somewhere under the scorn. But I'm a fast learner. Doing the same thing over and over again and expecting a different outcome will get me nowhere but right back at the beginning again. I don't feel the need to get Evan's praise or acceptance. It's just really fucking annoying me that he finds fault in every little thing I do, no matter what. The desire to prove him wrong is what's running high now. To get the information I need to help us, but also to shove it straight up Evan's ass.

"What about the rest of the plants? And the targets from Armand's list? We can still move forward with that—"

"The fuck did I just say?" Evan spits, his cheeks turning crimson, his eyes going wide. "This—" he points to Kai's body in an exaggerated manner "—is your new mission. Fuck the rest of it. I'll figure it out without you."

"No, you won't. Not calculating the next moves to make to send the right message. You need someone with more finesse—"

"Finesse?" He motions to Kai's body yet again. "The same finesse that got you discovered and chased by a fucking Hound? That finesse?" His teeth clench as he looks me up and down, disgust clear in his eyes. "No. We need you away from whatever it is we're doing. When everyone's looking toward the explosions, you go the other way and figure out what the fuck is going on with Project fucking Titan. I'll handle saving Harvest since that's clearly too big a mission for you."

Big mouth for a guy who knows I can punch it clean off his face. He probably also knows I won't do it. Killing Evan will not benefit me in the slightest. In fact, it will likely get me quartered and burned to ash to make sure I don't survive the onslaught. Despite how much I want to lash out, how much I want to bite back and rip Evan a new asshole, I take it. I take it in front of his lackeys, in front of the Sisters, in front of everyone.

Heat floods my cheeks. I inhale a shaky breath through my nose before releasing it. If nothing else, it's something useful. It's something for me to keep my hands busy that isn't tagging along after someone else. It isn't grasping at straws trying to figure out where I fit in. I'm the only one with knowledge of Project Titan and have seen the documents and what they're doing in University. Not Jericho, not Bennie, not any of the other Compound moles that Evan has access to. Me. And Gabriel.

I swallow my pride, tilt my chin up to Evan, and say, "I'll let you know what I find. You know how to reach me if you need me for anything else."

Without another word, Evan rolls his eyes as he turns and walks away, leaving me with Kai's body.

"Would you like me to signal Jericho?" Miryam asks me, keeping a healthy distance from me and the corpse.

She eyes Evan's retreating back before looking back at me. Evan already signaled him, but it can't hurt to send another.

I shake my head. "I'll go to him," I tell her with a tight smile as I lean over and take Kai's dead wrist in my hand.

With a grunt, I pull her up and throw her over my shoulder. This gives me an excuse to sneak into Jericho's flat. He gave me his entry code after all. It's about time I use it. First, I need to sink Kai in the bay. Maybe she'll do some good and bring some fish back to us. It'll be the first time she's been useful in her miserable fucking life.

9

Both a good and a bad thing about The Compound, and the Hounds specifically, is their bureaucracy. The entirety of Seven Hills, really, but The Compound especially. Regimented, orderly, and everything scheduled to a T. Even genocide. Of course, it's not going to say that on any calendar. But the rollout of the mission was assigned out on calendars. I know. I saw it. On top of regular duties for all of the Hounds, I usually know where Jericho is at any given time.

Working in intelligence, he doesn't do a ton of strike-force work. His usefulness is interpreting and analyzing data. It's only voyeuristically intrusive into people's lives instead of physically intrusive like Gabriel is with his raids and with the rest of The Compound and law enforcement. However unwilling others are to admit it, what Jericho, and by default Jaxon and his team, does puts them as the head of the beast—the brain—instead of the fists. It's why Jaxon is on such a short fuse with the general, assuming that fuse is even still sparking after the last raid. He's supposed to be the one providing smart intelligence by which The Compound works. Lately, it's been stupid thanks to us.

I make my way to Jericho's apartment, my old apartment building, by deep night. I follow the trails he gave me to memorize, making sure to avoid surveillance in the right places. Before I know it, I'm in his building with hardly a hammer to my heart. There's no guarantee he'll be home. He could be running something for the rebels. He's not required to check in with me, after all. Although he and Bennie usually do as much as they can. Or he could just be out. He does have a life beyond me.

Jealousy, white hot and furious, rushes through my veins. Not because he could be with someone else. Jericho is free to fuck whom he pleases, especially considering our situation. I certainly wouldn't hold that against him, for all our weird relationship is worth. No. Jealous for his freedom. His ability to move about the city and live like a normal person. As normal as a Defect can live. All I can do is grit my teeth through the life I'm currently living and quietly climb the dozens of flights of stairs to Jericho's floor.

The hallway is quiet at this hour. I sneak to his door and quickly punch in his code. Print unlock is tracked. Not closely, but the last thing we need is for The Compound getting some kind of alert that my prints popped up somewhere they shouldn't when I should be dead in a meat locker in University or wherever the fuck my corpse was supposed to go.

The lock throwing back is like a slam in the late-night quiet. I wince as I push the door in and slide through the smallest crack I possibly can.

There's a light on in his living room and over the stove in his kitchen, lending some coziness to an otherwise sterile, hyper-modern space. Once the door clicks shut behind me and the lock snaps back into place, I breathe a little easier. I still have no idea if he's home, or if he is, is he alone? Tromping through his apartment and yelling his name wouldn't do me any good for a number of reasons.

I step lightly as I move farther into his space, the smell of him washing over me like a balm. If it's something he uses in the shower, what he washes his clothes with, or if it's simply the smell of him, it's hard to tell. Whatever it is brings me a level of comfort I haven't felt in a long time. Even the brief moments we've spent together haven't felt this home-like. There's familiarity here. Routine. Even for the short time I was assigned to The Compound, I settled into my new home quickly enough until it was ripped out from under me.

When I get to the corner hallway and find a light on in his bedroom with no one around, I relax even more. His bed is still tightly made, the bathroom light is off, and it's quiet in his flat.

"Jericho?" I say into the silence, my voice not quite a whisper but my bravery not abundant enough to say anything in my normal speaking voice.

Nothing but the subtle humming of the kitchen equipment is my response. I'm alone in Jericho's apartment. An emptiness settles into my chest, a yearning wrapped in hope that he would be here. It was likely he would be, but him being gone isn't outside the realm of normalcy either. I would have liked to touch him. Hug him. Fuck him. That'll have to wait.

I sigh and meander around his space, touching things he touched, sitting in places he sat. I have all the time in the world, because what the fuck else am I going to do? Evan yanked me off of everything I was working on to figure out the details of Project Titan. Jericho is my first stop for that. It's through him I can signal to Gabriel and additional people in University to help me figure this fuckery out.

Lying in his bed is as close to a hug as I'm going to get right now, so I settle into his duvet and inhale deeply of his pillows. I wish he knew I was here. That I could get a hold of him somehow other than like this or through Evan or the Sisters. I feel like a creep, but I know he won't mind. At least not after his initial shock.

A bone-tired weariness settles in as I lie here, but my Defect abilities don't require much sleep nowadays. I get a couple of hours a night, max. It's enough for my body to repair itself. My sleeplessness was starting just as I had to get my ass out of The Compound. The number of hours I have in a day now would have been much more useful then. Now, time is interminable, never-ending, and so incredibly empty.

I've been alone for most of my life, but I never really felt it until now.

I must doze, because the click of the door snaps me to attention. The first thing I see is the bedside clock reading six. Shit. I've been here way too long. Luckily, it's still dark, but it's morning now.

People are up and about, and my chances of being seen have just exponentially increased.

At first I stay put, my heart thudding but calming quickly as Jericho's voice filters through his space. Panic ratchets back up when a second, unfamiliar voice says something back, and it doesn't sound like it's coming through a tinny handheld speaker.

Fuck it all.

Footsteps land heavily on the floor as I scramble up and straighten out the bed as best I can. Opening the closet door would make noise, so I scrap that idea. Leaving his bedroom isn't going to happen either. I toe the underside of his bed. My foot disappears under the mattress. I drop to my knees and find space enough for me to shimmy underneath and at least get myself out of sight. Not knowing if this is going to be a bedroom visit or something that stays on the other side of Jericho's apartment, I'm about as hidden as I can be.

"Is the Sisters' cache not enough? The Compound's already suspicious. I have to be careful what guns I move out of the armory and how the catalogue is doctored," the voice says from down the hall.

Footsteps move closer before feet appear in my line of sight. When Jericho speaks, his voice settles over me like a calming touch.

"The Sisters are arming an entire district. They—" He abruptly cuts off. The pause lasts only a moment before he continues his sentence. "They need as much as they can get. The Hounds are planning to go building to building. We need enough to at least cover the guard in each building."

The closet door nearby opens with a depressed whoosh. Clothes shuffle, hangers clatter, and the door closes again.

"They have five hundred at my last count," the other distinctly male voice says, closer now. "How many people can they possibly have?"

"If you read the reports you'd know that answer already," Jericho says back, an edge of irritation in his tone.

A door clicks and a fan turns on. Someone is in the bathroom.

There's only one booted foot by the doorway. It's likely Jericho who has excused himself.

"I have enough competing interests and levels of logistics to deal with. Those kinds of details are outside my pay grade," the other voice says, the volume pitched louder to talk through the door to Jericho.

The toilet flushes and a door opens again.

"You're the one who said the less information I know, the better," the non-Jericho voice says. Jericho's scoff of a response makes me picture his indignant face perfectly.

"Right," Jericho says, his tone even. "You are getting information. You're just not reading it. That's on you. Read it and let's see if we can get more munitions down to Harvest."

"Hey, I know what I can do!" the other voice chimes in, chipper and slightly sarcastic. "I can have my team start digging under that old prison island in the bay. Maybe we'll find some old criminal's stash there. Off the books and ready to use!"

I still don't know who this person is, but I can picture a generic sarcastic face well enough. I can also picture Jericho's deadpan look back at him.

"I'm going to bed. Think you can find your way out?" I can practically hear Jericho's eyebrow rising.

A scoff hits my ears as fabric rustles and footsteps walk away. "I'll do what I can, man. But my story isn't changing. The general is already crawling up all our asses. I don't have a lot of room to move no matter how much Harvest still needs."

A short, terse exhale sounds before the front door clicks open and then closed. Silence hangs heavy in the room for a moment before Jericho's heavy footsteps walk away, the bolt throws across his front door, and he walks back to the bedroom.

"You can come out now," he says softly and only a little impatiently.

I exhale deeply, the little rabbit breaths I was taking were not cutting it, and shimmy out from under the bed. My gaze lingers on his boots as I stand, allowing my eyes to meet his face last. I can't help the little smirk of a smile that pulls up my lip.

"I hope I wasn't too obvious," I tell him while desperately maintaining my composure when I want nothing more than to throw myself at him.

Jericho glances at the bed and back before he says, "The duvet was messier than when I left it. Anyone else breaking in wouldn't go to my bed."

"Technically, I wasn't breaking in since you gave me your code." I step closer and closer until my body presses into his and his hands cradle my chin.

"Technically," he says with a smile before he leans down and presses his lips to mine.

For just a second, I forget why I'm here and what I need to tell him. The danger he's in. Instead, I revel in his touch, in the quiet thrum of his body. How, for just this moment, I can forget that we're all completely fucked.

A cold slice of reality shoves between us when we eventually part, and it's like a kick to my teeth. I want more from Jericho. So much more. To forget. To feel. This is too important. Too catastrophic. Without ease or hesitation, the words fly from my mouth.

"I killed Kai," I say, my voice little more than a whisper over my lips.

Jericho freezes, his hands lingering at my chin. They start to shudder before he drops them to his sides.

"Tell me." His face is a mask. Stone and unreadable.

I start with Gabriel and the changes I noticed in him but ignored, before I move on to Kai and our brief chase through Olympia and her eventual expiration at my hands. Evan's reaction, my reassignment, and now I'm here trying to push the ball back up the hill and struggling something fierce.

"You and Bennie can't get these new shots. Whatever the hell the general is calling them, who knows what it'll do anyway let alone how it'll react with your actual side effects. Have you heard anything about this?" Panic tries to claw its way up my throat, but I swallow it down.

The clock has always been ticking. Now, instead of a gentle tick across time, it's a thundering boom on its way to zero hour. The general is going to slaughter everything in his path and will proudly stand atop a mountain of bones if he has to.

Jericho shakes his head as he stares into the space just over my shoulder. "Hints. A new healing agent that will help us should things turn sideways." His eyes snap back into focus. He looks at me, his brow pensive. "It doesn't surprise me he's starting with the Hounds, or that Gabriel was patient zero. Shit."

"I need to get into University. Find out what the fuck they have there," I say with a shudder in my voice as I plop onto the edge of his bed.

"That's too dangerous. We have to go through the channels—"

"Jericho, the channels are dissolving. You and Bennie need to get out. We'll move your families into hiding so the general can't target them. You can't get those shots. It will kill you, and then it's all done. The rebels will likely do little more than flail, and everything will be for nothing."

They're catastrophic thoughts, but I can't help but think them. It's bad enough Gabriel is going through it. I can't have Jericho and Bennie go through it too. I just found them. I can't let them go so soon. His gaze hops back and forth between nothing, his mind likely going a mile a minute trying to figure out a better course of action. Action that keeps the current ball rolling as-is in some fashion.

I don't think that's possible. We had a few months of work. It's going to have to be good enough. Evan has already started the more tactical scare tactics with the explosions and calculated assassinations. As much as I hate to admit it, now may be the time to ramp it up. Start targeting University in earnest to derail whatever super Defect serum they're developing.

"The mayor is losing his grip. We're pretty sure the general knows about Armand knowing about the plot to kill him. For as much of a politician as Armand is, the man's shit at lying. At least when it's his ass on the line." Jericho sits next to me as he exhales and rubs his forehead.

"As soon as you and Bennie disappear, if the general didn't already have suspicions, he'll know. He'll dig through all known associates of yours until he picks off every member of the channel. Before you two run, make sure everyone knows. People can grab what they can and go into hiding with us. It'll tip the whole mission off its axis. If the general isn't a fucking moron he'll say fuck it to the mission's timeline and try to eradicate Harvest as soon as possible."

"Or," Jericho says, his eyebrow hitching, "he'll continue with the mission because he doesn't want to look like a megalomaniacal maniac to the greater public. To his inner circle?" Jericho shrugs. "Too late. But if he wants to be the leader of whatever's left, people have to actually like him or he'll be next in line for a coup. He's smart enough to know that."

"That means Armand stays where he is," I reply with a heavy sigh, as I knot my fingers together. Jericho places his hand over mine and intertwines our fingers. "He's the lynchpin holding both sides together. He'll be our last line of defense with information coming out of The Compound aside from Gabriel, and he'll be the last person fending the general off from us, again, aside from Gabriel."

"You understand he won't survive, right?" Jericho turns to me as he says this, and my heart drops.

Gabriel's words ring loud in my ears, how worried he was. Something is wrong with what he was injected with. It may actually be eating him alive. Fear twists my heart and my breath bubbles up in chokes.

"Both sides are itching for Armand's head. I hope he understands that." Jericho finishes his thought, and I deflate like a balloon.

"I know," I say on an exhale. I really do. Harvest and Service aren't going to see him as some benevolent savior any more than the general is going to let him keep being the mayor. "He doesn't, or has convinced himself that's not the case. He's too self-serving to think anything else."

"You understand my concern with Gabriel being our only line of communication into The Compound, right? With the channels down, things are going to get messy. Unless he defects completely, we shouldn't rely on him once we pull out."

Jericho's gaze burrows into the side of my head, but I keep my own gaze planted firmly on my hands. Nothing he says is wrong. I know it. He knows it. I just don't want to hear it. Something is happening to Gabriel because he's taking a bullet for us.

"Do you still trust him?" Jericho whispers, his voice husky.

His words brush against my cheek. I turn to stare into Jericho's gorgeous face. The thick plush of his lips, his pensive brow, the soft curve of his jaw. I understand his apprehension with Gabriel, despite everything, but it's starting to grate on me.

"Yes." I stand with a huff. "I do. I should go ambush Armand as he gets to the office. I don't want this getting through the channels without you massaging it."

Without looking back, I take a step forward only to have a warm hand wrap around my wrist at the same time as Jericho says, "Lottie."

The sheets rustle as he stands, but I don't look back. Tears rim my eyes and I hurriedly blink them away. Everything feels like sand falling through my fingers. I don't understand how it's all gone so wrong, so fast.

"Look at me." Jericho's voice is raspy, nearly a growl.

My mind wants to ignore him, dig my heels in and keep walking. But the thrum of his tenor vibrates into me, hums through my blood, and demands I turn. As I do, I blink my lie detector on. Jericho blares blue. I blink it off just as quickly and curse my body as I lean into him, desperate to be near him.

"We'll figure this out." He brushes my cheek as he says it and slides his thumb along my jaw and across my lower lip. I rest my hand on his wrist and revel in the heat pulsing off his flesh. "We always do. Alright?"

I nod, and he presses his lips to my forehead. I close my eyes with the feeling. The softness of it, the tenderness. I want to stay here forever. In Jericho's arms I can convince myself everything is fine. My body is ready to ignore our impending crisis and push him on the bed, but today my brain is stronger.

"How long before you think you'll pull out?" I whisper to him as I stare at his lips.

"Forty-eight hours at most, assuming that serum isn't waiting for us this morning," he says with a twitch of his lips. I must have a look on my face because he jumps in with, "The news will be traveling through the channels by the time I get to my desk."

"I'll meet with Armand and alert the Sisters," I tell him.

Jericho nods and presses his lips to mine, urgency lingering just behind it.

"I'll see you soon," I tell him as I step back and make my way out of his apartment.

Movement around the city will be harder at this time, but not impossible. I pull out my unconnected handheld and check the time. Good. I'll be able to catch Armand exactly where I need to.

ARMAND IS AS PREDICTABLE AS A CLOCK. I WAIT AT MOST ten minutes behind the support pole next to his parking spot in the University headquarters garage. The same spot every day at the same time. It's a testament to his hubris. As someone who made a living following people's routines in order to kill them more easily, Armand should know better than to be a high profile person with such a predictable life. Of course, it wouldn't behoove him to change it now. It'll tip off the general. It's only been a matter of weeks since all that came to light. He's been really sure in his security as mayor for so much longer than that.

I have about a half hour before people start arriving. A quick scan of the garage tells me the same. Only a handful of cars dot the spaces while the stale scent of spent plant oil lingers in the air, car exhaust baked into the cement itself. I check my handheld as he clears the entry gate. Headlights drag along drab cement walls as he slowly rolls to his spot only feet from me.

An opening car door echoes in the empty space, and I shift behind the pillar. The thump of it shutting quickly follows before it's silenced by the tapping of his shoes on the ground.

I take a deep breath and lean around the pillar. "Routine will be the death of you." My voice is barely above a whisper, yet it sounds thunderous in the cavernous room.

Armand jumps and whirls around, eyes bulging. He scans the

shadows for a second before his gaze lands on me, and his shoulders sag on an exhale.

"I told you not to do that," he mutters, his tone scolding as he presses his hand to his chest.

My finger presses into my lips, and I motion toward a nearby maintenance closet. I would have preferred our usual meeting spot in the building, but this couldn't wait, and I have no other way to contact him. I jimmied the lock on it earlier, and I know it's big enough to fit the both of us, if not comfortably. Armand's eyes roll as he grits his teeth and walks toward me. I try to ignore the slight, but it burrows in. As if talking to me has become an inconvenience.

"This is too much of a risk," he whispers as I shut the door behind him. "Whatever it is, it should have waited until our usual meeting. Your insubordination, especially now, is concerning."

The control of ages comes over me as I settle into a set of shelves with various rags plopped onto it. "Not for this. The channels are pulling out."

That stops Armand in his tracks. He turns wide eyes on me and pulls himself back, as if what I just said is offensive, and he needs to physically distance himself from me.

"Not possible. They're necessary for our success," he says, aghast.

He means for *his* success, but I don't correct him. "Plans change, Armand. We have to adapt if we want to survive this. The channels won't survive if we keep them in place with what the general is doing."

I update him on what I think is going on. Armand is already aware of Project Titan, but as I tell him about the general administering something that's giving Hounds Defect abilities like mine, the color leaves his face, turning him a sickly gray.

"I'm going to make my way into University and see what I can find out while Jericho pulls the channels out. It's the path of least resistance. If you start poking your nose in there the general will know something is going on." I lean back, trying to give myself some space.

"And he won't when how many Compound residents just up and

disappear?" I try to respond, but he keeps talking. "No. Everyone stays in place. That's what's the best for this mission right now. Update me when we're *scheduled* to meet again. None of this rogue nonsense. No change in plan."

Armand places his hand on the analog knob, and I smash my hand into the doorframe, my arm blocking his exit. My boss has a few inches on me, and while he's the one who orchestrated my training over the years, he does not have my training, and he damn well knows it.

"This isn't your call, Armand. The channels are being pulled. We're going to have to manage without them. *This* is what's best for the mission. *That,*" I motion to him with my head, "is what's best for *you.* I know you liked the security and control of the channels, but I'm going to need you to stand on your own two legs for a little while. You're still in a beneficial position. We're hoping everything will work out."

His face hardens, his gaze sinister and penetrating. It makes me want to whither as his eyes bore into me, but I stand strong. My knees won't buckle. At least not in front of him.

"What's good for me is good for the mission," he hisses, his sour breath hitting my face. "Do you think the rabble will be able to run this city on their own? Of course not. Without me, this city crumbles. I've been the one holding it together for years. I'm the one who's been greasing the wheels. I'm the one making sure people survive. There is no Seven Hills without me, and I will be absolutely fucked if I let you save some grunt in The Compound over my well-being. *They* are not important. *I* am," he says with a press of his finger into his chest.

It's not anything I haven't known about him. My entire existence revolved around making sure Armand stayed on top by any deadly means necessary. But to hear him say it so boldly, to so willingly throw fellow Defects on the flames just to warm him, is a kick to the teeth as much as him handing me over to the general himself. Never, in all the years I've known him, has he said something like this so plainly to me.

He leans lower, our noses practically touching. It takes everything in me not to shudder at his nearness.

"Do you think I give one single shit about the plebs in Harvest?" His voice is a harsh whisper.

No, of course I don't. Armand's entire involvement in this operation has centered him. The general's plan to violently overthrow the mayor was enough for Armand to side with whoever he needed to in order to save his own ass. That doesn't mean I hadn't hoped that there was a shred of decency still in him. That, out of everything, he at least thought fucking genocide was a bad thing that needed to be stopped.

I was wrong.

"I care about them because I will be their god when they find out I was the one who saved them. I stopped the mad general from destroying the city and the people in it, and I will continue to rule as I've done since I took office." His eyes scream as he speaks, and a sneer flirts with his top lip. He keeps his chin tilted up, forever looking down his nose at me, at Harvest, at everyone.

Rule. It's a telling word choice.

"Am I making myself clear, Lottie? You don't want me to make any rash decisions, now, do you?" He leans away from me, his eyebrow raised and looking at me as if I'm a child that needs to be reminded of its place.

No one is safe with Armand. That much is clear. Even the general knew it more than I did. More than I cared to admit. The only person who means anything to Armand is Armand. He will sacrifice us all to save himself. If he isn't already scheming with someone else to make a deal with the general only to stab him in the back too, I wouldn't be surprised. It's something we need to plan for.

He takes my silence as acquiescence and says, "Good. Channels stay in place. The mission goes on as normal, and we will continue to communicate through the Sisters and our regular meetings."

He sniffs, straightens his jacket, pulls open the door, and lets himself out. I'm left in a closet, my hands shaking. I desperately try to keep my mind from unraveling. Armand is even more of an enemy than I thought, and now we have a second front on which to fight. We definitely don't have the manpower for it, but if we don't take out Armand too, his stranglehold will only get worse. I can't begin to imagine how hard he'll choke the city, especially those who deigned to work against him, however he feels like defining that.

The last question is whether he'll believe I'll follow his orders. If I know Armand, the answer is yes. If the side of him he just revealed to me is anything to go by, the answer is no, and he'll be teeing something up faster than I can get back to Jericho or Bennie. He's too determined to maintain power. It's in our best interest to prepare for the worst. That bar seems to be sinking lower and lower lately.

Shit.

I would say things can't get any worse, but I know better.

Okay. Next step? Get into University and see what the fuck they're cooking over there. I slowly open the door, glance around at the still empty parking garage, and shuffle my way out. I can break into the main University building easily enough. Where I need to go, I'll need Gabriel. I don't think Armand knows where the experimenting is happening. I sure as shit don't. Time for Gabriel to be more than a channel of information.

11

EVERY DAY, LIKE CLOCKWORK, GABRIEL MAKES HIS WAY TO headquarters at seven-fifteen for a seven-thirty meeting with General Courts, followed by an eight AM mission meeting. It was the first bit of information he passed along, and my Defect computer brain absorbed it like a sponge. It's still early enough. The few people who are out scatter along the sidewalk, making their way to work as if it's any other day.

I stand shielded behind a doorframe halfway down an alley. As if his steps sync to the ticking of the seconds on my handheld, Gabriel walks by the alley entrance, and I let out a little hiss between my teeth. We don't have any code or signals because we were never meant to interact with each other. The distance between us, both physical and metaphorical, is too large. There wouldn't have been a point. This is a risk I'm taking. A massive risk, but a necessary one.

It's faster for me to try and do this than run back to the rebels and have them activate crumbling channels. None of the moles within The Compound know about Gabriel except for Jericho and Bennie. Involving anyone in the channels anyway to get information to him would be too much of a risk. It's not that I don't trust Jericho to get the job done. Cutting out the middleman feels like the best course of action as the countdown clock ramps up.

All I can do is hope Gabriel heard something and comes to investigate.

He zips past the alley. Only a couple seconds pass—seconds that feel like hours—before he walks back into view, his eyes on his handheld as he taps through the screen. He looks up, glances around the street, taps his pockets, and shuffles into the alley as if he's looking for something. Which, of course, he is.

He just doesn't know what. His hand moves to his sidearm. One finger comes out and flicks the strap holding it in, allowing him easier access to pull it out quickly. I don't know what he thinks he's looking for, but I peek out from my doorway, making sure to catch his eye before I move back into the shadows. The alley is empty. If I were to move out to meet him, anyone passing by the entrance would see me. What we don't need is someone asking Gabriel who he's talking to in a random alley.

"Shit," he hisses under his breath. The telltale click of the button on his holster fastens the sidearm back into place. "I had a feeling, but I wasn't sure."

Gabriel looks back toward the street before stepping closer. I make room for him on the wall as he nestles next to me, our arms touching. The usual office wear of black trousers, fitted black shirt, and a tactical jacket hug his body, leaving only his hands, neck, and face exposed. He looks good, if not a little tired. Bags sit hard under his eyes, yet when he looks at me he smiles wide, something like relief in his features.

I sigh as I say, "I wish this was a pleasure visit, but it's not."

I tell him about the enlightening conversation I just had with Armand, precipitated by my killing Kai and what I discovered there, and how we're going to move ahead with the withdrawal of the channels.

Gabriel nods as his hand slides on top of mine, and his fingers gently rub my skin. "This doesn't feel right, Lots. Armand has been too anxious. I think he's itching to do something." Pain flickers across his face. He tries to smother it, but he's not fast enough.

I look at him. "You've gotten it too, haven't you? It's what you were alluding to the last time we saw each other. Don't think you hid your stamina from me either."

"Can't hide anything from you," he says, as the corners of his mouth inch up, the pseudo-smile avoiding his eyes entirely. "Literally. This—" He motions to his body with his free hand. "—we weren't expecting to be so intense. It took a little getting used to. Jericho helped when it was safe for him to."

"Good to know you two are getting along." I want to stay on this train of conversation. It's so seemingly innocent. So innocuous. But I know I can't.

"That's a stretch, but yes. The enemy of my enemy is my friend."

"I'll take what I can get. That includes you smuggling me into University. I want to get in there and see what's going on."

Gabriel shakes his head. "Too risky. Not to mention it's . . . awful. You don't want to see that."

I swallow hard and squeeze his hand. "If you can tell me what you were injected with was safe, and I have nothing to worry about, then fine. I'll take your word for it. If you can't, it's better if I can see it." I tap the side of my head, reminding him what the side effects can do. "It's easier to smuggle me in to see than try and smuggle information out. Less of a trace."

A muscle in his jaw twitches, and his throat bobs as he swallows. "Not today. Too much going on. Meet me tonight at three at the back of the University campus building. You have all the surveillance logged, right?" I nod. "That'll be the best time. No one will be around. I can explain it away as doing extra work for the mission or something. I'll figure it out."

"You better go," I tell him with a knot in my throat. I don't want him to go, but it's safer if he does. "Don't want anyone to get suspicious."

Fabric rustles as he turns his head and looks at me. His gaze drills into me, roving over my face as if to detail every trace of me. "How soon do you think they'll move out?"

I shrug. "ASAP. Armand will be pissed, and I'm afraid of what he'll do. Things are going to get bad."

"He won't do anything if he knows what's good for him. It'll tip off too many people that he was in on it," Gabriel says with less conviction than usual.

"You don't know Armand," I mutter. "But I hope you're right."

He reaches out and cradles my chin as he pulls my head to him. His lips press against my hair and linger there as I close my eyes, reveling in the feeling. Without another word he lets me go, pushes away from the wall, and marches out of the alley with his head high and determination in his step. No one would dare question Gabriel. Well, almost no one. With how much he's losing his footing, Jaxon could just get desperate enough. Time will tell.

For now, I have nothing left to do except impatiently wait for the dead of night.

I OPEN my mouth and gasp, but only whispers of air get through. My vision is black, and I claw at my throat, desperate to scratch holes enough to breathe. Slowly, the black fades, but breathing is still a struggle. I roll to my side. Outlines solidify into human form. I struggle in another gasp and cough, my lungs wringing out with each heaving choke.

Heat floods through my body and sweat plasters my clothes to my skin. I push myself up to my hands and knees, and the room spins. Something gray and dingy flashes past in a smudge of barely-there color before I reach out to stop it, only for my hand to press into something soft. I yank it back, my vision focusing enough for me to see what I leaned on.

A scream crawls up my throat, but I slap my hand over my mouth, afraid someone will hear me. A corpse lays huddled on its side, its nose and the corners of its mouth crusted with blood. Its cheeks are sunken, the eyes open and milky, staring at nothing. I scramble away, only to hit more softness. More cold flesh. More unseeing eyes. My hand presses into a coagulated pool of blood. I yank it back before I can get my bearings enough to get my feet under me.

The silence is deafening, a ringing quiet that makes my head throb. My internal computer flickers on, the orange adding a lie of life to this dead storage room of bodies. As my gaze lands on faces, profiles flicker to life, giving me details of the dead.

All ages, all genders, all Harvest.

I scramble to my feet only to find bodies piled waist high in haphazard stacks. Some face down, some with dead eyes staring. Not a single chest moves. No noise to tell me anything in this room other than me is living.

Through the bodies is a narrow pathway. I turn to leave, run and find out where the fuck I am, only to find myself in the street without having taken a step. Pops of gunfire ring in the distance, but the street is just as quiet as the dead-filled room. As I walk, I find sawhorse cordons blocking streets with armed forces at the tops of the throughways. Every guard wears full head gear with oxygen lines running to the back of them.

Protective masks to block out a pathogen. The biotoxin has already been released.

No.

Impossible.

It's far too soon.

My boots stomp into the ground as I run down the street at a pace, my lungs filling with as much air as they can take. I run without caring who can hear me or who will chase me. No shaking equipment rushes after me. No hollers greet my back. It's just me and the street and the dead quiet of Harvest.

From one blink to the next people line the curb, and I stumble to a stop. They're all dressed in Compound gear. Clean, pressed, new Compound gear, telling me these aren't Harvest or Service folks who fished clothes out of trashcans. These are Compound members.

I move closer only to have a cry stop in my throat. Jericho stands along the curb. As does Bennie. They're beaten and bloody and are barely upright, but they hold on. Other faces dot the curb, some I recognize from around The Compound. Others I don't. All insurgents to the regime.

Conspirators.

Conspirators who failed.

The line of heads throw back, blood spraying the sidewalk and nearby wall of the building as the gun reports hit me a millisecond after bullets hit their targets. A scream rips from my mouth as Jericho's blank gaze stares at his killer. His head wobbles and his body collapses. Bennie drops to her knees first before falling forward into the street. Arms flail and bodies twist as they crumple into each other.

Movement in the corner of my eye, from where the guns fired, draws my attention. When I look, the people are nothing more than black smudges on the background. The guns I know they have aren't discernible. When I reach out to snatch the closet one, it dissipates into smoke.

Gabriel is nowhere to be seen, no matter how hard I look for him. I'm nowhere to be seen, as no one seems to see me. Until Armand steps out of the mist, points a pistol at my face, and fires.

12

I JOLT AWAKE WITH A GASP, THE DREAM A VISCERAL reality I lived not too long ago. Only it wasn't Armand putting a bullet in my head. It was Gabriel. And it wasn't a real bullet, thankfully. Sweat coats my face and sticks my shirt to my chest. I take big, heaping breaths trying to calm my racing heart. It was just a dream. I repeat the mantra, but I know better.

My dreams post-truth serum aren't just dreams. They're prophetic in their own weird way. Before, it was just me on the receiving end of a bullet while others watched. It was also the Sisters making their presence known in my covert life. Now, my loved ones are dying, and me along with them. Defects. Because not even we will survive a real gunshot to the head.

I rub my face into my pillow, soaking the fabric in lingering tears while I take slow, measured breaths. My eyes glance up and the middle of the night stares back. It was late afternoon when I decided to lie down. I don't think I've slept this long since before my reassignment to The Compound. Maybe sleep is cumulative with these Defect abilities. I store it like a snake stores food, sleeping fully only every so often and it being enough for me to function. Whatever it was, tonight was apparently the night to slip into a restorative coma. I'll need it for what I'm about to do.

I throw the haggard blanket back and swing my legs over the bed. Sleep still hangs heavy on my eyes, but I rub it away, wakefulness already buzzing in my veins. It's quick work getting dressed, moving out of the safe house, and toward University headquarters.

The air is damp and crisp. Thick mist hangs around buzzing lights, giving the city a hazy quality. When it's this late, and I need to make my way through Harvest or Service, I use the streets. It allows me at least the illusion of freedom, if little more than the ability to see the sky every once in a while.

Once the brighter lights of University crest the next hill, telling me I'm about to cross a line, I duck into an alley and drop into my trusty sewers. I hope when this is all over I never have to traverse one again. If we end up having to leave Seven Hills, at least that won't be a problem.

I pop up again a couple blocks from my meeting point, under a bridge and in between a couple of cameras. From there, I dodge my way to where Gabriel told me to meet him only to find him waiting. I check my handheld and exhale a sigh of relief to see I'm not late. He's just early.

I double check the timing on the camera before sprinting across the street. He must hear me before he sees me because he stands straight, his gaze scanning his surroundings until it lands on me. His shoulders relax, and his face softens only a fraction. As soon as I'm in arm's reach he grabs me by the hand and pulls me to him. He grunts as I land against him, a small wince curling his lip before he runs his hand along my jaw and cups my head. I reach for him as he lowers himself to me and our lips touch in a tender moment that I miss so incredibly much. Not that we had many intimate moments before, but at least it was just a secret workplace romance. Now, he's cavorting with a dead woman.

Air sucks through his teeth in a wince of pain, and he lurches away from me, leaving me cold and wanting. My heart patters to attention at the twist of pain on his face.

"What is it? Are you hurt?" I ask, keeping my voice low as I reach out to him.

The muscles in his mouth flex as he purses his lips and pulls himself straight. A movement that's a struggle. When he focuses on me, there's glittering pain staring at me, but the corners of his mouth twitch, and he shakes his head.

"Later. Let's get this done," he says with a nod toward the door.

I want to stop him and demand answers, but he has already pulled an ancient-looking analog key from his pocket and sticks it in the door handle.

It takes everything in me to not push him on it, despite knowing that something is very wrong with him. Instead, I say, "Didn't think they made those anymore."

Fuck. I might as well ask about the fucking weather. Especially since I know they're still made. I use one when I see Armand.

Gabriel snorts as the lock clicks, and he slowly pulls the door open. "Seven Hills is prepared for a lot of things." He holds up the key and sticks it in his pocket. "Power outages, unlawful entry, whatever they want. We can get in anywhere."

That pulls me up short. I already knew everyone's access codes to everything are stored within Compound databases. I saw that for myself. But a key—an actual metal puzzle piece—isn't detectable. It's not going to log into any database. Someone can get in and out, like we are now, while staying as off the grid as someone can be in this city. It's The Pit-level analog, and not just Armand is utilizing it.

I follow him through the door and gently close it behind me. "Wait. How often do you use stuff like that?"

We step into darkness bookended by bright lighting on the ceiling. Gabriel turns to me and smirks. "About as often as your body count."

Horror washes over me at the sheer volume of violations The Compound perpetrates on the regular. Until it hits me. "Which one?"

He looks over his shoulder, a wry smile on this face, and makes a little gun with his hand. "Let's move. We don't want to fuck around in here."

My mind attempts to flit away to places where we can fuck around, but I focus on the task at hand. I should have known Gabriel meant my Armand body count, not my Pit body count. The latter never fazed him unless it was Jaxon. Even then he dropped it quickly.

Who fucks who and how much doesn't faze most people in Seven Hills, but that doesn't keep people from being assholes about it.

We maneuver through sterile hallways far more pristine than the torture hellholes below Compound headquarters. No water stains on the ceiling or cracked tiles. This University building is well-cared for. As if this space is kept in a way that's conducive for what it's meant to be used for: research and development. Not a secret enhanced interrogation dungeon.

Then the smell hits me and promptly knocks all those thoughts out of my head. Putrefying death. Like meat turned over and left out in the sun. A gag punches its way up my throat, and I retch before I can slap my hand over my mouth.

"They must have had someone out. It's not usually this bad," Gabriel says as he rests a gentle hand on my arm.

"What the fuck does that mean?" I hiss as I pinch my noise. Except that only allows the smell to hit from my mouth. I choke back another retch.

We push through another door, and Gabriel doesn't have to answer me. I see the answer for myself.

Sequestered in a corner of the room under plastic draping and hooked to myriad tubes and liquids is a person. I only recognize it as a person because my brain tells me it's not likely anything else. It's prone on the bed, half of it tucked under blankets that used to be white but are now speckled with reds, browns, and yellows. Its upper half rests against a reclined mattress, its head turned away. Its skin is pocked with oozing blisters and rotted flesh, blackened and crusted as if it's already started to decay.

Another gag rests in my throat, but I'm too horrified to get it up. This is what the general has been doing in his spare time. These are his experiments. This right here, prone and dying, is Protect Titan.

Then it hits me just as hard as the smell did. This is what's happening to Gabriel. When I look at him, he's staring at the person on the gurney, his gaze far away and his jaw twitching.

"Is that what'll happen to you?" I choke, the knot in my throat thick and twisted.

Tears well in my eyes, but I blink them back as quickly as I can. The grief pressing on my chest is the weight of Seven Hills itself. But fury is right behind it and will burn the entire city to the ground.

Gabriel huffs out a humorless chuckle and shakes his head. "That's a few months past now. One of the earlier tests." He turns and stares me down. "After you died, but before the general started giving us loyalty shots. Every time that happens, the top secret University fucks working on the project tweak the serum and try it again. And again. And again."

"On human subjects," I reiterate. I knew this is what they were doing. I saw the report. But reading something like this pales in comparison to seeing the atrocity first hand. "He'll bulldoze through the entire district in order to bulldoze through another, won't he?"

"He thought the last batch was good enough," Gabriel says, ignoring my question. He pulls his sleeve up to his forearm. An angry red welt the size of my hand says it all. "Not quite," he says with another sardonic huff.

I knew it without him telling me, but seeing the reality of Gabriel's situation sets off a hurricane of emotions inside me. I want to break every bit of glass in this room. Find the general, drag him out to the middle of the street, and put a bullet in his head. None of that will stop Gabriel from turning into the lump of rotting flesh on the bed.

"C'mon." He pushes me from the room, the smell all but forgotten as my mind spins. "There's more to see."

We walk past banks of computers, screens black for the night. The subtle hum of hidden servers fills the space of the empty lab. Half of it sits shrouded in shadows, their censor lights likely disabled so long as we're down here. Every little thing is a tell for human presence. How often the lights come on and off not being exempt from that log.

Gabriel opens an analog door, nothing more than a beam across its middle that pushes it open. On the far wall sits a bunch of viewing windows, thick glass between us and what's on the other side. Dim blue light washes over tables where fabric sits pinned to the table top. It sits a step above me, giving it some height. I have to walk closer to the window to get a better look at what I'm seeing.

As soon as my brain processes the sight, I let out something between a gag and a gasp and stumble backward into Gabriel's waiting body. He gently rests his hands on my arms as my breaths come in rabbit gasps, and my mind files every sliver of information I'm looking at.

It's a person on the table, flesh pale, almost gray, and they're naked as a newborn. The skin on their chest is peeled back, exposing their whole insides: ribs, stomach, gallbladder, lungs, heart. All of it. It's not fabric that's pinned to the table, but the person, split open and exposed. Even from where I stand I can see the heart beating in the chest cavity. Eyelids flutter but don't open. A machine off to the side spits out a slow heartbeat, far slower than what it should be.

"It's a Defect. A true Defect. They've been here since before you came to The Compound. They're kept alive and dissected so University can keep studying the side effects. They then make tweaks to the serum based on whatever the hell it is they're collecting here," Gabriel says as he motions to the horror show in front of us.

"How long has this been going on?" I ask him, deep down knowing the answer.

"About a year. As soon as Defects started popping up after we all got that truth serum.

I straighten, pulling my back away from his chest, and turn in his arms to face him. His hands fall away, leaving cold spots where the heat of him just was.

"How long have *you* known about all of this?" I ask, motioning around, my voice soft and, to me, weak.

An eyebrow twitches and the corner of his mouth lifts almost imperceptibly. "About a year."

"You've been doing this to people," I point to the cracked-open human on the other side of the glass, "for a *year*? Letting them experiment on people like this for a *year*?"

"What the fuck was I supposed to do, Lottie? Huh?" He lunges forward and closes the little distance between us once again. "I didn't fucking like it, but I like living more. You of all people should know what surviving means in this fucking city. If you're not on Olympia, you're a fucking sleep away from death. Every. Single. One of us."

The notion hits me like a truck. I never thought of it that way. I had the privilege of not thinking of it that way. I willingly accepted the path Armand set out for me all those years ago. I know, deep in the back of my head, that once I was in it, there was no getting out. Not with the information I had. No way would Armand allow me to go be some desk schlep in University if I decided I didn't like being his right hand.

Maybe if I thought beyond the end of my own nose I would have realized it. What am I doing here? What is all this for? To save a bunch of people whom Seven Hills has deemed no longer productive members of society and no longer worth our limited resources. Why did *I* die? Because I was deemed no longer useful.

Gabriel and I took different paths through our adult lives, but they are so incredibly parallel. He ended up in the same exact position I did. Once he learned where all the bodies were buried, unless he wanted to end up with them, he had to fall in line. For him to lay it out so plainly to me, I feel like I've been slapped.

I must have a shocked look on my face because he follows up with, "Yeah, I had the same reaction when I learned I was disposable. Seven Hills belongs to Olympia. The rest of us just rent from them until they can't siphon anything from us anymore. It doesn't matter how high anyone in any district climbs their respective ladders. All that matters is Olympia."

Maybe Evan was right. As I look around this room of death—as Armand's control of me attempts to get stronger, as Gabriel deteriorates—I can't help but wonder if we should just blow it all the fuck up.

Saliva clogs my throat and swallowing it feels like needles all the way down. I nod and inhale deeply, then nod again. "Show me more."

Time passes in a blur as Gabriel flits me around, showing me one experiment after another. One *human* experiment after another. Sure, there's care for survival here. Not survival of the many. Just survival of those at the top and the people needed to make sure they live comfortably.

Gabriel explains the security for this room is on entry only. The rest of everything in here is off the grid so as to not be traceable, like my existence. As he moves through the information on computer screens, I log each and every piece of it in my Defect brain. Every trial, every name, everyone involved. The people with access to this room are all part of it. Sure, they could be like Gabriel, just trying to survive in a city that desperately wants them dead. It doesn't make what they did to do that okay.

It doesn't make what Gabriel's done to survive okay. It doesn't make what I've done to survive okay. We're all marked for death in our own way. Some of us are just more aware of it than others.

What all this does is gives me places to go. People to see. Things to blow up. The tentacles on this monster are much larger than I ever thought, and it's going to take a lot to sever those heads.

Gabriel's handheld beeps. A push alert, something that goes out to all citizens of Seven Hills when something important needs to be shared. Weather warnings, for instance. The way Gabriel's already pale face goes even paler tells me it doesn't have anything to do with sandstorms.

"You need to get out of here. Now. Go to ground and stay low until I can get down to you," he says, still looking at his screen, his eyes roving over something.

"What? Why? What's going on?" I gently place my hand on his arm and stare at his face, clocking every piece of that too for my steel trap memory.

Slowly, he turns the phone around so the screen faces me. My body goes cold.

Staring back at me is my own face with a 'wanted' alert. Highly skilled, highly dangerous. Cash reward for capture. Dead or alive. Preferably dead. Enemy of Seven Hills. For high treason, conspiracy to kill the general, conspiracy to kill Armand, and conspiracy to overthrow the government of Seven Hills.

"Oh fuck," I mutter.

Something from the channels withdrawal must have tipped Armand off. He wanted everyone to stay in place. They weren't going to, obviously. There must have been a broken link in the chain somewhere who told Armand what was happening. This is his revenge. He must think this gets him on the general's good side. Maybe it'll save him from being overthrown by his own police force.

Good fucking luck, buddy. Points for trying, the fucking asshole.

"There's more," Gabriel says as he swipes across the screen, showing me faces that make my stomach drop even lower.

Bennie and Jericho, wanted just like me.

"Known associates who are currently MIA," Gabriel says with a hard sigh.

"You're not listed. That's something," I add with roughly zero conviction.

"Yeah, we'll see for how long. Let's go. Before anyone starts showing up and the shit really hits the fan," he mumbles and places his hand on my arm to guide me out of the research room.

I catch the time on Gabriel's handheld. We're not far off from the start of the work day. So many thoughts and feelings flash through my head that it swims. None of this is good. Not a single shred of it. We're all fucked. I hope Bennie and Jericho got out in time. I hope Gabriel stays alive a little longer. I hope I'm the one who can put a bullet in Armand's head.

13

WITH A QUICK KISS, GABRIEL LEAVES ME AT THE ALLEY, and I make my way back to the entry point a couple blocks away. I keep my head down, my own analog handheld out to blend in better with the few people popping up on the streets. I make sure I'm out of range of the cameras on each block, but human eyes are unavoidable. I don't have to go far to drop myself into a sewer hole like the good little gremlin I am, and I hear the news talking from connected handhelds along the way. We spent too much time in the general's dungeon of horrors, and now I'm exposed with a price on my head.

Once I'm safely underground, I pull up the blast notification that went to every citizen of Seven Hills with a device on the network, courtesy of Gabriel and the VPN through which he sent it. My photo is from my University identification, a picture of me in a full face of makeup, my hair done. It's not that I don't look like my photo, but makeup is great at warping a face just enough that the average glance won't catch the similarities. Easy enough since I haven't worn makeup in months. Only the people who actually know what I look like will know what to look for. That pool is small, but deadly.

Bennie and Jericho are another matter. Their photos must be from their Compound identifications, which look recent. Both of them will be more readily identifiable, especially by the Hounds. I'm a ghost people were too afraid to look at directly when I was around. Them? I'm sure there are people who can construct their features from memory. That's a problem. Assuming they've already made it to the safe house, we'll have to discuss a makeover.

As I march my way south, I can't help but wonder how much longer these tunnels are going to be safe. Armand doesn't have all of our information, but he has enough. Enough to make moving around the city difficult. That ticking clock is an explosion of seconds in my head that match my footfalls. Despite the darkness, I see the horrors from the University lab clearly in my mind's eye. Gabriel's revelation rings loud and clear through my head.

We're all a step away from death. We're all things to be used by the rich of our world. We literally have nothing to lose.

No more playing it carefully. No more playing it safe. The gloves are off. Armand sided with the general the second he thought the rebels and I no longer had anything to offer him. The second he realized he didn't have control of us. He never really did, but he was able to convince himself he did. Now, that's blown. When Armand was on our side we had access to University and even some limited Compound resources. He's taken all of that and put it in the general's court, leaving us weak and quivering.

Like I said, Armand had some of our information. Not all. That's for a reason. A reason like this. Need to know because protection of the cause is paramount. Let him make assumptions about us. He'll be all the more surprised by how hard we will bite back.

Never mind how the general will cut off his head anyway. I'm sure Armand will convince himself that won't happen. Or he'll think he can get to the general first. They'll work together for now, but that won't be a lasting peace, and they both know it. The enemy of my enemy is only my friend for as long as it benefits me to keep him there. We have to make sure that benefit runs out for both of them.

This isn't even to consider the very real idea that the general and Armand may expedite the mission. Why wait? Especially if they know the rebels are getting bolder. They know I'm here now. They know it's where Bennie and Jericho will run to. We're all Defects. If the general is building his Defect army, some of whom I've already seen, it may not be a hard sell to plow forward. Olympia will already be scared after the bombings in their backyard. Why not capitalize on that?

I round a corner. When the final tunnel before the underground entry to the safe house appears before me, I sigh in relief. No issues getting down here, but who knows how long that will last? Before I get the door open far enough to get my nose through someone flings words at me.

"Where the hell have you been?"

Evan's tenor rings loud in the closed space, and I reel from the question.

"Which is it, Evan? You give a shit about what I'm doing or you don't? I can't keep up with your feelings about me," I tell him, trying to keep my face neutral. I'm not sure how successful I am.

He holds up his handheld with a picture of my face on it. "How the fuck did this happen?"

"Armand happened, Evan. Yeah, it's all well and good to have such a big man on the inside until that big man is more interested in his own self preservation than saving anyone. He betrayed us. Now, the whole city knows I didn't die, and we are all the more fucked for it." I make sure to speak to him and his acolytes behind him.

"Armand knows where this safe house is." Miryam sidles up next to me. I nod. Myriad emotions pass across her face before she nods back and looks at Evan. "We'll initiate contingency plan A. We'll be moved out within the next couple of hours."

There's always a backup—and a backup of that backup—lined up. There has to be. Where we're standing is *my* safe house. *A* safe house. There are many more nestled on the streets of Harvest and Service. They will pick up and move somewhere else, somewhere Armand doesn't know about.

"Did Armand have access to any of the sensitive information?" I ask her. She shakes her head. "You're sure?"

"For all his appearances of wanting to help, he never lingered long, and he was never left alone. Someone always escorted him in and out of the house, and he's only been down here a handful of times. Each visit was logged just in case of an event like this," Miryam says as she tries to swallow a shudder in her voice.

"Is there anything I can do?" I ask, holding her gaze.

She shakes her head again, this time with a watery smile. "We're already half done. When the equipment and provisions are moved, we'll send someone to escort you to the new location so it can be mapped."

"As if that isn't a liability too," Evan mutters.

I lean toward him. "Excuse me?" I tap the side of my head. "This is how your insurgents move around the city. It's how they planted that bomb. It's how they'll plant more bombs without being detected, assuming we can even keep using the tunnels. It's the one thing the general and his fucked up project don't know about."

Evan blanches and leans away from me. "What do you mean?"

I motion to his handheld and the wanted poster on its screen. "Armand knows we move around through the sewers. Do you really think he didn't hand that information over to the general? The only upside is he didn't have specifics. If the general is willing to eradicate an entire district to keep the people on Olympia fat and happy, what makes you think he won't bulldoze through the sewers?"

He paces away from me, pressing his hand to his forehead, before he turns around, his face twisted in rage, and hurls his handheld at me. I dodge out of the way, and it shatters on the wall behind me, sending glass and bits of metal scattering.

"You're the one with the relationship with him, right? He fucking listened to you! What the fuck didn't you do that made him do this? The entire fucking network has collapsed!" Evan shouts, spittle hitting my face.

Miryam moves a step away, and Evan's henchmen keep a respectful distance.

"It would have collapsed anyway," I calmly tell him, doing my damndest not to scream back. He's afraid. I get it. He gets this moment to lose his head, but not another one. We don't have that kind of luxury now. "The general was administering his new serum to everyone in the Hounds, which would have included Jericho and

Bennie, and eventually anyone else in The Compound who was on our side."

He moves his lips, likely to say something to the effect of 'so the fuck what,' but I keep pushing through.

"The serum is poison. It's killing Gabriel, and who the fuck knows how it would react to someone who already has the Defect side effects it's forcing into people? It was only a matter of time before they would have had to make a choice anyway. Try to stay on the general's good side and play along while hanging themselves in the process, or flee and expose themselves anyway. It's a lose/lose situation. We decided to willingly dismantle it before the people in it literally dissolved."

Evan simmers in his rage, his hands balled at his sides while he vibrates with fury. Like a whip, he lashes out and yanks something off a nearby shelf and hurls it at the opposite wall. Miryam screeches and ducks out of the way, but the rest of us barely flinch.

"Evan."

All heads turn toward the voice that makes my legs wobble. Jericho walks toward us tentatively, his hand raised to hip height, urging Evan to calm down.

"It would have been nice if everything stayed the course, but it didn't. Everyone made the best decisions they could at the time. All we can do is adapt and move on, and that's what we have to do now," Jericho tells him, looking him dead in the face.

Evan may not listen to me, may not give two fucks what I have to say or what my excuses are, but he listens to Jericho. He sees Jericho as a voice of reason. Probably because this is where Jericho is from. He and Bennie have roots here. I don't. I'm an interloper who thinks she knows better, whether I actually do or not.

"Your family?" I ask, my voice soft as I ask the impatient question bubbling under my tongue.

"Safe. Bennie is with hers now. She'll meet up with us later," Jericho says with a nod. "Lets get everything cleared out and make sure when the Hounds raid this place," he looks to Evan again and holds his gaze, "*when* that happens, all they find is an abandoned house."

Jericho takes the initiative and moves to the control room, but places a gentle hand on my arm as he passes, followed by a light squeeze to let me know he's there. He's safe. His family is safe. For this brief moment, everything is okay.

I stay out of everyone's way as they shuffle equipment and provisions around. Jericho says he'll keep an eye on the tunnel entrance while I make my way to the attic. I sit myself in the empty, stuffy space and watch for anything out of the ordinary.

It isn't long before footsteps on the stairs draw my attention. Jericho's head emerges through the hatch. A long sigh releases out of me. I deflate. My shoulders sag when he walks toward me. His arms around me are a balm on my soul, his heat more comfort than I've had in years. I rest my head on his shoulder and wrap my arms around his hard body.

"How are you?" he whispers onto the top of my head.

Tears collect on my lashes. It's such a simple question, but one I don't hear often. I honestly didn't know I needed to hear it now, but as a sob knots in my throat, I realize how desperate for comfort I've been.

"Gabriel is dying," I tell him. He squeezes me tighter.

"I know," he mutters and rests his cheek on my head.

"What do you think the general will do to him? It was supposed to be his bullet that killed me." A tear tracks down my cheek, and I rapidly blink, trying to push the rest away. If I dissolve now, I don't think I'll be able to pull myself back together.

"Hard to say. He took the new serum, so that should buy him some time, but it's the general. Don't forget Jaxon and how hard he's been gunning for Gabriel's job. This could be the thing that gets him an in, assuming the general is desperate enough." The safety of his body disappears as he pushes me away and holds me at arm's length. "He would be pissed if you worried about him now. He'll figure it out. Gabriel always does, the resourceful fuck. He didn't get to where he is without that."

A small smile flickers across his lips. I try to smile back, but I know my lips crumple. The sob pushes itself through and bursts out of me in a torrent. Tears flow in a waterfall down my face as I gasp and collapse to my knees. Jericho falls with me, wrapping his arms back around me, cradling me while I cry giant wracking sobs into his chest.

The pressure, the pain, the guilt I've been living with for nearly two decades crashes over me, and I can't hold it back anymore. There's nothing to dull the feelings. Nothing to help brush them aside. Just me and my thoughts and the reality I'm facing down. I can't hide anymore.

I fucking hate it.

All the weakness I feel, how helpless I am right now. There isn't time to have these feelings. To lie down and cry. This safe house is no longer safe, and I'm risking both Jericho and myself by having a breakdown here. Jericho doesn't make a move to snap me out of it. He doesn't try to pull me to my feet and move us out of here. There's just the empty, stuffy attic, my withering tears, and us.

Time passes. I don't know how much. Probably not enough. I don't want to hitch myself up and get back out there. I want this to be fucking over. I want things to go back to normal. Except normal was a fucking facade. It was fake. Gilding on a dumpster. I was just too convinced of its reality to see past it.

Gentle steps sound up the stairs, and I take a deep breath. My sadness tapers, and the tear-stained swelling of my cheeks is already deflating. As much as I've come to enjoy my powers, they're making me feel less human by the day. Maybe I should think of it another way. They're making me feel more human. It's because of them I've been able to brush off the Seven Hills shackles. I've broken through the mirror into the real world.

"It's time to go," a soft, feminine voice says.

A Sister, probably, but I don't look.

"Be right down," Jericho mutters to her before those same gentle footsteps tap away.

I inhale deeply, letting the dusty air fill my lungs to bursting.

When I exhale, I push all the bullshit away. I feel lighter, purged somehow. Deeply, immensely sad, down into the marrow of my bones, but it's a fire instead of a weight.

Jericho's arms tighten around me, and he presses his lips to the side of my head. His subtle breath rustles my hair. I close my eyes against the feeling, wishing yet again to stay in this moment forever and knowing the impossibility of that.

"What you're feeling, load it in a gun, and fire it at the right people this time," he whispers, his words flowing over the shell of my ear, absorbing through my skin, and settling into my brain.

Course correction. I did Armand's dirty work for too many years. It's time to wash my fucking hands.

I rest my palm on Jericho's arm and squeeze him back before I push myself to my feet. Jericho stands with me.

My face must say what my mouth doesn't because he smiles at me and says, "Good."

Part of me curses myself for being so raw and readable. The other part says fuck it. I'm tired of hiding. I'm tired of existing in the fucking shadows.

Jericho motions to the hatch. He holds onto my fingers as he guides me down the stairs and back to the basement. We have tunnels to map and a whole shit list of people to kill.

14

WITHIN AN HOUR OF US CLEARING OUT THE FINAL remnants of our lives in the safe house, the Hounds rumble down the street and descend on it from the outside and through the tunnels that Armand knew. Jericho watched the road from a nearby rooftop and reported back. None of the rebels went into the tunnels to observe. Too risky. The less attention we draw to the underground, the better. The Sisters were careful and didn't show Armand much of them, but the Hounds aren't just goons. Well, most of them aren't. They'll figure out our symbols soon enough, making the tunnels unusable. Hopefully, it won't be too soon before we can do some real damage.

Someone mentioned taking out some of the tunnels to try and get ahead of The Compound, but that was quashed pretty quickly. We still need those tunnels. Plus, we have the leg up there. We actually *know* them. Even if—when—the Hounds finally start sniffing around down there, even if they learn the schematics of it all, it won't mean the same as it does for us. For us, it's home territory. A map will only tell them so much.

Bennie's family, Jericho's, Evan's, everyone directly connected to us, are all safe, squirreled away in a Sister safe house until we handle things. Assuming we handle things and don't turn Seven Hills into a pile of bodies. Both thoughts can be true, and that terrifies me.

It's been radio silence from Gabriel. Not like he'd be able to work through the network to get any information to us, what with the network being disabled and all. I feel like if the general had any inclination that Gabriel was in on my escape, I would have heard about it. It's a weakness on Gabriel's part. I wouldn't put it past the general to dangle Gabriel in front of me, use him as leverage to see if I would choose myself, the mission, or Gabriel.

Unfortunately for the general, I wouldn't throw the mission away at this point, as much as it kills me to even think that. Even if I'd be willing, I'd get taken out before I could. The destruction in front of us is too important. It's truly a matter of life and death for so many people. A single life isn't worth so many deaths. Not now.

My heart clenches as I think these thoughts, and I choke back the tears. I'm done with that. I got my good cry in. Now, it's time for action. Evan's action. Everything he's ever wanted to do, the gloves are off now. We've wasted no time and have set to retooling our tactics as soon as the old safe house was in our dust. It's only been a handful of days, but we've managed to plant several bombs across Olympia and University, and have taken out three more Hounds on the mission team. The general and Armand mean business, and so do we.

Bennie jogs in, dirt smeared across her face, a stern set to her mouth, and her newly buzzed head on full display. Once our faces were released, Bennie's hair was too much of a recognizable liability, and it was the easiest way to change her looks, aside from no longer wearing makeup. She punched a wall for it, for the work and the care she put into her hair, but eventually stuffed all that anger into resolve, said fuck it, and demanded a chop.

Jericho is no different. He's on the other side of the room working through the various security feeds and talking with one of Evan's people. His own bare scalp is on full display, buzzed down to fuzz. The only other thing he could do is grow facial hair, which he's working on now, a fuzzy shadow blooming across his cheeks and chin.

I brush a hand across my own shaved scalp—my head now constantly cold—and send shudders down my back at the fuzzy feeling. I couldn't very well let them morph their looks alone, could I? I pull a black beanie from my back pocket, a donation from the Sisters, and pull it on top of my head.

"The charges are in position on target one. Liam stayed behind to see it through. The rest scattered to gather equipment for the next drop," Bennie says, her tone casual yet firm. All business.

I love it, but I miss her lightheartedness, her energy. She still has plenty of it, but it's put to darker use now. Just like me. Just like Jericho.

I unfurl the rudimentary paper map of the city, something dug out from underneath University long ago. The city hasn't changed much since this was originally crafted, and we added our own flair to make up for what the map lacks. Drawn in haphazard marker are newer buildings, mainly in and around Olympia, and scattered throughout University and The Compound. We're going part strategic, part terror campaign.

Because time is not on our side, and we have no real idea how fast The Compound is going to move, we're taking a multi-pronged approach. We peppered them with little hits. Now we're going for the big ones. Big target number one is the parking lot for the city's ambulances. With emergency medical disabled, it'll leave residents of the Upper Hills vulnerable and exposed.

The second big target is localized power disruption. Olympia will be going dark. As will The Compound. Compound headquarters will likely come back online fairly quickly, but that's not the point. It's the inconvenience of it. The awareness that we can do these things plus the added discomfort of the people squatting at the very top.

"Can you proof this, please?" someone asks of Bennie, as they walk up to her.

The girl is young. Young enough to still be in school, but I wonder how much schooling she's actually seen. Her skin is a deep brown, like Evan's. She's likely seen more time in the fields than in a classroom.

Bennie nods and hands the paper back. "Looks good. Run it, then burn it."

The girl nods, her stare hard and determined, as she turns and marches away. She and a small group of her friends approached one of Evan's rebels after we relocated and asked to help. At first he scoffed. They're kids, still a few years off from graduation. They insisted. They'd been playing with older tech and discovered a way to highjack airwaves and broadcast messages through the Seven Hills systems. Evan stopped scoffing after that. He gave them room to set up, and they've been our covert broadcasters ever since.

It's hardly been a week, but they've managed to rattle enough people in University that I'm hearing reports of walkouts from upper floors who didn't know what was going on under their feet. They're even getting a bit more . . . creative with their storytelling. Expanding fact into fiction using the information I gave them from the secret University lab. The general's monsters are ready to take over the city. With enough detail, and the right tone of voice, we can get under people's skin. From what I'm hearing over area handhelds and what people are reporting in, it's working.

Seven Hills needs the land down here, so bombing campaigns wouldn't be to their advantage. No sense in blowing up their food source. I don't know what protocols The Compound has for anything like what we're doing, if they have any. If they don't they're scrambling and trying to come up with something that will appease their primary base, Olympia, while dealing with their current trouble, us.

We're about to make them feel a whole lot less safe, and slip The Compound's grip on stability even more.

As for me, I'm finally picking up my gun again. Well, not *my* gun. That's stuck in the basement of Armand's office. I was never allowed to take it with me. Check in and check out. I never really thought about the whys before. Now, I understand. Lucky for me, we have plenty of contraband Compound firearms here, including a rifle that's close enough to what I was using that the learning curve should be short. We're no longer afraid a hit from me would be a tell. Now, we'll use it as a calling card. Big target number three, targeted powerful assassinations.

Bennie looks at me as I grab the rifle from its rack and pocket a handful of bullets. I don't need much. Just the tools required to get the job done. In and out. She looks at her watch, then back at me.

"You got an hour. Are you going to make it?"

I nod. "Of course. I'm leaving in a minute."

If I run at full tilt through the tunnels, I'll get to my target point in twenty minutes. Still, no sense in cutting it close. I've been practicing, and I have a feel for the rifle well enough, but this will be my first real shot with it. I want to be calm and prepared, not rushed.

She places a warm hand on my arm as I pass by, and I rest mine on top of hers. The heat of her sinks into me, a reassurance, and I hope mine does the same. A brief smile flickers across her face as I continue on, knowing I need to get out of here if I want to give myself time to prepare.

As I pass Jericho, I lean into him and ask, "Anything yet?"

He's shaking his head before he turns to me. "Nothing. Gabriel's been elusive, and we're working blind." He grabs my arm, halting me, a rougher touch than Bennie's. Insistent. Urgent. He leans into me, his voice a whisper, as he says, "If you think you can find anything, do it."

He means finding Gabriel. We've been trying to figure out where the biotoxin is being held. That was never information I had, and neither Jericho nor Bennie knew either. The people we've collected who scattered out of University are equally in the dark. Which means it's either in the sub-basement where they're developing the Defect injections, or The Compound already has it. If the latter, we'll have to up our game even more because the general will not hesitate to release it well ahead of schedule if he has to.

I nod. His gaze lingers on my face a little longer, a penetrative look that I want to get lost in. Instead, I keep walking, allowing his hand to slip off my arm. Every time we leave a safe house could be the last time, so each glancing touch, each lingering gaze, is something to be treasured.

I tuck it away in my mind, file it into a folder of things never to forget, and make my way to the tunnels. My pen light guides me to my spot in University that will allow me to do my job. To help mitigate potential ambushes from the Hounds, we changed our usual routes, passing through more circuitous tunnels that the Hounds might not think we considered. At least we hope.

The thumps and splashes of my feet running along the damp ground echoes through the tunnels. I can either move slow and quiet, or fast and loud. At the rate I can run, it's fast and loud. If there is anyone down here with me, any errant Hounds sniffing around where they don't know better, they won't be able to catch me. Assuming they're not all jacked up on serum and can't keep pace.

If the Hounds were smart, after today they'll make a list of potential targets and protect the hell out of them. Or not. It depends on how useful the general thinks each person is to his cause. This scientist, the one I'm about to put in my sight, is the lead on the new Hounds serum according to the intel Gabriel passed to Jericho before he pulled out. Using his intelligence resources, Jericho then connected some dots to others within the Project Titan program and created a lovely little list for us. The scientist is the one who tells everyone else how to alter the serum and why. Without him, development of purposefully engineered Defects stops.

Hopefully.

It's worth a shot.

Literally.

Either way, what he's doing is hurting people. Killing them. And for what? So the general can have his controllable super soldiers and gain a tighter hold on the city.

The first link in the chain is about to be gone.

The trick is getting him out of a building or a car. He drives in, parks underground, stays inside all day, gets back in his car, and drives home to park in yet another underground parking garage. A worker from Service noticed he goes to lunch down the street from the University building every month. Meets his wife, maybe. Or someone else. Who he meets is irrelevant. His bare head is what I want.

I'm perched across the street from the main entrance to the University building, on the roof of a coffee shop and some offices.

The street is empty for an afternoon. Likely because people are starting to get nervous. Whispers run up and down this city, and they're getting into people's ears. Our attacks have helped.

Good. They should be afraid.

I figure I'll let the guy have a last meal. Enjoy his monthly outing with whomever. While I wait, I scan the buildings around me, clocking what's where. The main University building towers over me, but I'm squatting under an overhang, some kind of equipment, and shouldn't be visible to anyone looking onto this low roof from above.

A couple people meander by during my waiting period, but the street stays mostly empty. Until I see him. Dressed in a sharp suit, his balding head with hair growing out along the sides. He walks with his hand in his pocket, the other arm swinging. He could be anyone. Just another worker droning on in the machine that is Seven Hills. But he's not. He's an orchestrator. An accomplice to pain and suffering.

To torture. And willing, at that. At least from here he looks at ease, his shoulders back and straight. He's confident. Unburdened. Like someone who has been given permission to solve a problem by any means necessary.

Unfortunately for him, so have I.

I line up my shot, the scope already zeroed, my target in my sight. Time is not on my side, and the longer I take to pull the trigger, the more I risk getting exposed. I take a breath. On the exhale, once I hit that natural pause in between breaths, I squeeze the trigger.

The thump of the rifle as it kicks back into my shoulder is a welcome nudge. The report of a bullet released from its holding cell. The splatter of blood as a piece of the man's head goes flying, and he crumples to the ground.

I pull everything back, shoulder my weapon, and retreat. My job is done. The first scream echoes through the tunnel of buildings along the street. It's quickly muffled by the thunder of booms coming from the direction of The Compound. Specifically their emergency depot.

The detonations rumble through my legs, traveling through the ground and up through buildings to get to me.

There won't be anyone coming to save this poor scientist. If he is still alive—that's a *big* if—he won't be for long. There isn't anything The Compound has that could cure a gunshot wound to the head.

Calling card deposited. Not that there's anyone else in the city who would do what I just did. Since the entire city knows I'm still alive, and someone just took a head shot in the wide open, those dots won't be difficult to connect.

Good. Let people be scared. Let them cower. When they learn The Compound can't keep them safe, when the general is only out for himself and the power he can grab, we'll have all the more people on our side when we take them out.

One by one if we have to.

The stairwell dumps me out into an alley, and I make quick work of tucking myself back underground. His family would have gotten our letter by now. The detailed information about what he was doing and the body count he amassed doing it. If they didn't know what he was up to before, they'll know now.

They'll know his death is on the general's head. All of the pain and suffering to come in Seven Hills will all be laid at the general's feet. And Armand's. I can't forget about him.

There's so much more to do. Right now, I have to make my way to Gabriel. I have to get to him somehow and find out where the biotoxin is stored. If anyone knows where it is, it's him.

It's a risk, but everything is a risk. It's information we need to know. Instead of heading south back to the safe house, I head west to The Compound building and into the viper den.

I don't have access to Gabriel's flat, but I do know how to get into Compound HQ and up to his office. The risk is higher than old me on a weekend, but if I don't do it, we'll have no idea where the biotoxin is. Short of sending people to search every inch of this city, which would be a colossal waste of resources, Gabriel is our only shot. I feel I owe it to the rebels to at least try to get this information. If nothing else, it'll make me feel like I'm doing something worthwhile than just fucking up all the time. Funny. That little voice in the back of my head is starting to sound less like Armand and more like Evan.

What I do have going for me is I have the schematics of the building already in my head, along with security timing thanks to Jericho. For someone who isn't a mutant, this would be impossible unless they had a vault for a memory. Too many moving parts. For me, I flip through each piece of information I need as I need it, moving a step at a time, and suppressing my overwhelming desire to scream in frustration.

I bite my tongue, grind my teeth into dust, and make my way through The Compound headquarters stair by stair, inch by inch, avoiding people and cameras and whatever else this surveillance district can throw at me. It's the middle of the day and my risk of exposure is high, but only by the people who know me well enough.

It's amazing how people's eyes skate right by when they clock me as something not worth looking at. What I'm wearing isn't particularly haggard, but it's older Compound gear scavenged from some benefactor in the district. A black beanie covers my head—my *bald* head—and I am makeup free. Lucky for me, most people don't pay that close attention, so the few I do come across in the stairwell as I make my way to the top floor don't give me a second look.

Granted, it wouldn't hurt to smear some dirt across my face or something. The Defect powers are fantastic at keeping my face looking refreshed, no matter how much sleep I get. No bags, no blemishes, not a single eyebrow hair out of place. It's doing us that little favor. But right now, I hope it doesn't make me look too good, too close to my wanted photo. If nothing else, my cheeks are more sunken, the angles on me sharper. I'll take whatever I can get.

When I get to the top floor—the floor that holds all of the Hounds brass and thus the people who would be the likeliest to recognize me on sight—I pause at the door and press my ear to the metal. Silence greets me. I wait until the next security clearance window and open it only as much as I need to squeak through before closing it again.

The hallway is empty.

Lucky for me, Gabriel's office is only a few strides away. I take them, counting the seconds I have left to get through the door. I press my ear to metal again and listen. The tap of fingers on a keyboard filters to me, but nothing more. No rustling, no mumbling. I think it's just him.

I hope it's just him.

Cold metal presses into my sweaty palm as I wrap my hand around the handle and slowly open the door, the click a resounding boom in the quiet space. Gabriel's office opens up to me. The large picture window, sun streaming in, the executive desk on the far side of the room with him sitting behind it.

"I thought I said don't fucking—"

His gaze landing on me cuts his sentence off at the knees. Shock, awe, fear, and anger swirl across his face in a slideshow of emotions as I close the door behind me.

"Lock it," he says without hesitation.

With a single finger, I throw the lock into place, securing us into this temporary sanctuary.

"Tell me you're fucked up on Pixels, and that's why you were stupid enough to come here." Gabriel's eyes are wide and his mouth hangs open.

Bags hang heavy under his eyes, and his cheeks are hollow. There's no visible bruising, but he's covered to his neck and wrists. Hardly any flesh is visible. I desperately want to see him. All of him. See how much time he has left.

"Sober as an explosion," I say with a wry smile.

"Yeah," he says on the breath of a chuckle. "You guys are making quite the impression." His gaze lands on my shaved head, but he doesn't say anything about my missing hair.

"That's the point." I step closer as Gabriel comes around the desk to meet me. "I—"

He grabs my face, cradling my chin in his hands, and presses his lips to mine, smothering my words before they ever had a chance. I welcome him in, our tongues tangling together, desperate and wanting.

"You shouldn't have come here," he says, his lips trailing his words down my neck. "I'm on thin ice as it is."

His hands wend their way under my shirt, flesh on flesh, and I gasp at his touch. "How'd you explain the bullet?"

The one that was supposed to kill me. The one from his gun.

"Blamed it on a mole who already left."

My ass hits the desk as he whispers against my stomach. Soft lips caress my skin as his hands push my shirt up my body, and I eventually pull it over my head. I tug at his shirt. At first he resists, clamping his arms tight to keep me from pulling it up.

The puff of air he releases against my abdomen, and the soft "fuck it" he mutters against me, tells me to take it off just before his body relaxes and allows me to pull his shirt over his head. Tattoos climb along his arms, over his shoulders and down his chest, leading my eyes to the sores blooming across his torso, and I gasp.

He remains kneeling, green eyes staring at me—through me—as my gaze traces the bruising across his body. Deep maroon gashes slash across his chest and stomach, across one shoulder, fading onto his back where I can't see. Images of the person hooked up to tubes to keep them alive in the basement of University flash through my mind. Gabriel's future. Tears prickle my eyes as I find his gaze again. A subtle smirk quirks his lip, the gallows humor just touching his eyes.

"Would you believe me if I said it's not as bad as it looks?" he asks from between my legs.

"No, I wouldn't. Especially when you already insinuated weeks ago that it's killing you," I mutter, my tone even and vacant.

My gaze blurs, my eyes unfocusing as scenarios fly through my mind of what Gabriel is going through. What the general is putting him through. The sacrifices he's made for this cause. It's more than what anyone has done. Fear simmers in a knot over my heart. Gabriel is minimizing what's happening to him, and I want to burn the building down to avenge him.

Fingers hook into my pants and pull them down, my bare ass hitting the cool wood of the desk. A gasp rushes from my throat, stopping my thoughts in their tracks.

"Then let a dying man enjoy his last meal, won't you?" he says, as he trails kisses along my thighs.

A choked laugh that could also be a suppressed sob erupts from my mouth. I watch him take my boots off, then my pants. Through tear-blurred lashes, I reach a hand around and unhook my bra, laying myself bare for him to feast. No doubt Gabriel is convinced of the security of this room, otherwise I wouldn't be splayed out stark-naked on his desk as he dips his face between my legs.

"Keep your voice down," he mutters as he slides his tongue along my slit.

Another kind of choking noise clogs my throat as Gabriel devours me, licking and sucking and flicking his way around my cunt as he consumes every piece of me. I rest my legs on his shoulders as he wraps his arms around my thighs, anchoring me to him. I lean back on the desk, giving him better access, and revel in the feel of his tongue sliding between my folds, probing my core. Of his shadow-speckled cheeks grating against my inner thighs, adding delicious friction to his touch.

He slides a finger in, then another. I choke, and my head rolls back as I fist his hair. I pull him closer to me, my legs wrapping tighter around his head as my orgasm builds. Gabriel probes and licks me to my peak, my mouth hanging open as the yelps crawl up my throat. Just before I can get my first cry out, Gabriel's free hand finds its way to my mouth and slides his fingers along my tongue, stifling me. His thumb holds my chin while his fingers massage my tongue, sliding back and forth in my mouth as he finger-fucks me to completion.

When he's done, he pulls his fingers from me and licks them clean. He lets my mouth go and stands as I slide off the desk and attack his trousers with vigor. He blindly unlaces each booted foot while I fumble with his pants. They're barely past his ass when I push him into a nearby chair and jam my legs to either side of him. It's a tight fight, but he doesn't seem to mind, and neither do I.

His hands roam my body, over my breasts, up my neck and back down again as I position him at my opening before seating him as far as he'll go. The shudder that runs through his body vibrates through mine as he fills me, stretches me to take all of him. Little puffs of air escape his mouth as I wrap my arms around his shoulders to hold him to me as I ride him to completion.

As my hips writhe against him, his lips trail down my chest and his mouth finds a nipple, his tongue swirling around the hardened peak before teeth nip at the sensitive flesh. Electricity pulses through me, and I gasp, my pussy soaking him as I ride.

I can't help but think of the assholes who will sit in this chair. The general. Jaxon. Anyone else who is still on board with this mission. What they'll be sitting in. Gabriel's hands grab my ass and pull me into him, guiding my hips as I grind against his cock. Let them sit in our leavings. That I was here right under their noses and they were none the fucking wiser.

My orgasm builds, my body flushing hot as I crest the hill. I lean back, and Gabriel presses his face between my breasts as his pants grow faster, punctuated by moans as we build together. I squeeze around him, and he goes rigid, pouring into me as my body jerks forward, the waves from the orgasm rolling through me.

The pleasure ebbs, and I place my head on Gabriel's shoulder, our bodies slick and sliding across each other as he wraps his arms around me. We sit like that for a moment, or an hour, or a year. I don't know how long. We breathe as one, comfortable in our silence as I feel the heat of him against me. I savor this moment, our fucking subdued in comparison to before. The roughness is draining from him, being eroded by the serum that's slowly killing him.

A shudder slashes through my breath as I try to hide a sob, but skin to skin with Gabriel, he doesn't miss my reaction.

"Thank you," he mutters into my chest, where my heart is thundering under his touch.

I can't help but laugh, a little breath of a thing. "For what?"

"For this," he says with a squeeze of his arms around my body.

He pulls away just far enough to look at me. He drinks in my features, his gaze clocking each piece of me. I graze my fingers along his cheek, memorizing the feel of his scruff against my skin. Maybe this is what death does to someone. It softens their edges. Waters them down. Puts things into perspective.

"Even though it was fucking stupid of you to come here," he says with a quirk of his lips.

Or maybe not.

I huff and pull myself from him, my knees stiff for a moment before my healing kicks in and blows the soreness away. When he slips out of me, a trickle of cum follows. As I slide off the chair, I feel it slip from me and land on the fabric. I try not to smirk as I pull my clothes back on, knowing one of those fuckers is going to sit in it and not have any idea. Childish of me, but it's just one more insult to their injury.

"I had to," I say, as I pull on my boots. "I need information and only you have it."

He pulls his shirt over his head, covering his beautifully bruised body. "And you thought you could fuck it out of me?" he asks with a laughing huff.

"The fucking is a bonus," I tell him before my tone goes serious. "We need to know where the biotoxin is. We know it's not in University, which means it's probably here. There are still a few months before its release, so I know it's being stored somewhere."

Gabriel's face goes slack, his gaze far away as he looks away from me and runs a hand down his face. A sardonic laugh rumbles out of him as he walks to the other side of his desk. "Lots, it's already been deployed."

Ice floods my veins as the room goes wavy. "There's still months left. What do you mean "deployed"?"

He sits in his chair and leans back, nothing but business on his face once again. "A few days ago. After you and the others were exposed." Gabriel shrugs. "General Courts said fuck it and pushed everything up. The attacks only encouraged him. Snuff the rebels before they can do even more damage. I didn't know until it was already done. With the channels gone, I didn't know how to get the information to you." He motions to me. "You took care of that, at least. Assuming you can get out of here without getting caught."

"What the—what—"

Words escape me. The very thing we were fighting against has happened, and none of us knew about it. How the fuck could this have happened?

I scrub my hand over my face, my eyes wide and not seeing a damn thing. "How? Maybe I can stop it."

"You can't—"

I slap my hand on the desk, a snarl across my face as the scream rises in my throat. Gabriel puts his hand out as if to push the noise down. I have sense enough left to not hand myself over to the general now.

"Fucking tell me."

"It's in the water," he mutters.

The room spins. I take a couple of stumbling steps backward and plop into the chair he and I just fucked on, uncaring about anything other than what he just told me.

"A bacteria. Mortality rate is upwards of seventy-five percent. Anyone left standing will be eliminated on sight," Gabriel says with a sigh. "Everyone's been drinking it for at least a day."

"I don't—" I can barely untwist the knots in my head to form sentences. "How does it stay contained? We all drink the same water."

Gabriel shakes his head, and I swear under my breath. Of course we fucking don't.

"Harvest and Service have their own water stores, each district with containment underground and their own treatment facilities. University, The Compound, and Olympia all use desalination treatment and have their own stores." He shrugs. "It's easy enough to contain it to just Harvest."

"What about the fields? What's watering those?" I ask, afraid of the answer.

"Water that's tanked in from the Upper Hills. To make sure our food sources are as clean as they can be," Gabriel says with a sarcastic smirk.

"It was all for fucking nothing," I mutter, my hand covering my mouth.

"No," he says, as he shakes his head and leans forward, clasping his hands over his desk. "University has an antibiotic on hand, just in case there's any cross contamination."

"Where?" I sit up straighter, my hopes rising.

"At basement level where I took you. There's a refrigeration unit on the far side of the lab. It's in there. Don't sneak. Just blow your way in. All or nothing now." His throat bobs as he swallows, his gaze hard.

"We'll need diversions." I look at him, hard. "Evan's good at diversions."

"Hurry up. Harvest doesn't have long. Days at most. I'll take care of things here," he says with finality.

I nod and pull out my handheld to check my security timing. I work on autopilot, standing and making my way to the door, before something clicks. Something sharp and sudden and gut-wrenching. I only have seconds, but I turn to Gabriel and rush him, plowing my lips onto his.

The kiss is brief and hard, desperate, and needy. He holds my head in his hands as I press my hand into his thigh. When I pull away, I beeline to the door without looking back. I can't. I can't afford to break down on his office floor, and it's all I want to do. That seems to be all I want to do lately, and it's a struggle to keep it all together.

The hallway is empty as I make my way back to the stairwell and shut the door quietly behind me. I'm two floors down when a door swings open, leaving me with nowhere to go, and my fight response revving high. Until I see the face of the Hound who just pounded into the stairwell staring right back at me.

"You!" Jaxon spits as he lunges for me.

16

ALL ELBOWS AND NO GRACE, I EASILY BLOCK HIS THROW, his fist grazing the edge of my hand. But that glance of his fist hits noticeably harder. I swing my arm out and land my knuckles against his chin. Jaxon doesn't even blink and throws his elbow into my jaw, shooting pain up the side of my face.

The rush of it bends me in half just long enough for my face to take the full force of his knee. Blood explodes across his leg and on the floor, and my head reels from the hit. The pause he takes to revel in his mastery—I can practically feel the sneering smile radiating through my back—I use it and lunge for his legs, hurling the two of us down the stairs. I need to disable him, or I'm not getting out of this building.

Part of me thought that Jaxon wouldn't take General Courts's new Defect serum simply out of self preservation, especially if he has access to the lab under University. The other part of me knows he'd be the first person to get in line to receive it, ever the kiss-ass desperate to climb Courts's ladder.

"I can't fucking wait to bring your head into the general's office myself," he sneers, as blood trickles down the side of his head.

I inhale and want to scream at the pain lancing through my ribs, knowing something is broken, but I can't stop. There's no time. Our bodies are a tangle of limbs and teeth coated in blood as we wrestle with each other. My shoulder digs into a stair as I push his face away, his strength matching mine, evening us out in ways that make my skin crawl.

My skills far surpassed anything Jaxon ever had. When I started mutating, it gave me even more of a leg up. Now, it's neutralized us both. As he wraps a hand around my throat and squeezes, my vision going spotty, for the first time I think he might actually get the best of me.

Until I see a gap in his arms that will fit my own nicely. Before my strength saps even more, I pool my reserve and jam my hand up under his chin, sending his teeth crashing together and throwing his head back. Defect or not, his body still takes the hit. Jaxon stumbles back, his vision unfocused as I gasp for air.

I can barely get my legs under me, but I manage to shuffle far enough away to get his shin in a good kicking range. My foot flies out, right into his tibia, and his leg snaps like a hearty branch. His yell rips through the cement corridor of the stairs. I only have seconds before someone investigates that, assuming they can hear it at all if they're not in the stairwell. It's not a chance I can take.

This will disable him and allow me to run off. His leg will need to be reset before his body heals it properly, otherwise it'll heal fucked up and he won't be able to walk again.

Sweat beads on his forehead and across his upper lip as he moans and holds his very broken leg. Bone pierces through his pants as blood pools on the landing. I want to hit him again. Bludgeon him to fucking death. But I can't. I'm dead if I stay.

Against my better judgment, I turn and make to keep heading down the stairs until I hear the slide rack on a gun. I turn around to find a barrel pointed at me, Jaxon's hand shaking with the effort it's taking him to hold it up. His disdain for me is so great, so pervasive, it's a shot he's willing to take.

"Say goodbye, bitch." He winces, the words a struggle as he says them.

"Goodbye, bitch," a baritone answers.

Both our heads turn to the landing above us.

Gabriel stands there, his sidearm out and pointed at Jaxon. The flash of gunpowder goes off before I process what's happening. A high-pitched squeal resonates inside my head. Jaxon's head whips back, the back of his head exploding out behind him, blood splattering against the wall. His hand drops, and his body goes slack. For just a second, I wonder if what I'm seeing is real.

Until Gabriel presses his hand to my shoulder and through my warped hearing yells, "Run. Go!"

He shoves me. I stumble down a stair before I catch myself. I take one last look at Jaxon's dead body—at the blank look on Gabriel's face before the slow build of a smile takes it over—and run. He's wanted to do that for years. Now, he's finally had the chance. One more of the general's sycophants gone, and the world is all the better for it.

As far as I know, Gabriel has the general in his pocket. If he can convince Courts of his non-involvement in my faked death, I have no doubt he can spin a story for his boss about why Jaxon needed to be shot in the head. Not that the general will mourn that as a loss. He was probably stringing Jaxon along anyway, waiting for him to fuck up yet again and hang him out to dry. The man probably got some sick joy out of torturing Jaxon. Otherwise, why let him keep failing like he has? The general reveled in Jaxon's squirming and got off on how his subordinate twisted himself into knots to please him.

Fuck both of them.

I take the stairs all the way down to parking level and dodge through the cars, heading for the alley. Just as I duck behind a pole, I lock eyes with someone who makes my blood run cold, then boiling hot. I know he saw me. I can feel it, his gaze plowing through the cement pillar I stand behind.

The general.

Each step he takes echoes like a ricochet around the underground parking structure. Like the sound of a bullet, only there isn't the soft meat of a person to absorb the hit. No splatter. No crunch. Just the *tap tap tap* of a predator moving closer.

This could be the moment. I can kill him. Right now. I'd put money on him not having taken his modified serum. He's seen what it's doing to people. To Gabriel. No way would he risk that for himself. He wants to survive his master plan to take over the city. I'd overpower him in a heartbeat.

"I wouldn't try anything, Charlotte," he says, his voice echoing like the tap of his shoes. "You are still human, and I don't need bullets to disable you long enough to get you to my lab and pry you apart piece by piece. A taser will do the job well enough. You're enhanced, not infallible, as I've learned."

The urge to engage is high, but I know he didn't get a good look at me. He only thinks he saw me. He's pretty sure he did, hence the monologue. I'm not about to draw him into a battle unprepared. Plus, I don't know what kind of failsafe he has in place in the event of his death. Things are already horrific, and it's my first priority to get back to Harvest and warn people of what's coming.

"You and your thugs are terrorizing Olympia, making my job all the easier." A huff of air escapes him. I know he's smirking even if I can't see his face. "You even sent Armand running right to me, the fucking rube. He's been useful, if nothing else. Thank you for all of this. Really. You've been an immense help."

He's just trying to get into my head. We have eyes and ears everywhere. Olympia isn't just falling into the general's arms like some fainting maiden. We're getting information out there about what he's doing, and it's scaring the shit out of people. Not just about what he's planning for Harvest, but The Compound. His Hounds. Flyers have been going up all over the city when a Hound goes down, detailing who they were and why they were targeted. We're not letting people look away. No one is safe. That's the terror we're trying to instill. In the general's Seven Hills, everyone serves him or they're fertilizer.

Not everyone is buying what we're selling, but enough are. So, I know he's spinning bullshit.

A car pulls through the entrance to the parking area, the engine roaring through the cavern and the tires thumping along the seams in the cement. I catch his reflection in a nearby car window and watch him look over his shoulder. I take the distracting opportunity to dodge away from the pillar and behind a nearby car, creating more distance between us.

From where I now squat, I'm watching him from an angle, just behind his shoulder and far enough away that he won't be able to reach me. He takes another step closer to the pillar, thinking I'm still there.

"If you turn yourself in now, I'll give those closest to you the antibiotic. Spare them the death that's coming."

He takes another step. I don't believe him for a second. There would be nothing holding him to his word that he'll do anything for anyone if I take his hand and we walk into the sunset. I slide behind another car, leapfrogging my way away from him as he moves closer to where he still thinks I am.

"What about if I tell you it'll keep Gabriel alive?"

That halts me in my tracks. His voice is smaller, less substantial where I'm squatting, but it sounds significant nonetheless. He still thinks I'm behind the pillar, and he moves a step closer to it.

"I was honestly surprised when he volunteered for the latest generation serum, and it's unfortunate that it's eating away at him. He's such a good solider. It's a shame to lose him." A low, throaty laugh echoes around the parking area, and it sends shivers across my skin. "Don't worry. There are others just as willing to step into his shoes."

Tears bead on my lashes, and I cover my mouth with my hand as I choke back the sobs. Everyone is expendable, even Gabriel, who General Courts still believes is loyal to him. Armand has proven that, and now the general has too. It shouldn't surprise me, but the realization is a punch to the gut. I want to punch him back.

I can't. Not yet. We have to get that antibiotic and save as many people in Harvest as we can. My hands itch with the revenge of it all. Instead, I slink lower and move back another car, away from the general.

"Too bad you were just a fuck to him," he says with a chuckle as he takes another step closer to the pillar, his voice sounding more echo than firm the farther I get from him. "That's all you ever were to anyone."

My blood boils with his words. It takes everything in me to keep moving away, toward the exit and toward the alley so I can get back to the safe house. Me attacking the general is exactly what he wants. He wants to prove to himself and to whoever else will listen that I am the animal he thinks I am. I won't give him the satisfaction, no matter how much I've thought about that very thing.

As I move back another car, the general gets close enough to touch the pillar. He leans into it, thinking he's being quiet, before lunging around to where he thinks I am, only to find nothing. He'll keep finding nothing as I move back and back and back to the alley and into the sewers.

Each step I take, my soul shreds. No matter how clean my hands are, they're always coated in blood. I allow the darkness and the dripping quiet of the sewers to absorb my wracking sobs as I blindly make my way south. The release of escaping capture not once, but twice, catches up to me. Also the fear of what my presence on Compound property could mean for Gabriel. Perhaps the general will only think I was there to try and plumb more secrets from them. Or maybe he thinks I was there to beg for Gabriel's good grace. I sniffle and keep moving, away from the what-ifs and toward something more certain.

The University lab underground, the torture rooms under The Compound, all flicker through my mind like a movie, each scene tattooed across my brain in vivid detail. All possible futures for Gabriel. I refuse to believe he doesn't know it. He's worked with the man for so many years, he should know how the general works. Nothing goes to waste, including Gabriel's mutilated body.

I allow myself the time to wade through my feelings, a minute at most, because it's too dangerous to be so unaware now. Anywhere. The sewers are safer, but not entirely safe. Not since Armand fucked me over. Now anything is possible. I want to be prepared for it.

I sniff again, swipe my wrist across my nose, and pick up my pace to a sprint. There's no time to waste. We have to get that antibiotic, then bring everything crashing down.

17

"IS ANYONE SICK?" I ASK, AS SOON AS I SEE SOMEONE, anyone, through the doorway of the safe house.

They turn to look at me, confusion on their faces, before a Sister steps into view and asks me to repeat myself.

"Anyone. Anywhere in Harvest. Is anyone sick?" I reiterate, as my anxiety grows.

There are only a handful of people around, but I have their attention. One person stands from their desk, holding themselves tentatively, looking at me like I might lunge.

"I-I'm sure someone is sick somewhere. There are thousands of people in Harvest," the Sister stammers, the worry growing in her eyes by the second. "Why? What's wrong?"

I waffle with telling them now or waiting until I can find Evan. The more I can mitigate people consuming whatever the fuck the general released into the water, the better.

"Don't drink the water. The general already released the biotoxin." The Sister's face goes pale, and the others in the room gasp. "It's bacterial. Gabriel didn't know until after it had already happened." The Sister wobbles, and I put my hand on her arm to steady her. "We're going to get that antibiotic. I know where it is, and we will blow our way in there if we have to. In the meantime, boil all the water you intend to use for at least five minutes. No cooking, no drinking, no bathing in it without boiling it. You hear me?"

The Sister nods. I turn to one of the others in the room. "Go find Evan. Now."

They nod and run off as Jericho walks in. "I thought I heard your voice. What is it?"

I repeat everything to him, and then to Bennie who walks in behind him.

Bennie's jaw sets. She looks like she's about to light something on fire. "I have to go tell my family." She points at me, her stare hard and unmoving. "Don't you fucking leave without me on that breach team." She turns to Jericho. "I got your parents. I'll be back soon."

Jericho steps closer and places a gentle hand on my arm. My shoulders relax a fraction with his touch. Just his presence is calming, but there's no time to wallow in it. We have shit to do.

"You see Gabriel?" he asks.

I nod and tell him about my collision with Jaxon and my almost-run-in with Courts in the parking garage. "He told Gabriel the biotoxin was released days ago, but who knows if that's true."

"There's no reason Courts would lie to him, right? What sense would that make? Unless he thinks Gabriel has been in touch with the rebels. I'd put money on that being the last thing he thinks, considering Gabriel," he says to reassure me. "Fuck."

At this point nothing can reassure me.

"I don't know if we can stop it in time, Jericho," I tell him, a waver to my voice. "We were supposed to stop all this before it even hit."

He steps in front of me, blocking my view from the rest of the room and putting my focus on him and his reassuring aura. "Adapt, right? We adapt. Pivot. Attack. Got it?"

He pulls me to him and wraps his arms around my shoulders. It's a comfort being wrapped in his warmth, a momentary pleasure before we literally blow shit up.

"Why is it always you who brings the worst fucking news?" Evan bellows as he storms into the room, the nervous-looking tech I sent to fetch him following at a safe distance.

My blood boils. Rage builds inside me like a storm about to rip through the city. I'm fucking tired of Evan's criticisms and his nagging. I'm tired of being the source of his rage and his punching bag. Stress is only so much of an excuse.

"Would you rather I sat on it, Evan? Huh? Would you rather have watched people die around you and not know what was happening?" Fury wrinkles across his face. He opens his mouth, likely to scream again, but I shut him up quickly. "You would have held that against me too. Withholding information. Being responsible for killing so many people. I literally can't fucking win with you, and I'm done trying. Do you want to actually help me or not?"

The muscles in his jaw twitch, and he barely opens his mouth to speak. "It's under my—"

"No, it's not under your anything. I know where we need to go, what we need to get, and what we need to do to get it. It's under my command because I have all the information. I'm not playing a game of fucking telephone again so you can fuck it up and somehow blame me. Eat dick, Evan." My words come out in a torrent, stumbling over each other as I try to get months of frustration out. "People are going to die. Soon. So check your fucking ego, and let me do my fucking job."

"And what do we need to get that job done? Where is the antibiotic?" Jericho asks, as if I didn't just bite Evan's head off.

My gaze lingers on Evan's face for a moment before my eyes roll as I shift my attention to Jericho. His presence calms the rage seething inside me a fraction.

"It's in the basement lab in University. Gabriel took me there. I know where to get in. We don't sneak. We explode." I look back at Evan. "Something you're good at, charging into a place with guns blazing."

"We need explosives and firearms. I'm on it," Bennie says, her voice jarring since she had just left, before turning around and grabbing a nearby tech as she leaves again.

I didn't even see her come back in, and I barely catch her gaze as she heads back out again. I assume her and Jericho's families are safe for the time being. Jericho brushes my arm before he follows Bennie out the door, presumably to get a small team together and gather supplies.

"While we're doing this, dispatch a notice through the handhelds to start boiling water effective immediately and send runners to every door to reiterate the message," I tell Evan, as I hold his gaze.

His shoulders are still tense, but he's gnashing his teeth less. That's something. "I don't have enough people to do that and go on this raid. There are too many people in Harvest."

"Try," I implore him. "Pay some kids from Service. Do whatever you can to get the message out in as many ways to as many people as possible." He stares at me for an uncomfortable moment, his eyes never leaving my face. "I'm not working against you. I never have. If you're going to trust me at all, do it now and *help me*."

He takes a deep breath before turning and muttering to the people standing at his shoulders. He reiterates what I just said and sends a couple off after Bennie and Jericho while the others go in a different direction at a run. When the conversation is over, he turns to me, his arms crossed tightly across his chest.

"Show me what you want to do," he mumbles, his lips barely moving, as if he's resigned to his humble position of having to listen to me for once.

I turn to a computer bank and pull up a map of Seven Hills that spans a cluster of five screens. The Upper Hills clump at the northern end of Seven Hills. Olympia squats in the only natural green left on this end of the city, wrapped in trees and gates and blinding-white mansions well preserved despite the conditions all around it. The Compound wraps around Olympia, because of course it does. It's the protective forces for all of Seven Hills, but its primary job is keeping Olympia free of riff raff. University is to the east of The Compound and south, the farthest south of the Upper Hills and our closest target.

We can't start there. We have to start in Olympia.

Evan goes a couple shades paler than his sun-drenched skin would otherwise go. It's the only emotion he shows when I tell him about the diversions I want to create. We've already hobbled emergency services. What's left will be closing ranks around Olympia first, leaving the rest of the Upper Hills exposed. Hopefully exposed enough for us to barge into University headquarters to grab the antibiotic.

I point out homes in the wealthy district, close friends of Armand and the general. People who petitioned me and who Armand encouraged me to accept. I don't tell Evan that. It's not information he needs to know. Still, my cheeks flush all the same. Armand's maneuvering of me over the years grows clearer by the second as I remember bed-filled basements and the smell of sex in the air. I was Armand's right hand. Sometimes it was my job to scratch backs, so to speak. Funny. I never considered myself a prostitute until this moment, and my hate for Armand grows even greater with the realization.

"Anyone specific in mind?" Evan asks with an obvious nudge to his voice.

I know who he wants me to say, and I gladly give him the fuel.

"The mayor." I glance at Evan from the corner of my eye. "Don't kill him. Yet. But scare the shit out of him."

"The general in there?" He motions to the screen with his head.

"I'll have to ask Jericho or Bennie. I don't know where the general lives. I assumed The Compound, but Armand doesn't live in University, so I don't want to assume." I sigh as I take in the map, the only home I've ever known. We're about to blow the shit out of it. "The focus is Olympia, but the attack needs to spread out. Hit them everywhere. Draw them away from University headquarters so we can get in and grab the antibiotic."

"I have some stuff built," Evan says, looking at the map much the same way I just did. "I'll get people on the rest. Do you want a single barrage or a rolling attack?"

"Rolling. Make them think it's over then hit again. And again. And again. Try to get emergency response vehicles or whatever else they're using if you can. "

"You know that's unreasonable, right?" Evan asks. I turn my head to look at him. "Getting *just* the vehicles."

I swallow hard, a scrape like razor blades sliding down my throat. I don't need reminding, but I do. This is a war. We can't cherry pick who lives and who dies. The act of saving lives costs lives. No wonder the world before us went to shit. No one comes out on top when that's what we're working with.

"Try," I tell him, my look resolved. "Emergency response isn't our enemy. They're just doing their jobs."

"So were we," Evan says, a stark reminder yet again of our situation.

Perhaps it's best not to think about it, not to see it all as a clear one-for-one exchange of life. No one wins there. We can try to do what we need to do without obliterating Seven Hills and everyone in it. It's holding an armful of eggs and trying to keep them from falling and cracking. It's impossible. Saving everyone in Seven Hills is impossible when half the city views the other half as less than human.

The terror campaign and the reminders we've been leaving around the city made a small dent. But people like the comfort of their homes. They like their peace. Especially those in Olympia. What's some farmers to them when machines will do the same job and ensure their tables remain full? Flyers don't change minds like that. Action does.

So does death.

Bennie and Jericho come back into the room, followed by a couple of Evan's men, their faces expectant and waiting.

"We have work to do," I tell Evan before looking around the room. "Lets get it done sooner rather than later and end this fucking thing."

18

Hours.

That's how long it takes to rally the numbers we need, create the bombs we need, and relay the slap-dash plan we concoct. Fear and survival motivates. Unfortunately for us, The Compound is working on home territory the same as us. What we do have going for us is our targeted attack on Compound members. There isn't a constant flow of Hounds to use, and no reserves to draw from. So taking out even ten Hounds and Compound members closely tied to the mission works in our favor. That's ten fewer people we need to worry about, but still a whole district's worth of concern.

We're a small breach team, me, Bennie, and a handful of Evan's men. Jericho is with the drop group scattering bombs throughout Olympia where they still have access. Credit to The Compound, they're wising up and welding sewer covers and drainage grating down. Credit to us, it's a lot of ground to cover, and The Compound keeps getting spread thinner and thinner. We dispatched a team where that's their entire job, to keep an eye on our entrances to street level and mark what's still available to us. This is where kids are useful and not put in direct harm's way. Observe, mark, report.

Evan stays behind despite his rumblings. As much as I empathize with his desire to go in guns blaring, he's considered leadership, and we can't put all those eggs in one basket. Hence, why it's just me and Bennie, Jericho and Evan elsewhere, and the Sisters scattered even more. Continuity of governance, whatever governing we're actually doing.

Another siren blares through the air as we huddle in the shadows behind University headquarters. One of only a small handful of emergency vehicles left to help the people of the Upper Hills careens down the street.

"How are we on time?" I mutter over Bennie's shoulder.

She looks at her handheld. "We're seven minutes in," she whispers back, her voice echoing around the space enough for the rest of us to hear.

Just as she finishes her sentence, a boom like thunder rumbles through the air and a shudder runs up my legs. From Olympia to University, bombs dot the streets, scatter around buildings, ready and waiting to further rock the world of the Upper Hills. Another rumble, louder this time, rents the air. I can't help but smile. Smoke and the smell of burning things hits my nose as sirens scream. The handful of people with us who are still connected to the Seven Hills grid tell us of the emergency messages popping up through the system, working through a network of VPNs to keep security off our tails.

Stay inside. Stay away from windows. Find shelter immediately.

If only they realized nowhere is safe. Not while the people of Harvest are at risk.

One more boom sounds close enough to pop my ears. I look at the building looming over me. It sways with the aftermath of the explosion. Exactly what we were hoping for. Right on cue, a much closer siren blares. A piercing, eye-bugging siren from within the University building I know all too well after all these years.

Fire alarm.

The best way to get people's attention and get them out of the building. Only a small handful of people will end up coming out this door we're all hovering near, and their rallying point is around front of the building. The fewer road blocks we have to deal with, the better.

As if I saw the events in one of my dreams, the metal door bangs open and a smattering of people file out. Some look annoyed at being disturbed. Others look concerned, their eyes darting around them as they shuffle behind their coworkers.

We're prepared to blow the door in if we have to, but everyone leaving the lab is so focused on getting themselves out of harm's way that they're not paying attention to anything else. Plus, the noise of the sirens and the explosions hide the shuffling feet of one of Evan's men nicely. He's able to grab the door before it shuts and slams the knob off with the butt of his rifle, ensuring it won't click shut again. For a super secret laboratory, the door is not nearly as reinforced as it should be. I guess that would draw too much attention to its secrecy. Subtlety, for once.

To the general's credit, he has been subtle. Sneaky and subtle like a snake sliding through overlong grass. No one can see him until he's on their heels, and then it's too late. We're not too late. We can't be.

If there's anyone else in the lab, they're about to get a big surprise. Then I remember of course there's still people down here. The lab rats the general keeps hooked up to life support so they can be studied. As we breach the door and make our way in, Evan's men clear out the aisles to make sure we're alone. With Bennie at my rear, I get a glimpse of someone strapped to a table. Like the last person I saw down here, their skin has practically rotted away, but their chest still moves up and down. They don't acknowledge us as we move through the space. Not that I would expect them to.

I blink and Gabriel's face replaces the anonymous person's on the table, his green eyes still intact, staring into me. Begging me to end his life. I blink again and it's back to someone I don't know. Bennie pushes into my shoulder, reminding me we have to keep moving.

Her fingers wrap around a strap on my vest, partly to keep me close and part to not lose me as I shuffle us through the cluttered space. Bright lights overhead expose us far more than I would like. I'd have preferred the dark, but I'll take what I can get.

The refrigeration unit is on the farthest side of the lab. As we pass another bank of tables I see it. Relief flutters through my heart just as gunshots pierce through the quiet. We duck behind a table, our backs to cool metal, and we look at each other, frowning. Rifles continue firing as bullets zip through the air. We're on a side of the lab without an exit.

"Looks like they stationed Compound people here," Bennie says as she leans into me.

"I'm not surprised. You think they're Hounds? They're in the lab, after all," I ask, as I try to peek around the table leg.

Evan's men appear to be drawing fire. I'd prefer to keep eyes off of us until we can get what we need, but we need to know what's happening, where, and how much.

Bennie leans around the other side of the table before wrenching herself back. "Can't tell through their kit, but I'd be willing to bet. Which means they don't have long. I don't care how well they're trained. It wasn't enough against the Hounds."

"Then let's go," I tell her while motioning to the cold storage with my head.

Bennie nods back. We stay low as we maneuver around a table and make our way to the door of the refrigeration unit. Of course, when we get there, we both see it's not just a door anyone can open. Even in this super secret underground laboratory of death, people need old-fashioned keys to get into certain rooms. Why wouldn't they? The general siloed the hell out of the mission team when I was there. It shouldn't surprise me he does the same down here. The Hounds being here now is either an inconvenient coincidence or the general was getting paranoid about his secret lab. My money is on the latter.

A bullet hits the reinforced glass over our heads. We both wince and hunch into our shoulders before recalibrating and figuring out what the hell to do.

From what I can see from the lack of random keys hanging around, all we can do is shoot our way in. Which means the noise will likely draw the Hounds. I look at Bennie. She glances at the handle over my head before looking at me.

"I'll cover. You get in, get the fuck out, and then we can beat the Hounds back," she says, as she turns and presses her back to mine.

Reports ring around us, bouncing through shouts and yells and groans as flesh takes bullets. I point my rifle up, settle my finger on the trigger, and fire. The heat and propulsion of the bullet tears through the handle, but doesn't make a dent where I need it to. I look back over my shoulder at Bennie, and she nods.

"Keep going," she tells me.

It wasn't enough to draw the Hounds' attention. I fire once and wait for the go-ahead from Bennie, making too-slow dents in this seemingly impenetrable handle of this fucking door. Finally, my last bullet rips through the handle and tears it out of the door, leaving a gaping hole that releases the lock and allows me to push the thing open.

Bennie places a warm hand on my knee, and I still. The metal clang of the handle giving way still rings with the report of bullets, and I know from her touch that it's drawn attention. She hunches a few inches lower, and I follow her lead, trying to keep out of the line of sight of the advancing Hounds.

She pats my leg. "Go. Now."

The pause is little more than a second before I open the door and scoot my way through. The temperature drops a solid forty degrees. My muscles clench against the shudder trying to wrack through my body as I stay low and make my way along the shelves, searching for the barely-pronounceable name Gabriel told me. I'll know it when I see it. There are shelves stacked over my head, but that means standing in full view of a window. A reinforced window that's already taken one bullet with only minor cracking, but I don't want to test how strong the glass is. The thing is, I might not have a choice.

When I finish searching the lowest shelves that would keep me hidden, I slowly raise my squat position one shelf at a time, searching for the precious gold that will save the people of Harvest. There's a subtle tapping on the door. I'm surprised I can hear it over the gun bursts and shouts of the rebels and the Hounds. It echoes loudly in the small space. I know what it means without words. Hurry the fuck up.

"I'm fucking hurrying," I mutter to myself, knowing full well Bennie can't hear me.

My head is several inches above the window line, unnervingly exposed to the firefight, when I see it. The antibiotic that will help thousands just sitting there for what? Just in case the toxin seeps into the wrong water and infects the wrong people? In case a Hound drinks from the wrong bottle?

Fucking assholes.

I grab boxes, tiny glasses rattling around inside, and hope they don't break before we can get them to Harvest. I stuff them in various cargo pockets littered across my body and in concealed pockets just under my vest.

A resounding thud, followed by cracking glass, makes me jolt. I fumble the last box, but salvage it just in time. I don't see the second bullet, but I see the spiderwebbing that fractures out from its impact point all the same. Bennie's head peeks up and she fires off a couple of shots before ducking back down again.

Honeymoon's over.

It's just two rebels left standing against half a dozen Hounds, and they're not looking too great. We have no choice but to power forward if we want to get out of here. At least Bennie and I have a better shot against the Hounds than the rebels. Bennie knows more of their tricks than I do, and between the two of us we have preparedness to spare. Time to meet them head on.

I lean out of the safety of the bulletproof room, the barrel of my rifle first, and fire a shot at an advancing Hound, nicking them in the neck. Blood squirts from the wound, and I give myself a nanosecond to celebrate. The person slaps a hand to their neck and stumbles, pulling the Hound behind them with them in their panic to stop the flow. That Hound stays behind while the remaining four advance.

Bennie moves down a row of tables before popping up and firing off a couple of shots. One Hound takes a bullet to the vest. It knocks him off his feet, but I know we don't have long. A rebel jolts up from behind the advancing team and nicks a Hound in the arm. Another man comes up behind him just as the first disappears behind his cover and fires more indiscriminately, managing a pop to another Hound's torso.

If we can get out the door, I can grenade this place, but I'm not going to do that until the rest of us left standing are at least out of range. I take another shot at an approaching Hound, and it wings their helmet. Another one and the bullet blasts through their eye protection. Their head snaps back, and they drop to the ground like a sack of grain.

I duck behind the tables and make my way to Bennie who springs up just before I get to her to fire off a couple of shots before dropping again. I pull a flash bang from my vest, wave it in front of her, and she nods.

"Get the rest of the rebels to the door. I'll hold the Hounds off and then blow this place up." I say it in as low of a voice as I can, the quiet gaps in gunfire more resounding now that the Hounds are down two people.

Bennie gives me a resolute nod and starts creeping her way back to the rebels and the door. Meanwhile, I maneuver around, trying to get a glimpse of where the remaining Hounds could be, just as one pops up and fires. I know the caliber of my gun, and I know these desks are metal, but thin metal. I press the butt of my rifle to my shoulder and aim where I believe the man to be squatting. With a squeeze of the trigger, the report makes me blink, and I brace my body against the kickback. The bullet smashes through the side of one of the tables, ripping a hole hardly larger than it was round. The angry, muffled swearing that fills the ringing silence tells me exactly what I need to know.

I pull the pin on the flash bang, count to three, and throw it before dashing for the door. The bang is thunderous and the plume of smoke flowing out of the canister fills the room quickly. I don't have a lot of time.

Ahead of me, the metal door bangs open. No one else is in sight. Good. I'm about to rush after them when something snags the corner of my eye. Something I sorely needed to be reminded of but wish I could forget.

The Defect hooked to life support. Their chest shudders in little fits and the machine they're hooked to beeps, but that's the only sign they're still alive. If they're aware of what's going on, they don't let on. I could let the grenade do its work, but they're behind a wall and glass that is likely bulletproof. It would be a cruel death, and I've had enough of cruelty.

The press of the rifle against my shoulder feels like the weight of the world. I sight the person—General Courts's victim. The shudder of my breath sounds ragged in the crook of my arm. My finger shakes as I press it lightly against the trigger. I close my eyes as I pull it the rest of the way.

I barely hear the report. When I open my eyes, their head has turned away from me, and their life support signals to the room there's no life left to support. Tears sting my eyes, but I don't have time. There was barely any time for this, if I didn't fuck it all up already.

Yells push through the dissipating smoke. The sound of pounding footsteps tells me they're moving closer. I pull the grenade off my vest and pull the pin as I move closer to the door. I hold it a second longer than I should and throw it later than what is likely smart. It goes off feet from me, half a second before I can get the door closed all the way. The pop of the grenade burst is anticlimactic, but the screech of the Hounds coming after me is all the confirmation I need as I close the door the rest of the way and dash for the nearest sewer drain.

They knew who they were up against. If any of them survived, and it's likely at least one did, they'll be coming for us sooner rather than later.

19

No one waited for me. That was the plan. If they got out, they got gone. Heroes die for nothing when they're on our side of the line. Tiny glass bottles clink as I round a corner to the nearest sewer opening and make my way down. What I should have done is give Bennie or a rebel at least some of the antidote. I didn't even think of it. Now, I'm kicking myself for it. I'm sure they're kicking themselves too because they're empty-handed until I make my way back to Harvest.

Assuming I even do.

As I traverse a newly-carved route through the sewers, I know there's no reason I shouldn't. The Hounds meeting us in the lab was bad luck. The only forewarning they should have had was the bombs going off. Someone with two strategic brain cells to rub together would have realized, at the last minute, what we might have been after. That's assuming they wrestled that information out of Gabriel.

A lot of assumptions are being made, and it makes me anxious. Something isn't sitting right, but I can't quite put my finger on what.

As I turn a corner, following the subtle signs spray-painted on the walls, a boom knocks me into a wall before it snuffs my hearing, and the air gets sucked right out of my lungs. My head spins as I grope along the wall, my legs buckling no matter how hard I try to stand.

My muscle weakness wanes within seconds, my hearing roaring back in, until another boom goes off, closer this time. The heat of it sprays across my body. Smoke slides into the tunnel, slithering along the damp ground and wrapping around the edge of the wall like a hand. Over the ringing, the pounding of footsteps greets my ears.

They're down here. With me.

I have to run.

I stumble back the way I came, my body still working overtime to fix what the bombs hurt. The general wouldn't be so stupid to take out the entire sewer system just to spite us. Especially since he's moving forward with killing all of Harvest. There aren't enough people in Service to rebuild the infrastructure. No. This is a diversion. This is him knowing where we are and making damn sure we don't get to where we're going.

I don't have night vision, but I sure as shit don't want to turn on my pen light and draw unnecessary attention to myself. So, I move by memory, my hands out to keep me from thumping into walls. The way I see it, the way the side effects lay it out for me, is a sort of schematic. I follow its lines for as long as I can. That turns out to only be a couple turns before another bomb goes off, and I stumble into the wall. Something cold and wet leaks onto my ribs. Some of the antibiotic bottles just broke. If I don't get these to Harvest as soon as possible, I'm going to lose them all. Then what? The people we lost while we were up there died for nothing. The effort, for nothing.

I refuse to be nothing.

My first thought is to head to street level, but that feels too obvious. Smoke me out underground and drive me up. I'm about halfway home, somewhere between the southernmost section of University and the northern most edge of Harvest. The chances of Hounds or anyone else from The Compound waiting for me up top are far too high.

I keep running south, weaving my way through the tunnels and hope to the Sisters a bomb doesn't go off as I turn a corner. I'm off my main path, detouring around and going out of my way to avoid the more commonly traveled routes. As bombs go off, they pop my ears and rumble the walls, but they're far enough away that I can skirt them. Which tells me they know the path we travel, and that's where the bombs are. They also haven't outfitted the tunnels with any kind of surveillance, so they must be working off of timers. I wouldn't be surprised to find out the Hounds in the lab were cammed, which means they knew when I left and are likely basing the explosions on which point I should hit as I run.

Smart.

Just not smart enough.

Until I turn a corner and get blown back a dozen feet with the explosion of another nearby bomb. My ears ring, a high-pitched squeal that churns my stomach. The air whooshes out of my lungs as my back smashes into the ground, and I choke on the little air I can suck in. My bones ache. My flesh aches. I groan as I try to roll over, but my body screams. My insides feel like they've been pulverized.

My brain recovers long before my body starts to, and panic sets in. I have to move. Now.

The screaming pain quickly dulls to a rough ache. I move my hands down my body, feeling for any major wounds. More wetness soaks through my chest. As I slide my hands under my vest, I silently curse at more lost antibiotics. I'm not aware of any lab in Harvest that can replicate what I have left, but that doesn't mean it doesn't exist. If anyone would know, it would be Evan or a Sister.

"Report on street level," a deep voice commands.

Fuck!

My muscles still throb and my joints creak like I just aged twenty years from that blast. I pull myself to my feet as quietly as possible and stiffly shuffle on my way.

"Report underground east," that same voice says before he pauses. After a moment he says, "Report underground west."

They're moving in a phalanx both at street level and in the tunnels trying to blow us out. Fuck, I hate being right.

"Roger. Keep heading south," he says.

The sounds of their footsteps grow louder, and I try to match mine to theirs to hide my movement. Tunnels carry their sounds. They're not trying to be quiet. The bombs killed any element of surprise anyway. No, they want us to know they're coming. Like a fucking wrecking ball.

If I move too quickly, I run the risk of drawing their attention. They don't know how close I am or am not. It's clear the bombs are ahead of them, putting them any of a million points ahead of me. The fuckers have been busy. I'll give them that.

I can't tell how close they are to me, but I hear their mutters, the taps of their boots on the grimy cement. A handful of yards. The street team is likely within a few feet of them over their heads. From here, I can't tell how far out to either side they span, and it's not worth finding out. Assuming it's as far as they can go, trying to get behind them is out of the question. I have to get far enough ahead of them to get to street level without being spotted. I'm afraid if I stay underground, I'll lead them right to the safe house or inadvertently to another safe house I don't know about. Getting out of this rat maze is my best option.

I keep my ears tuned behind me and my eyes on the schematics my side effects project as I let this Defect intuition guide me home. My pace increases as their voices grow more distant. The booms of the explosions become less effective, meaning our paths are diverging.

By the time I'm only a handful of blocks from my safe house, I make the call to head to street level. If I'm judging right, I'm far enough ahead that I can scoot out from under them without being detected.

I hope.

Cold metal rungs press into my palms as I grip the ladder and climb. I press my ear against the cold iron of the manhole cover and wait, hoping I might be able to hear if the Hounds are nearby. All is quiet on the other side. Slowly, so incredibly slowly, I press my shoulder into the cover and slide it out of place. The crack is barely enough for me to see through, but enough for me to assess my surroundings. There's a building in front of me. To either side sit empty streets. Behind me, it's another building.

I quickly press my way through the sewer hole and settle the iron back into its place as quietly as I can. I'm somewhere on the east side of Harvest. The streets are quiet.

Too quiet.

My stomach twists with what that could mean, none of it good.

Nautical twilight settles over the sector, smudging everything a blue-gray that strains my eyes. It's little consolation knowing if I'm having a hard time seeing, so would anyone else. I stick close to walls, lingering under overhangs if I have to. Being out in the middle of the street, out in the open, is not a place for me to be. The air is charged, the lungs of the city holding its breath for something to happen. There's a snap coming, and quick. I don't think any of us are ready for it.

My heart is in my throat as I scan the streets and keep my eyes on rooftops and in seemingly empty windows. The Compound doesn't have the manpower, let alone the special operations unit of the Hounds, to station people in buildings for extended periods of time on a whim. It's not an effective use of their resources. That doesn't mean they won't do it.

I pass by a nearby sewer grate just as the low rumble of a bomb sounds from below. They're still marching south, which means I have to pick up my pace.

The dilapidated door of the safe house is a welcome sight, plain and unadorned, the building looking abandoned. I scoot around to the back of the building and tap the code onto the metal doors in the ground with my foot and wait.

And wait.

And wait.

I tap out the signal again. There should be someone posted nearby when people are out, someone waiting for a signal like mine to let people in. No one comes. The longer I'm standing in this overgrown yard, the more agitated I get. There are buildings all around me hemming the small yard in, but that's little reassurance. I have the cure, what's left of it, and The Compound is heading south. I don't know how far south they're going to go.

It's only a matter of time before the general realizes what I grabbed. When he does, he'll be on us in full force, assuming he isn't already. I don't know how long I was in the tunnels, but it wasn't brief.

After my fourth attempt at signaling, someone finally throws the lock back and creaks the door open. I don't recognize them, but their gaze is haggard and shellshocked. Their hair is a mess, and sweat glistens on their face.

"You Lottie?" they ask as they slowly blink and sway on their feet.

My hand darts out and catches their shoulder. They put their hand up and nod.

"I am. I have the antibiotic. How bad is it?" I ask, as I step down the stairs. I close the door behind me, locking it into place.

We're standing in a small carve-out under the house that leads into a longer tunnel that runs into the basement. It's lit with a lone, bare bulb halfway down the hall. The rebel motions me to follow them as they click the light off. Another light farther down the tunnel, well away from the door, beams in the darkness and guides us to relative safety.

"Three dead already." They look back over their shoulder at me, their eyes blazing. "All children so far. They keep going down, and they're not getting back up."

THE SMELL HITS ME BEFORE THE SIGHT, AND I DO MY BEST to hold back the gag clawing its way up my throat. I round a corner and come face to face with a triage unit, beds practically stacked on top of each other in this cramped basement room. The smell settles over everyone like a pall, nowhere to go except here. My stomach roils with it. The majority of the bodies in the beds are children, with a few older residents of Harvest mixed in. Those rushing around trying to help the sick don't look so great themselves, their skin sallow and sweat beading on their brows, much like my escort. At least they're on their feet.

"Oh, thank you," a Sister mutters as soon as she sees me and rushes over. "Please tell me you have the antibiotic.

My hands blindly find pockets as I stare into the sick room, pulling out tinkling boxes of glass one by one. One box is a total loss, every bottle smashed beyond salvage. One box I'm able to pull half a dozen bottles from it before tossing it in a nearby bin. The rest I hand over to the Sister in a heap.

Someone comes up behind her, someone I don't recognize and much more put together than the likes of the Harvest folks. From University, maybe. Judging by the way she picks up a bottle of the antibiotic and nods, muttering "this will do," I imagine she has more knowledge about it than I do.

Buried in a pocket on my leg is a handful of needles. It's likely not enough, but they can be sterilized between uses. I hand them to the Sister who hauls off after the University person, ready to start dispensing doses to the sick.

"Oh, thank fuck," a familiar voice utters before strong arms wrap around my neck and pull me close.

Bennie's familiar scent comes over me, and I nuzzle into her, reveling in the security of her arms for just a second. It feels safe here. Then the stench of the sickroom wafts over me, and I'm brought back to reality.

"I'm glad you got back. The rebels too?" I ask, as we pull apart.

Bennie nods. "You had me going there for a second. With how long it was taking you, I didn't think you were coming back."

She smiles as she says it, trying to make the dark thought light, but it doesn't reach her eyes. I know the feeling. It hurts my heart to let my mind linger on it for too long.

"I wasn't sure I was." I glance around the room and try to peek through the doorway, but I don't see him. "Has Jericho come back yet?"

"Yeah, I think I saw his team not too long ago." Bennie motions to the doorway I just looked through.

I grab her hand and guide her in that direction, talking as we move. "The Compound flanked me down there. That's what took me so long. I think those Hounds in the lab were miked or scoped or something. They knew it was us, and they tried to smoke me out of the tunnels."

Jericho's head finally comes into view, soot staining his cheeks, but my heart sings all the same. Before I can get to him and grab his attention, he looks in our direction and his eyes beam for the briefest moment before going serious again. I have haggard look on my face, I know. With Bennie in tow, I don't need to hold up a sign. I motion with my head in the direction I'm moving, toward our ever-evolving command center. He maneuvers his way through the crowd to meet me at our next doorway junction.

"Were things dicey for you on your way back?" I ask him, still holding strong to Bennie's hand. We move as one down a short hallway and to a tightly packed command center lined in screens.

"No, it was quiet. I assume you did, though," he responds.

I nod. I reiterate what I just told Bennie and let her fingers slide from my grip so I can point at a screen. "Street level and underground. They had bombs set up on our route and were trailing them south. They knew we hit the University lab and they followed us. Where they'll stop, I don't know. Assuming they even do. We need to round up all the Defects and set up a perimeter to head them off. Move the tank blockers into place to disrupt street flow before they get here, assuming we're not too late already."

"I hate that term," Jericho whispers, as he stares at the screens.

"What, Defects?" Bennie asks, a quirk to her lips. "What else should we be called? Evolved?" She puts up a finger, and her face goes indignant. "Oh, I know. Mutants. How about that?"

"Touché." A smile flutters at the corner of Jericho's mouth.

Under normal circumstances I'd ask him what's wrong, but all things considered it's a stupid question to ask. Literally everything is wrong. Everything is falling down around our ears, and we're barely capable of staunching the avalanche to stop it.

"How many do we have?" I ask, afraid of the answer.

"Fifty, maybe." Jericho sighs and looks at me. "Better than three." He glances at Bennie, and she shrugs. "I'll go alert Evan. He'll be able to round them up faster, assuming none of them abandoned their posts already."

"To go where?" Bennie asks. "Into the Wastes? Out onto the sea on a raft? There's nowhere to go. Our families can die here or they can die out there, but at least here is home."

Bennie's bottom lip quivers, and tears well on her lashes. She sniffs and furiously blinks them away. I thread my fingers back into hers. She gives me a tight squeeze before letting go and pulling her hand back.

"I don't think we have much time left either way," she says, as her gaze slides across the screens.

She's likely thinking what I am. There's a convergence coming. I saw it with The Compound today. It's only a matter of time before the gloves are all the way off, and we're in it up to our necks.

"So, let's try and fuck them up harder than they're going to fuck us, huh?" Bennie says with a rise of her eyebrow.

"Let's commence fucking then," Jericho says with a sly smile as he turns toward me.

His hand travels down my arm, lightly grazing my skin and sending the little hairs prickling. It's not a suggestive touch despite what he just said. Simply a reassuring one. A bit of levity nestled inside a catastrophe.

He disappears through a door, heading toward Evan to round up the rest of the Defects while Bennie and I lasso a crew together to set up road blocks. We enlist everyone who can manage. As long as they can haul things, light or heavy, they can help.

"How's your family?" I ask, as we leave a room of people shuffling around, getting ready to join us.

"Managing," Bennie says, as she guides me to a garage around the back of the building. "They're not as sick as a lot of others, but they're not great. They'll get rationed low doses of the antibiotic. Hopefully, it'll be enough."

She laughs and shakes her head as she pulls up the garage door. "My mother is ready to tear someone's head off, she's so angry. My dad tried reasoning with her, but now he's just as pissed. Puking and shitting his face off, but pissed all the same. He's ready to fight, even if it means just pushing some buttons."

"Sounds like you," I tell her with a smile. She hands me barrels that only those of us with mutated bodies would be able to lift.

That's the kind of resolve we need. This is an all-hands-on-deck moment. The Compound is coming for all of us, Defects or not. Bennie's tone is light when she speaks, but I'd be stupid to think she's ignoring the darkness descending on us.

A truck backs into the space in front of us, its tailgate down. It parks, and I start loading.

"Got it from somewhere. What about your folks? What do they

think about all of this?" she asks innocently enough, yet I flinch with the reminder of my parents.

They're not something I talk about often, but I guess she deserves to know.

"I imagine they're on Armand's side. They were all for me doing what I did for him. Until I started coping." I look at her as she hands me a pallet, and she nods. "Despite my proximity to power, the reputation I was gaining was unbecoming. So, to protect themselves, they distanced themselves from me."

"And if Armand falls?" she huffs as she hands me another barrel.

"Whoever's left standing, so long as that person meets their standards." I snort just thinking about it. "Don't expect them to cozy up to the likes of Evan. Too low." I whisper the last part, and we both smirk.

After my "death," I only spared a brief thought for my parents. I was growing to be a burden by association. They were likely relieved when they found out I was gone. I'm sure that turned to horror when they found out not only was I alive, but a rebel Defect who was trying to stage a coup. A part of me wants to go to them when this is all over and try to mend that bridge. The other can't be bothered. I was never a child to them. Just a pawn to be used to further their own ambitions.

"But seriously. We take the general out, then Armand, who's left? Who runs the city?" Bennie asks, as she hands me a giant knot of twisted steel.

"I'm not sure we've gotten that far," I say with a shrug. "I wouldn't put it past Evan to storm University and take the mayor's seat once everyone is out of the way. I think Armand technically has a lieutenant, but he's been the mayor for more than a decade. Pretty sure he and everyone else around him have been treating it as a lifetime appointment."

"What about us?" Bennie asks, a slight smile twitching her lips.

"Like you and me?" I motion between us with a frown, hoping she's not saying what I think she's saying.

Bennie lifts her eyebrows in a knowing look. "And Jericho. And

Evan. And representatives of The Compound and Service and University."

I wait for her to add Olympia, but she doesn't, letting the silence fall between us, punctuated only by scraping metal.

She must sense what I'm thinking because she adds, "Olympia could get absorbed into The Compound. Everyone else actually serves a function. They're just squatting on a hill siphoning resources. They can be put to work. Maybe reallocate some of *their* resources."

A chuckle bubbles up my throat and pours from my mouth. "I'm sure they'll love that."

Bennie shrugs and steps out of the garage before rolling the door back down. "Status quo hasn't worked for most of us. Time to change it."

Gabriel's words flicker through my mind, how we're all something to be used until we're dead. How we're all just waiting to die. A knot tightens in the back of my throat at the thought of him, at what he could be doing now. What someone could be doing *to* him. I shake it away the best I can. The people on Olympia don't care about him. Or me. Or Harvest. They care about themselves. I laugh at the idea of those rich fucks doing manual labor to earn their keep, but I know, deep down, Evan will drag them from their houses and chain them to machinery if he has to. Assuming he lets them live.

"You good?" the driver asks, peeking around the edge of the truck.

Bennie and I nod before we jump on the back bumper. The driver's side door slams. A couple seconds later we rumble forward, bumping over the curb and rolling down the street to our first blockade point. Other Defects should be waiting for us to unload and disperse.

It's hard to picture what Seven Hills will look like completely upended. The powers that be, be no more. Perhaps Armand's lieutenant will step in. Or maybe they'll be too afraid in the face of the rebel army. Once General Courts is gone, there might be someone under him willing to step into his shoes. Gabriel won't do it, and

Jaxon is dead. I don't know the people of that district well enough to know if there's anyone else willing or able. It's something I can ask Jericho. If there is another power play involved in The Compound, he would know about it.

The truck rumbles to a stop at the first drop point, and Bennie and I jump down and start unloading. As expected, fellow Defects greet us and grab barrels and knots of twisted metal and dash off, running at speed and carrying weight no normal human can. But there are only a couple dozen of us here. Jericho stands on the next block, pointing away from him and speaking to someone.

"Lottie and I will take West Ash to Lake. Remember, you don't have to completely block the street. The point is to slow the vehicles down. All this needs to be stretched as best we can. Got it?" Bennie speaks with authority, yet there's caring in her tone. She's firm but doesn't bark orders.

Without question people listen to her, grab what they can, and spread out. There's a knot of metal halfway back on the truck bed. I jump to the platform and grab it before jumping down again. I follow her lead, a natural position it feels like. I don't want to lead people. I've never lead people. Judging by the way Evan treats me, both when it's just us and around others, it'll be hard to undo any of that. Plus, very few people trust me for very good reasons. Bennie, though? She exudes trust and falls into a leadership role nicely. Same with Jericho.

I'd envy them if I didn't feel such relief that they're around to take on those roles.

We move quickly, placing pieces along each narrow block, working as if the Hounds are nipping at our heels. Which they are. I can feel their teeth. The air is thick with tension. There's an electricity pulsing around us, the coil wound taut. Something is going to break, and it's going to be soon. I have a feeling a lot of us aren't going to make it out unscathed.

21

IT'S JUST LIKE ANY OTHER MARK. ANY NUMBER OF TARGETS I've had over the years. Sure, they look human. They blink and breathe and walk. They bleed. But to me, they were never anything more than an objective. At least that's what I told myself as I shoved more Pixels up my nose and fucked until I went cross-eyed.

It's what I try to tell myself now as I line up my sight, aiming for the sweet spot between the armor and the helmet. The Hound's collar is up, and it's a tricky shot, but I've made worse. My breath shakes, and I exhale. Pixels would be the best and worst thing for me right now. I need my head on straight, but I also need my hand to stop shaking.

The barrel rests on top of the cement ledge, helping me steady the rifle. Each shift of my finger as I try to pull it against the trigger rattles the gun and causes me to shift. Fuck. I haven't been this nervous since I first started with Armand.

I would figure the truth serum side effects would calm my nerves, release whatever chemicals in my brain needed to be released in order to make this easier. As I learn with the side effects, the things it fixes are physical, not mental. It helped me sweat out my Pixel addiction in no time. The itch for it, the craving, the *need* still exists. It can't erase my memories of how it made me feel, nor my longing for those feelings.

Instead of making me numb, then euphoric, the side effects make me so much more aware. Vibrant. With that vibrant awareness comes the jitters. Like I'm wound too tight. I hate the feeling.

It's on me to take the first shot. At least then, everyone would know that would be one Hound down. One less person to have to battle against. All we need to do is make sure the Hound Defects die faster than they heal. A shot to the neck will certainly deliver that.

Doubt overwhelms me. Panic. Fear of an unknown future. Bennie's questions rattle around in my head. We stop The Compound, General Courts, and Armand. Then what? I'm not used to having answers. This shot will start the landslide of questions into the future.

This one single shot.

No. This is nothing like any of my other marks. Not even close.

My breath is loud cradled against the butt of my rifle. The air rasps against my face. It feels like an eternity has passed, but I know it's only been seconds. A scout alerted us to The Compound's movements a half hour ago. We scrambled to our positions, me atop a building with line of sight down the main avenue they're traversing. I've been here waiting for them to come into view—waiting to take this shot—ever since.

Jericho perches with me, farther down the roofline, acting as my backup. The second line once I take my shot. I duck, he fires, we trade, and on and on it will go until the bullets run out. I don't dare look at him. The encouragement, the eagerness, on his face urging me to take the shot is what I'm afraid to see.

Take the shot.

I set my finger on the trigger as the Hounds come closer. What armored vehicles they have left rumble down the road at a measured pace, infantry flanking the sides, monitoring places the people in the vehicles can't see. One big organism with dozens of eyes. I'm sure there's a phalanx underground too, wanting to cover as much ground as they can and catch any scattering rebels. They think they got us, but we're ready for them there too.

Slowly, I press the trigger, feeling it give under the pressure. Until the report echoes around the buildings and along the too-quiet street. Followed by another and another. The Hounds on the side of the vehicle hunker down while one falls to the ground under a spray of blood. A Hound *not* in my sight. The mount on the vehicle turns away from me and points toward a rooftop across the street.

Because it wasn't me who fired the shot. The butt didn't kick back into my shoulder. The report didn't snuff my hearing.

My brain scrambles as my finger lifts off the trigger without firing a shot. What the fuck do I do?

The percussive bang of the armor firing thunders in my chest, the feeling filling my heart to near bursting, the pressure in my chest expansive. I yank the barrel toward me and drop below the roof line. My back pressed to the concrete, I look toward Jericho and mouth, "what the fuck?"

Crouched down in a similar position, confusion ripples across his face. He shakes his head as a frown settles in. I peek over the edge of the roof just enough to see a pillar of smoke rising from the building across the street, and I curse whoever fired that fucking shot. More pops ring out, the *tap tap tap* of the gunfire flicks to an exposed nerve. Someone got fucking twitchy, and it may very well have cost us everything.

Jericho motions over the top of the concrete with his gun, his gaze firmly planted on me. We'll only have seconds to fire on them before they turn the big gun on us. I nod my confirmation. It's a risk we have to take. I move back into position, and Jericho repositions his crouch. The movement of the Hounds below us has stopped, the firefight raging. We don't have comms like the Hounds, so we make do with what we can see and guess the rest.

On three, we lurch our rifles over the cement. Jericho fires indiscriminately while I line the driver up in my sight and pull the trigger. No hesitation like I had before. I don't have the luxury. When the spray of blood splatters across the windshield, my sight finds the next available Hound. My finger presses on the trigger again. Someone else goes down. With the driver dead, whoever rides in the passenger seat takes a moment to get to the controls. We have at least thirty seconds before the turret turns toward us.

We pull back from the ledge, scurry to the other side of the roof, and brace. When the explosion hits, it knocks us on our asses, my teeth rattling. Jericho rests his hand on my arm. A trickle of blood snakes out of his nose, but his eyes blaze. I nod and sit up, staring at the gaping hole where I was just squatting, the building half a story shorter in that corner.

After a handful of seconds, the ringing in my ears stops, the ache from the blast fades, and my rapid healing sets in. I take a deep breath and compose myself, trying to slow my heart to something manageable, but adrenaline courses through my veins. It's unlike anything I ever felt working for Armand. Then, I was just dead inside. I'd compartmentalized everything. Now, I'm alive, thrumming with energy and ready to barrel through the Hounds' front line.

"We have to get away from this building," Jericho says and points behind me.

Stuffed under the cement overhang is a simple wooden plank. I'm nodding before I even look back at him. For a moment, my legs are wobbly, but I get them under me and hustle to our escape.

The gap between the buildings is too far to jump. We figured if we attacked from the roof, the Hounds would come up from the ground to meet us. Traversing the buildings is the best option to not have to dodge a bunch of bullets.

Lucky for us, the buildings in Harvest are packed in. The board is maybe twelve feet long and a half inch thick. I glance at Jericho when the thought settles in. *Will this thing support us?*

No time like the present. I wing it out and settle it over the ledges of our building and the one next to it. Jericho motions for me to go first, and I take a tentative step onto the wobbly wood. I move quickly and keep low, both to stabilize my center of gravity and make the smallest target possible for anyone who may be aiming at us from below.

The wood bounces under me, and I sway with it, the ground dropping farther away as I try to focus on it. Bad idea. I never considered myself afraid of heights, but as vertigo spins my head, I second guess that thought.

I breathe a sigh of relief when my boots hit solid ground, only to choke on my breath as I turn around to see Hounds swarming the rooftop.

"Jericho!" I scream, as I raise the rifle to my shoulder.

Someone at the back of the scrum fires first. My body drops to the ground, operating on autopilot. I pop up over the concrete edge the next second, finger on the trigger and pulling, trying to give Jericho enough cover so he can get across the board.

"I got you! Run!" I yell to him.

He tucks his rifle under his arm, in no position to try and fire and scramble across the board five stories up. I keep firing, my lone rifle hardly a match for the half-dozen currently pointed in our direction.

Jericho grunts and jerks forward, the board wobbling under him. I screech and grab the end of the board to stabilize it. He's only a few feet out. He can make it. He looks at me, pain swimming in his eyes, and grunts again as he jerks forward. This time I see the spray of the entry wound. My eyes go red. His throat bobs as he shuffles forward at a snail's pace, trying to stay upright and not lose consciousness.

I swing my rifle up and fire blindly, half-heartedly aiming for legs and arms and faces and anywhere else that isn't covered in armored kit. When Jericho is within reach, I stop shooting and whip my hand out. He reaches for me just as a bullet grazes my shoulder. I hiss against the pain just in time for a bullet to land its mark in my flesh, throwing me back and away from Jericho.

I see nothing but him. I lunge forward again, grab his arm, and feel his fingers wrap around mine. With one good yank, I pull him the rest of the way across the board and into me. We tumble to the ground while bullets whizz past us, only for me to sit back up without thinking and yank the board back to us, away from the Hounds.

We don't have long. They'll report our position and call for backup if they haven't already. All of the grenades and bombs and flash bangs are on the ground, scattered across the lower half of Seven Hills. Roof perches only have rifles. It's not the smartest move, but with limited supply, we didn't have much of a choice.

Jericho and I lie tangled together as sweat beads on my forehead. My muscles twitch and pain shoots through my torso as my healing kicks in. Clothes scrape against my body as Jericho painfully bends and grabs something from his leg. A blade flashes in front of me as bullets keep winging by. A bead of sweat drops off his face and lands on my lip. My tongue licks the spot where it drops without thought. Without care.

"Dig them out before I heal with those fucking bullets in." He motions to my own wound. "I'll do your shoulder next."

I look behind us to find the brick-fronted stairwell leading into the building, and I point with the knife he just handed me. On a silent *three* we scramble to a crouch and shuffle behind the more fortified wall, bullets pinging past our ears as voices yell and scream over the clamor.

Jericho leans his good side into the wall as he shimmies out of his gear and exposes a bloodied mess of body and shirt. I rip away the fabric to find the holes closing quickly. Flesh knits back together before my eyes. My hand shakes as I raise the tip of the knife to his skin.

"Now, Lottie. Do it quick," he grits out through clenched teeth.

I know I have to move faster. At the rate I'm going, he's going to have to slice all the way through me to get to the bullet, but the thought of tearing through Jericho's flesh turns my stomach. A bullet pings off a brick just over our heads and we both jerk into each other.

With a deep breath and as steady of a hand as I can get, I plunge the blade into Jericho's back. A stifled moan escapes him. His body tries to jerk away from me, but he holds himself steady, knowing he has to stay still. Tears bead on my lashes as I continue to dig through him, his grunts and whimpers of pain louder than the bombs and bullets flying around us.

Then I feel it. The delicate *tink* of metal on metal as the knife comes in contact with the bullet. Jericho gasps as I push in, scraping the blade against his skin before finally dislodging the wounding metal. Sweat glistens on the side of his face I can see and down his neck. He lets out a rush of air as he leans his head against the brick.

My stomach unclenches as I rest back on my feet until he pulls himself up and looks at me from the corner of his eye.

"One more. Hurry up," he demands.

I can't help but bristle at the order. The command. An involuntary kick of defiance built into my DNA. Of course I ignore it. I'm faster this time, and steadier, if not less nauseous at rooting around in Jericho's back for a bullet with a knife blade. The first bullet felt like an eternity. This one I can at least cut that eternity in half. As I work, there's a lull in the firefight. Echoing voices carry up the stairwell we're leaning against, bouncing around brick and metal.

This bullet is a little more stubborn, but I'm still able to pop it out faster than the first. Jericho lets out a shudder and swipes his hand across his sweaty face before he turns around and yanks the knife from me. He twirls the blade around, and I obey without words, showing him my back as I pull my gear away from the wound.

A muttered curse hits my ears when he finishes tearing through the fabric. "This is going to hurt, Lottie. I'm sorry." As if he's the one who shot me. As if the bullet is his fault.

I only nod and wrap my arms around my legs as Jericho drives the blade into my shoulder. A shriek escapes my mouth before I slap my hand over my lips to stifle it. Not like anyone would hear much of anything through the turmoil around us.

Pain blossoms across my shoulder, my chest, down my back as the blade digs into my flesh, scrapes across bone, and finally bursts with the released pressure of a bullet squatting in my body. A wave of cold sweat washes over me, a shudder wracking me as the release fades. He places a warm hand on my arm as I take deep breaths.

When all is said and done, it's only been a couple of minutes since I pulled the board back from the Hounds chasing us. It's too much time as the voices in the stairwell grow closer. I look back at Jericho as I reach for my rifle. He nods as he grabs his. The Hounds in the other building, the few left, have hunkered down in the corner we vacated, ready and waiting for us to show our faces again. Or wait for their comrades to storm in and take us out themselves.

Flesh and muscle and veins knit back together, revving my body temperature high while lighting my resolve on fire. I shoulder my rifle, ready my finger on the trigger, and peek through a gap in the brick to find my shot. When I have it marked, I pop up from my crouched position and fire before dropping back to the ground, the lurching of the Hound's head as my bullet throws it back imprinted in my mind.

Jericho takes one shot, then another, as I creep around the wall and take my second. Another shot to the neck. His fire keeps drawing the Hounds to him, giving me the chance to take the clean hits we need to neutralize this group before we're attacked by the second one coming up the stairs.

Just as I'm about to take my third shot, the corner I'm aiming at explodes in a plume of dust and debris. Chunks of cement and brick patter around us as we cover our heads with our arms to avoid a hard hit. My hands and arms take a beating, but it doesn't last long.

When the noise of the war from below comes roaring back, I peek around the brick to find the corner of the building, and the Hounds that were there, gone. Jericho and I look at each other, his face mirroring my own confusion.

"I think we captured the vehicle from the Hounds," Jericho says.

I nod just as feet pound up the final set of stairs, ready to pounce on our rooftop sanctuary.

I motion to the edge of the roof with my head, urging Jericho to check that out while I take care of the rooftop door. He nods and presses a hand into my knee, using my leg to help him stand before he crouch-runs to the edge of the building. I slide around to the door, grab a shard of cement, and jam it under the heavy steel just as someone slams into the other side, wedging the door onto the cement block. Thankfully the steel door is thick. There aren't too many bullets in Seven Hills that could pierce metal this thick, but I scramble to the door and press into it all the same, jamming it as much as I can.

But the Hounds on the other side are also Defects, and there are more of them. I don't know the extent of what General Courts's soldier serum can do, but I'm only one. My strength peaked weeks ago. It's something to behold, but the armada on the other side of the door manages to crack it open with each ramming hit on the other side.

A panicked cry tumbles out of my mouth as a hand comes through. I dig my boots in and shove myself against the door and the hand. The door grinds through flesh and bone, the sickening squelch and pained animal cries coming from a human mouth are something I will never be able to unhear, before the hand lands with a wet thump at my feet.

In my periphery, Jericho scrambles to the battered corner of our building and grabs the plank before rushing to me.

"C'mon," he says, as he grabs my hand and tries to yank me away from the door.

He rears back into me when I don't budge. I motion to the struggle I'm currently going through. "What about—"

"Now! We don't have time!" He yanks me away from the door.

He keeps hold of my wrist as we run to the far side of the building. I glance over my shoulder and watch the cement wedge hold for a few more hits before a kitted-out Hound barges through the door, stepping on the severed hand in the process.

"Go!" Jericho yells as he points to the laid-out plank between our building and the one directly south of us.

I clock the Hound running for us as I climb onto the plank and shuffle across as quickly as I can, Jericho at my heels. Just as we jump onto the other building and pull the plant back, the rooftop of the building we just left explodes in a plume of smoke and grit. The blast launches at least one Hound close enough to the edge of the roof that they go flying over it, their screams snuffed out by the blast.

"The rebels are covering us. Let's go," Jericho says. He takes the board and heads to the south side of the building for our next traverse.

I walk half-backwards as I stare at the ruins. The roof where we were just standing is gone, a handrail and some stairs visible through the gnarled bones of the building.

"Lottie." I spin around to face Jericho, my eyes wide. I stumble to a halt just out of arm's reach. "We've taken the block." A smile flickers at the corners of his mouth as he reaches a hand out. "Come on."

Relief, all-consuming but fleeting, falls over me like a wave, and I take his hand. We'll have to rendezvous with the others, see what their situation is like. This one, for the moment at least, is stable.

I take Jericho's hand and we traverse another rooftop, and another, making our way south to the rendezvous point.

22

WITHOUT OUR INTELLIGENCE NETWORK, KNOWING WHAT the Hounds are doing is impossible. Knowing what Gabriel is doing —if he's even still alive—is impossible. We took heavy losses, which doesn't surprise me. The Hounds were able to gain ground across multiple blocks before we hit them with all the firepower we had left. It leveled multiple buildings and destroyed peoples' homes. Luckily, we'd already evacuated those areas, but the ache is still there. A handful of blocks away, people scramble across the street, bags in hand. Someone holds a child as they run away from the encroaching war.

It's clear when we get to the rendezvous just how much our numbers dwindled, but so have theirs. All manner of bodies litter the streets. We've pulled our dead back to send them off appropriately. No one has come to collect the dead Hounds, and we're not going to touch those. Maybe the stink alone, and the signs of carnage, will deter any additional forces.

Once the fighting quiets down and the smoke dissipates, we pull the Defects back. Getting barraged and not allowing our bodies to heal will only make us as dead as everyone else. Mandatory rest. Get cleaned up. There are sentries posted above and below the streets as watch and runners waiting to get the message across. It's all we can do to keep fighting and not get exhausted and obliterated into submission.

I sit on the edge of my bed in a room that, for the moment, is mine until we have to move again. We're running out of places to relocate, and the Hounds are making returning to old buildings impossible as they blow through them. At least the sick are reviving. The antibiotic is working, for the most part. There wasn't enough to go around, and some were too sick to save. The death toll climbed higher before it leveled out. Those strong enough, those willing, revived with a resolve to beat the general. To push the Hounds back and tell The Compound and Olympia and University that they're worth life too, even if it means others have to die to make room.

I press the heel of my hand into my eyes and rub the images away. My brain is too tired to make sense of their logic, or what we're facing. It's not logical. It doesn't make sense. If it's us or them, we're going to save ourselves first because no one else will do it.

My soiled shirt sticks to my body and sends shudders across my skin as I peel it away. Dirt, blood, debris, and sweat all mingle into the threads, creating something that I'm not sure a good washing would even fix.

Leadened limbs don't even feel like my own. I see them moving, but there's a detachment between me and them. The weight of the world presses everything into me. I knew we weren't going to be able to save everyone, but the death toll still hurts all the same.

A gentle knock lands on my door. It's an effort to pull myself to my feet. Little pinches and pulls itch under my skin as my body heals itself at a rapid pace, draining whatever energy I have left. My stomach rumbles, and I press a hand to it, the adrenaline dump making room for feelings like hunger.

The door opens without a sound. Jericho stands on the other side, blood sprayed across his face, soot and ash streaked across his shaved head, and his shirt shredded and barely hanging on. He looks at me, his eyes roving up and down my body, before a smile twitches at the corner of his lips.

"Is that what I look like?" he asks, his tone light.

I can't help the inkling of happiness clawing its way across my mouth. "Yeah."

I step aside and let him in before I close the door behind him. I motion to the bathroom and say, "I was going to take a shower. Maybe I'll feel more human after that. How's your shoulder?"

He moves it around and shifts his head from side to side. "Pretty much healed. The rest of me, not so much. I wanted to see how you were doing."

I snort and shrug. "Ruined. A shower probably won't fix that, but at least I won't be covered in grime."

A knot forms at the base of my throat, an ache blooming around it as tears build behind my eyes. Without a word, Jericho steps toward me and wraps his arms around my body, the warmth of him an enveloping comfort that I sorely need.

With rapid blinks, I push back the tears, but my gasping breath still gives me away. Not like I need to hide anything from him. I never have. It feels like an out of body experience, as if the me feeling these things is different from the person I'm looking at in the mirror.

I haven't felt this deeply in years.

It's a dawning realization that's so sudden and so true it pushes a gasp from my lips. Jericho holds me tighter, his arms a welcoming embrace against the onslaught of emotions I'm wading through.

Drug free has not been a state for me for just as long. The two things, I'm sure, are intrinsically linked. For so many years I've been numb, unfeeling and uncaring. I had to in order to protect myself from what I was doing. I didn't have a choice if I didn't want to die at thirty by my own hand.

Now, the serum side effects, and all the consequences they brought before, shoved my crutches aside and forced me to stand on my own two feet. It's terrifying. It almost makes me yearn for the drugs and the sex again, just so I can escape the torment of my own mind. These images of Gabriel. The rebels being shot dead. The torture under University. My feelings for Jericho. It's too much, and I feel like I'm going to break under the weight of them.

Without a word, Jericho steps back, my hand in his, and leads me to the bathroom. The shower is a plain box encased by glass walls.

He turns on the overhead and lets the water heat, then steps up to me. He slides his hands under my shirt, toying with the hem as he presses his nose to the side of my head, a gentle nudge, and breathes lightly.

"Let me take care of you. Just this once," he whispers.

Just this once. Because I know nothing other than taking care of myself and pushing everyone away. All I can do is nod as he slides his hands up my body, pushing the fabric with it. He tosses my ruined top onto the floor and makes slow work removing my pants one leg at a time, supporting each leg as he steps me out of my clothes.

The subtlety of the gesture, the kindness of it, nearly buckles my knees, but I press my fingers into his shoulder to stay standing. He doesn't wait for me to return the favor, instead pulling his clothes off far faster than he did mine. My fingers trace along the ridges of his stomach, the etched lines of his muscles. All I want in this moment is his nearness.

He takes my hand and guides me into the shower, the steaming water a wincing balm on my skin, the heat of it cleansing. I reach for the soap, but he snatches it out of the holder faster than I can get to it.

"Let me do this," he says, his gaze hypnotizing.

Suds fill his hands as he rubs the bar between his palms. When he's done, he places it back in the holder and runs his fingers along my shaved scalp, grinding the tips in to massage my worries away. The rhythmic rub of his hands forces my eyes to close, and I press into him drunkenly. We both laugh, light and languid as he soaps my head into a froth before getting to work on my arms, my shoulders, my torso, my legs.

I wince when he hits the still fresh, albeit healing, wound on my shoulder. A finger brushes across the knitting flesh before his lips press to my skin, making the pain go away instantly. Heat rushes to my core and the familiar willingness grows as Jericho cleans every crevice, every inch of my body, washing away not just this day, but these weeks, these months. Making me forget, at least for now, everything but him.

Once the suds are little more than bubbles circling the drain, I grab the soap and return the favor, running my hands along the planes of his stomach, the taut flesh across his chest, the blades of his shoulders. I try to reach his scalp, but unless he crouches, it's not going to happen. We laugh trying, me standing on my toes and failing to return the thorough massage he gave me.

When all is said and done, our bodies free from the leavings of the day, Jericho trails his finger along my collarbone, following drips of water down my arm, across my ribs, and along my hip. With the day washed away, the terror behind us for the moment, desire wends its way through. Constantly hidden under worry and anxiety and pain, it sees an inch and takes a mile as my nerves spark to life under Jericho's grazing touch.

His growing desire pushes against my leg, needy and wanting, as I touch every inch of him, committing his flesh to memory because tomorrow . . . tomorrow is another day best left to the future.

Fingers trail down my stomach, brush across the short tuft of hair between my legs, and graze along my slit, teasing and tantalizing. His touch plays among my folds, probing deeper until he finds the little bud hidden within, waiting to be struck like a match. A gasp escapes my lips as he rubs a finger along it, brushing and caressing my need to the surface. I shift my legs apart, a not-so-subtle nudge for him to probe deeper, and he receives my signal loud and clear.

Jericho dips his lips to mine and brushes feather-light kisses along my skin, his tongue teasing at my flesh as his fingers sink lower. Lower. Lower. A digit circles my opening and I try, and fail, to hold back a whimper. I grab hold of his hard length, the water creating a slick for my hand to slide along his shaft in smooth, firm strokes.

Cold presses into my back before I realize I'm against the wall. Jericho stands over me as he continues to tease my opening, forcing my hips to buck higher and higher to grab his fingers. Finally, he grants my silent wish and plunges one finger inside me, then another. I gasp at the penetration, my head hitting the wall as my mouth opens and moans roll across my tongue.

He moves his fingers inside me, the delicious movement stoking waves of pleasure across my body. The squelch of my juices scream my readiness for more of him and drives me deeper into a lust-filled haze. I rub my thumb along his tip, the telltale drip of pre-cum a thick slick against the water telling me he's ready too as he sighs against my neck before nipping my skin with his teeth.

I rest my leg on his hip, angling myself so he can plunge deeper. With this cock in my hand, I stroke him closer to me. He slides his fingers out and places his hand over mine to guide himself to my entrance. Seated and ready, I slide easily onto his head, my body stretching to take him as he controls his thrusts, my body lowering onto him inch by inch.

Water pelts against his back and head, splashing onto my face. I barely notice it, and I certainly don't care as my other foot leaves the ground and Jericho takes my weight entirely. With one hand pressed to the wall and the other on my hip, my hands dig into his neck. We writhe as one being, a crashing wave of desire as he gently moves within me. A slow and steady rhythm builds my lust deep inside of me, ensuring an eventual explosion.

Our moans curl around each other, twist and knot together, growing harder and fiercer as Jericho drives into me. His slow, sensual rhythm dissolves into something frenetic and eager, and I take every inch of him.

His mouth finds a nipple, and I press his head to me, water hitting my lips as I cry out with each flick of his tongue. My legs squeeze tighter around him as he plunges deeper. Harder. His grip on my hip is bruising, but I arch into him, matching him thrust for thrust as he drives me to my peak.

When the bloom grows, heat floods my ears and my vision goes spotty. I hold onto his neck and seat him as deep as he can go, riding him until my world explodes. The orgasm takes me over, a firework display of pleasure running through my veins as I cry out, gasping for release as my body throbs. His arms tighten painfully until he goes rigid. I feel the pulse of his cock inside me, the jets of him filling me as he comes to his own finish.

We stand there for a moment, knotted together as our bodies come down from our frenzied fuck. He breathes into the crook of my neck, and I gasp into the open shower, holding him to me as if he'll float away if I don't. Before long, my feet touch the tile again, and Jericho reaches behind him to turn off the water. He grabs the towels from the hooks and wraps one around me before taking one for himself.

He scrubs the fabric across his head as I revel at the pulse of my fading orgasm, wishing I could hold onto this moment forever. But I know tomorrow is an inevitability, and this moment is fleeting. We have work to do despite our desires, and I curse the world I was born into. It's the world I have, and after we fuck, we have to unfuck the city falling around our ears.

Jericho reaches out and grazes a thumb along my jaw as he says, "We have a few more hours before we have to head back."

I nod and press my cheek into his hand. Now it's my turn to grab his fingers and lead him from the shower and to my bed, just big enough to fit us both. He smiles as he leans down and presses his lips to mine. A startled screech rips from my mouth as he wraps his arms around me and twirls while yanking me on top of him, the two of us falling to the bed in a heap.

A stolen moment of bliss before we're required to remember that reality waits for us just on the other side of the door. For right now, I welcome Jericho's wandering hands and the softness of his skin against mine as we pretend, just for a little while, that we're back home in our flat and the world isn't falling apart.

23

I SLEEP SO LITTLE NOW THAT I BARELY DREAM, SO IT TAKES me a moment to realize my vision is hazy and the world isn't operating in any way that makes sense. The street I'm standing on is dead quiet. Not a person around. A light flick of smoke tickles my nose as a haze lingers just over the ground. The quiet pop of gunfire echoes in the background. I whip my head around to try and pinpoint where it's coming from. The crunch of my boots against the ground is thunderous in this dead world as I make my way toward the noise.

My dreams used to be about the Wastes, about being consumed by the unknown. I guess that did happen, having to fake my own death and drop into an underground world I knew nothing about, and where I'm only grudgingly tolerated. Now, they're about the end of everything, not just me. The slaughter of Harvest, the death of my friends, and of everyone I've come to love.

I brace myself as I turn a corner and see a familiar sight. A row of people on their knees, Jericho and Bennie included, perched in front of a line of armed Hounds. Gabriel stands at the end, his helmet off, gun aimed at Jericho.

The former Hounds are all thinner, their cheeks sunken without access to The Compound's abundance of food. Gabriel included, because his body is destroying itself. A scream rips up my throat, the sound distorted as it leaves my mouth. No one looks in my direction.

Instead, the Hounds' guns fire, and my friends fall. General Courts appears behind Gabriel, a gun aimed at the back of his head. My lover's head snaps forward before his body crumples to the ground after the general pulls the trigger.

In front of me, like a ghost from my past, Armand blips into existence, the barrel of his gun pointed at my head, and pulls the trigger. I clock the tiny explosion of the bullet as the gun fires, then a gasp as I sit up in bed, my heart hammering and my breaths coming in staccato bursts. I press my hand to my chest, trying to quiet the thudding, when a telltale pop echoes through the building.

I shake my head and sit up straighter, wondering if I'm still hearing things from my dreams.

Pop pop pop.

A scream.

I shove at Jericho as more gunfire goes off. His eyes snap open then settle, the tiredness there winning for the moment.

"They're in the building!" I whisper harshly just as more gunshots echo through the hallways.

Whatever sleep still lingers in his bones disappears as he pulls himself off the bed. We dress quickly and quietly, my blood thrumming as I listen for the Hounds' movement through the building. At some point, Jericho left the room, and I only realize he's gone when he returns holding my rifle. He lobs it at me, and I catch it, take the safety off, and chamber a bullet. Rifles aren't going to be the best for such tight quarters, but if worse comes to worst, I can beat the shit out of someone with it.

A lightbulb goes off in my head when I remember the small sidearm I stuck in a drawer when we first relocated to this building. I rush to the dresser and yank it out, thankful for something smaller. I drop the magazine to check the bullets. Twelve with no additional. It'll have to be enough.

"Where's your family? And Bennie's?" I ask him, as we ready our firearms and keep our eyes on the door.

Jericho shakes his head, not looking at me. "I don't know. I told them to keep moving in case . . ."

His throat bobs as he swallows. He doesn't need to voice what he was going to say. In case he gets captured or killed. The Compound at least won't be able to get their families.

"I have a way of finding out, but that way isn't happening right now," he says.

I keep my rifle on the door and look over my shoulder. There's a fire escape outside the window that'll lead us to an interior courtyard where we can access an alley exit, but the chances of someone waiting on the ground for us is high. The chances of someone already being on the roof, or scoping the roof at minimum, are also high considering our last run-in with the Hounds. That makes a window exit out of the question.

"Do we go to them?" I ask him, my mind running a mile a minute as I try to figure out our best options.

I want to save people from whatever fuckery they're being hit with, but that won't happen if I take a chest full of bullets.

Jericho shakes his head. "Let them come to us. They can only get through that door one at a time. This is the one place we have an advantage."

So we perch, me behind a decaying island aiming my rifle around neck- and head-height, and Jericho in a far door on the other side of what used to be a living room, keeping a piece of the wall between him and a direct line of fire.

Waiting is a torment. Each rumbling bash of a door, every gunshot, sends my nerves screaming. No matter how many there are or how loud they get, my body flinches without my permission. Tears well in the corners of my eyes, and I rapidly blink them away. Scream after scream has my muscles vibrating. A piece of my soul withers away as the Hounds onslaught continues, and we stay here.

I keep telling myself *we're no good to anyone dead we're no good to anyone dead we're no good to anyone dead.*

It doesn't help.

Another *boom* reverberates through the walls followed by panicked, fear-filled voices, then more gunfire. I flinch with each shot. The silence that follows is a hand pressing down on my head, harder and harder and harder, until I feel like I can barely stand anymore. The general knows we got the antibiotic, and he's correcting the error bullet by bullet. The only thing I know for certain is their manpower is dwindling. We're a tightly controlled population to begin with. The general doesn't have bodies to spare. Unless they're Harvest bodies, of course. If the Hounds are moving building to building, it'll be a slow traverse. They won't be able to leave people behind to monitor in case anyone circles back.

My thoughts won't bring anyone back to life, though.

Boots land heavy on the other side of the door. I grip my rifle tighter, finger on the trigger ready to pull. For a moment everything goes silent, the world holding its breath. Waiting. Then the door bursts open in a spray of dry wood and metal as the knob goes flying, leaving behind the battering ram at its back.

My aim is careful and quick, making fast work of the Hounds scurrying to get inside. The person with the battering ram crouches out of the way as the attack team moves forward. My finger pulls the trigger. The first person drops before they spot us. As the second raises their rifle, barrel pointed right at me, Jericho removes them from the equation.

Only two more come barreling in behind them, rifles up and ready. Before either of us can get another shot fired, a familiar crackling voice fills the space.

"Fire one more shot, and I'll burn the building to the ground."

I freeze.

It's only then I hear the thumping on the roof, boot steps pounding above our heads. Metal creaks from the bedroom, followed by grunting and shuffling through a window. They're coming in from the fire escape, just like I suspected.

"With your own people in it?" I say back, not sure who I'm supposed to be speaking to.

It's the general's voice, but the speaker is invisible. I assume someone is miked with audio and visual.

"They'll be fine," he says, the haughty tone thick in his voice.

I know it's not him behind the kit on the Hound in front of me, but I want to slap them all the same.

"Put your guns down and step forward," the general says.

Jericho catches my eye and I frown, shrugging. What the hell am I supposed to do with this? We're surrounded, but both of us are injury free. Clearly the general wants us alive, but why?

"We're not interested in being part of your experiment," Jericho says, keeping his finger on his trigger and his gun up.

I'm still at the ready, but I'm not sighting anymore. Instead, I'm taking in my surroundings. There are at least eight Hounds in the room with us, all in full kit, all armed to the teeth. It's us they've been looking for. Everyone else just got in the way.

"You mean the one you blew up? Don't worry. You won't be. You're both more hassle than you're worth. Same with your friend. Aren't you?"

Sounds of a struggle erupt from the hidden speaker, followed by labored breathing and someone swallowing.

"Kill them all, Lottie!" Bennie screeches, her voice tinny and distant through the speaker before she screams. Her voice muffles, and the sounds of flesh taking hits rings through the speaker. Bennie yells a couple more times before her cries dissolve to whimpers.

I glance at Jericho. His jaw clenches, the muscles flexing. Tears pool on my lashes as I look back at the Hounds. My spine straightens and my arms lower my gun, no thought required. Confusion and panic flicker across Jericho's face as he looks at me and lowers his gun too. Someone snatches them out of our hands, but I don't clock who. I don't care. The general has Bennie. Somehow, he has Bennie, and I will do whatever I can to get her back.

"What was that you wanted to say?" the general prods.

I can only assume he's talking to Bennie.

"Don't fucking listen," she gasps. A clearing throat and a juicy spit is right behind her words.

A heavy object comes down against meat, Bennie's meat, and I wince at her yell. They don't stop.

A low chuckle flows through the microphone. “Yes, Lottie. Listen to me. You will obey every order my team gives you. You will not fight them. You will not try to escape. If you do, you and everyone you even considered a thought of caring for will die.”

“Stop beating her,” I mutter through clenched teeth. “Stop it!”

“Don’t worry, Charlotte,” the general sighs through the microphone. “She’s alive. Some people are just harder to train. You learn quite easily, don’t you?”

This is a game to him. One he must win at any cost. One he firmly believes he will win. The more he takes away from me, the less I have left to lose. He forgets that. I haven’t lost Bennie yet. I won’t lose her. I won’t lose.

I’m tired of General Courts’s threats. Say something so grandiose, so absurd, so often and the message gets watered down. Yeah, I know he’ll kill everyone. He’s said that a thousand times already. Shit or get off the pot.

Just not before we get Bennie. I put my hands up. Jericho does the same. Hounds snatch our wrists and pull them behind our backs before ratcheting them down tight to the point of cutting off circulation. I start to say something but know they won’t care. I wonder if they think these cuffs will hold us or if the threat of killing Bennie will be enough to keep us in line until a Hound comes at me with a thick beeping collar.

“The fuck is that?” I ask, moving backward on instinct, only to hit a solid wall of Hound behind me.

“A fucking muzzle,” the Hound says, their voice low and obscured by their helmet.

They lurch forward and the collar jams into my throat, pins I didn’t see pushing into my skin, puncturing my flesh. As soon as it’s fastened at the base of my skull, it clicks to life. The telltale hum of tech warns me before even more piercings punch through my skin, circling my neck as I gasp and wince at the pain. When warmth floods my veins and my knees grow weak, I know exactly what this fucking thing is.

I've had this shit before.

It's only a matter of seconds before my head hangs heavy, but I lift it enough to see Jericho in much the same position, whatever the fuck this shit is pumping through his body and keeping him weak. The general ran it through the Defects he tortured to keep them from healing. He ran it through me to make sure I stayed down when Gabriel captured me.

It's poison, whatever it is, and it's working. Hopefully not good enough for us to concoct something. Some kind of plan to get us out of this. If my dreams are any indication, this isn't going to end well. In fact, it may very well be the end.

The only thing we have going for us, the only element of surprise, is our contingency plan. If we get captured—me, Jericho, and Bennie specifically—Evan and his rebels are to burn everything to the ground. Go hog fucking wild. Save us, if he can, but I'm not putting my money on that.

The poison beats us up from the inside. As they jostle us out of the apartment and out of the building, each hit feels like a strike with fists and pipes and anything blunt someone can get their hands on. It's an ache deep into my marrow. The last time I had this shit, I thought it was just because Jaxon and Kai beat the shit out of me, and it stopped me from healing. No. This shit throws its own punches and they feel like steel.

There's an MRAP waiting for us on the street, and we're thrown into the back, our backs touching. My fingers brush against Jericho's and they intertwine. Pinkies and ring fingers twisting up, unwilling to let go. I lean my head against his upper back, and he rests his head on mine, our bodies spent with nothing more than injections.

It's only been months since the side effects mutations, but I grew to feel rather invincible over that time. Now that's being beaten out of me.

Fuck the general.

Fuck Armand.

I hope that's where we're being brought. If they knew what was good for them, they should have followed through on a kill-on-sight order. But the general has an ego, and Armand likes to patronize. It's too good of an opportunity to pass up. Plus, we'd make good bodies to use as an example.

No. We're being brought right to them, and fuck it all, I will fight with every last breath in my lungs or die trying.

24

IT'S A FAMILIAR SIGHT, THE UNDERGROUND LEVELS OF The Compound. A perpetual dampness clings to the air, settling cold into my bones. Gray ceiling tiles loom overhead, some broken, others water-stained. The floor looks damp, slick with some kind of residue, but as we're marched down the hallway, our boots tap dry tile.

My eyelids hover heavily over my eyes, and it takes far more effort than I care to admit to keep them open. My body is working overtime trying to heal itself from whatever I'm being injected with, and it's losing.

Jericho's feet snag on each other, and he stumbles, bumping into the wall. The Hounds holding him up snap to attention, jostling him as they try to stabilize him on feet that don't want to cooperate. We keep moving the entire time, a death march to a future we will never see.

My mind whirs, trying to comprehend my surroundings. Trying to think at least one step ahead, but I can barely walk, let alone think. This shit is muddling my head. The Hounds with Jericho step in front of one door as me and my entourage keep walking. Not to the room next door, but a couple doors down. So we can't yell to each other, maybe? Not like I can even open my mouth for how heavy my jaw feels.

A scream rips through the corridor. I flinch, the first real feeling other than pain I've felt since the apartment. Another scream, and another. Bennie's face flashes through my mind. A groan wends its way up my throat. We came. He can't hurt her anymore. That was the deal. I try to form the words, forcing my lips into shapes other than a flat line, but it doesn't work.

Tears prickle at the corners of my eyes and track tickling trails down my cheeks. I can't escape the thoughts forcing their way to the front of my drug-scarred mind. That our attempt to save Bennie just gets us all killed. To not take that risk meant we would have likely heard her execution through the Hounds' audio system. The general certainly wasn't shy about reminding us her life is fragile. At least with this, there was a chance. A slim one, but still a chance.

A hand at the back of my neck pushes me forward. I fall limply onto a steel table with a resounding crash. Pain barely registers. It pales in comparison to what I'm already feeling thanks to the drug.

Someone fists the back of my shirt and slides me up the table before breaking my wrist cuffs and roughly flipping me over. For a second, a brief, terrifying second, I think I'm about to lose my clothes. That *this* is the kind of torture the general has in store for me. Not medical. Violation of another kind. When everything remains in place and the Hounds grab my arms and strap me to the table, I breathe a small sigh of relief. At least for now my clothes will remain on.

With my wrists, ankles, and chest firmly strapped down, tight and suffocating like my wrist restraints, the Hounds file out and leave me alone in the dreary, rotting space. Alone with my thoughts, with the punctuated screams of someone I can only imagine as Bennie. With a body that's betraying me through no fault of its own.

No one will hear us scream down here. Not anyone who will care. This is a private part of The Compound, like the lab in University. Limited access. Limited eyes seeing the reality of the situation.

It isn't long before the tenor of Jericho's screams join the woman's, Bennie's. Deep growls and gut-wrenching yells ring loud and clear in my ears. The ceiling goes watery as my eyes fill with tears. My chest heaves as I listen to their cries, their pain, their torture. This is purposeful. The general wants to rip out my heart before he stops it from beating.

It's only so long before those tortured cries pull sobs out of me, vast, choking things that rob me of my breath. On my back, I swallow snot and spit, and I gag on it, turning my head as far as I can to hack it all out. Moisture tracks down my cheeks. I can do nothing except let it, my hands bound and me unable to even lift my shoulder to my face.

My fingers tingle, the circulation cutting off from the restraints. I flex my hands, but it barely pushes the tingling back. Between that and the collar around my neck keeping me weak, it's only a matter of time before I become too wasted to even lift my head.

The light click of the door precedes the shuffle of clothes into the room. A part of me wants to keep my eyes on the ceiling. Not give whoever just walked in the benefit of my reaction. The other part, the morbid part, is too curious, and it wins as I lift my head, a struggle unto itself. My heart plummets into my stomach.

It can't just be the general sauntering into the room, a look of triumph on his face. No. It's also Armand at his side, the lesser of two evils as far as he is concerned. Even in the end, he expected absolute fealty, unwavering obedience to his whims. He never cared about anyone but himself. Silly, stupid me for thinking otherwise.

Look where it got me.

What hurts most of all is Gabriel. Not because I think he's changed sides, or is somehow responsible for doing us in. No. It's because of the creep of the wasting disease beyond his shirt collar. The blackened marks of dying skin. He's in a short-sleeved shirt, undaunted by the sores on his arms eating through his tattoos. This isn't the last image I want of him. Those stolen moments in his office were more than enough.

The general takes a seat on a nearby stool, the only one in the room. Armand watches him with pursed lips, but says nothing.

"You were given everything," the general starts. I rest my head back on the table, relieved to no longer hold it up and not caring to give him the pleasure of my undivided attention. "Some of the best accommodations for your kind in University and then in The Compound. Food, clothing, drugs, sex. All you had to do was fall in line. I told you she was going to be trouble, and you didn't listen. Look at the trouble she's caused."

That last sentence I assume is directed at Armand, not me. The general always kept me at arm's length when I was assigned to The Compound, for whatever reason why. It did all boil down to him not trusting me. A spy for Armand, not an all-in Hound, all of the above.

"I'm sorry it's come to this, Lottie," Armand says, not addressing the general. "I really am. I've spent so much time molding you into the perfect soldier. I'm just sorry it's gone to waste."

Do I yell and thrash and spit their words back at them? Or do I lie here, purse my lips, and say nothing? I lean toward the latter, keeping my gaze on the ceiling. It's less effort. The cries of my friends have faded into so much background noise, little more than whispers in my ears. I try to bring the noise back to the surface, something to focus on other than the dumb words I'm hearing, but their voices continue to fade. More tears trickle down my cheeks as I blink.

"This was never a fight you were going to win," the general continues. "I want you to know that. As we speak, I'm rounding up your rebel cohorts, and they will be disposed of accordingly. Your little terrorism campaign didn't work the way you wanted it to, I can assure you that. The number of people running into my arms, begging for my protection . . . We've barely been able to keep up with demand."

He's lying. We've had too many positive reports for that to be true. The Upper Hills are made up of more than Olympia. There are plenty of working people in The Compound and University who wouldn't benefit from the tyranny of the general. It could turn too quickly onto them next. When there's no one left beneath them, they'll be next on the chopping block.

Still, I remain quiet, my arms limp at my sides, my eyelids blinking slowly. The ache of whatever the fuck this shit is weighs on me. I wonder if it'll put me to sleep before they get a chance to actually kill me this time.

Fingers brush at my hairline. I flinch away, the movement automatic, but Armand doesn't take that as a deterrent. No. He continues caressing my skin before tucking invisible hair behind my ear. Hair that was there the last time he saw me. Now, it's just a tuft half an inch long off my scalp.

"I thought of you as a daughter, you know," he tells me, his face impassive, his eyes vacant.

He stares at me, at the top of my head, but I don't think he sees anything. Not what's right in front of him, anyway. Maybe he's seeing me over the years, duty-bound and loyal. Someone who came running to him after a hit to report in. The excitement I gave him. The pride. It was a fucked up relationship, whatever it was. Now, with distance and hindsight, I'm glad it's over. For everything I've lost, for all the restraints holding me down, for the first time in my life I finally feel free.

"The world is better off with you not being a biological parent if how you treated me is how you'd treat your kids," I spit, the words sliding across my lips unbidden.

It's the first thing I've said since entering my final prison.

"You don't mean that," he says with another gentle caress that sends shudders down my back. "Everything I gave you over the years. You were at the top of the city. My right hand."

The snort that pops out of my nose echoes around the small room, pulling the general back. The stoic look settled across Gabriel's face flickers for an instant before it settles back into his wilting mask.

"I was a pariah, you asshole. No one wanted anything to do with me. I was *alone* because of *you* and the dumb decision of an idiot eighteen-year-old." I sneer as much as I can, as much as my weak muscles will allow. Holding my eyes open is enough of an effort, let alone emoting something that will have any impact.

No worries, though. Armand sneers enough for the both of us. He sticks his hand out to Gabriel, his arm crossing my body, and motions to him.

"Give it to me," he snaps.

There's a pause before the tell-tale clink of metal on flesh tells me Gabriel just handed his sidearm to the mayor. Armand wants to be the one to put a bullet in my head.

Rustling draws my attention as the general gives me one last look and steps up to Gabriel. "Make sure she's actually dead this time."

Gabriel gives him a small nod as the general shuffles past and out the door. Maybe he doesn't want blood splatter on his clothes. Or he has better things to do. Maybe Armand told him he wanted to do this alone. Who knows?

When Gabriel turns back to me, there's a glint in his eyes. He glances at Armand as the mayor readies the sidearm before he looks back at me, his eyebrow twitching up. The little hairs on the back of my neck stand on end. Thanks to the poison, it's the only thing I can lift on me at the moment.

Armand lowers the barrel so it's pointing at my nose. There's a slight quiver to it. I honestly wonder if this is the first time he has ever held a gun. The tunnel of death blurs as Armand's hand shakes. My eyes cross trying to look at it. Instead, I stop and slide my gaze along the gun, up Armand's arm, and to his face. If he's going to shoot me, he's going to have to look me in the eye to do it. The bullet won't land, but he's going to think it will.

"I hope you find peace," he says, a shudder to his voice.

The irony of his words isn't lost on me. My heart ratchets up as his finger moves to the trigger. Despite the serum pumping through my veins keeping me weak, a surge of adrenaline rushes through my body. My eyes widen, my awareness coming back to me. For a brief moment, I feel it. Strong.

I hold his gaze steady as his finger depresses the trigger far too slowly for both our liking, no doubt. But I hold his gaze all the same, until something smashes into the room. The report of the gun shoots a ringing silence into my ears, and I scream.

25

THE BULLET WHIZZES PAST MY EAR, TAKING A CHUNK OF IT with it and punching through the cold metal table I'm strapped to. Bodies file into the room, some black-clad, others cobbled together in whatever they could find.

Rebels.

Relief washes through me, coating my adrenaline in something calming before allowing it to kick into overdrive. Jericho's determined face and Bennie's worn complexion bring up the rear, guns drawn, eyes well over my head as people yell, fists fly, and feet scuffle all around me.

I try yanking my arms, but whatever surge of strength I have isn't enough for me to get off this table. Armand opens his mouth, starts making demands, until he's yanked away, the gun ripped from his grip. Gabriel snatches the mayor's lapels and hurls him into the nearest wall, a hand pressing into his back to hold him in place as a rebel locks his wrists together, then frisks him to make sure he's otherwise unarmed.

Jericho maneuvers to my side as Bennie fists Armand's jacket sleeve and yanks him out of the room with the mayor kicking and screaming all the way. The expletives. The demands. The pleading. The bargaining. So many moods of Armand as he's led away in handcuffs. In seconds, my wrists are freed and my chest is clear. My wobbly arms push me into a sitting position, and I rub at the spots where the straps dug in. I can still hear Jericho's screams as I watch him assess me. Without a word, he wraps his hand around the back of my head and pulls me to him, our lips colliding in a fervent, desperate devouring of a kiss.

"We came close there for a second," he whispers into my forehead as he presses his lips there.

"Your screams were real?" I can't help but ask, as I wrap my arms around his torso. "And Bennie's?"

"The rebels came," he says in avoidance of my question, which answers me all the same. "That's what matters."

He flicks the lock on my collar, and it falls away, landing in my lap. I toss it into the corner of the room and rub at my raw, punctured skin. I can already feel my body healing, stitching itself back together, and forcing the toxin out. It won't take long.

Gabriel walks back into the room, his face serious. "We have to find the general. Now. Before he activates any of his failsafes."

The elation fizzles out of the room as the three of them huddle around me sitting on the table. The Defect side effects work fast, but not fast enough, and I wince as I slide off the table and get to my feet. Jericho rests a hand on my arm to steady me, and I nod in his direction to let him know I'm fine.

"You're going to have to give us a little more than that," Bennie says, as she rests her hand on top of her holstered side arm.

Gabriel sighs and winces with the movement. "The general has a number of contingency plans in place in the event something doesn't go how he wanted it to go. They range from a message to the public to burn it all to the ground."

"Let me guess," Jericho says. "He's going to burn it all to the ground?"

"Likely. He'll know about all this within minutes. He has backups of backups of backups watching everything." Gabriel sighs again as he glances around the room, seeing something other than the dingy walls.

Bennie she taps the handle of her gun. "He's so sure of himself but paranoid as hell. I shouldn't be surprised."

"He was down here. You could have taken him out before he left. Why didn't you? That would have saved us the hassle," Jericho says.

I look back at Gabriel, but he just looks tired. Defeated, but not down and out yet.

"You gave a go-time for your plan B. I knew the rebels needed to take out the posts before they got here. If they didn't, and I put a bullet in the general's head, none of us would be talking right now. I made a decision, and it largely paid off. We just have a loose end to tie up." It's a reasonable explanation for the measured Gabriel.

I probably would have just shot the general in the head when I had the chance. Looks like Jericho would have done the same thing, and likely Bennie too. But Gabriel isn't wrong. Yeah, the general would be dead, but so would we and everything would just carry on as it was. All that death for nothing. No, he made sure it would count for something in the best way he could.

"Let's go tie some knots, shall we?" I push away from the table and march toward the door, each step steadier than the last, until fingers wrap around my arm and spin me around.

"I will lead," Gabriel says. He gently pulls me behind him, depositing me with Bennie and Jericho. "Jericho will take my six, Bennie my nine, and Lots my three. We move as one, and you stay on my heels. I'll get us through this building faster than any of you can. Shoot anything that moves. We can't trust anyone."

Jericho has a look on his face. Concern, indignation maybe. He's not doing too great a job at hiding it. As Gabriel glances at each of our faces, he lingers on Jericho while he keeps speaking.

"After everything, you still don't trust me?" He scoffs and shakes his head.

"Hard habit to break," Jericho says back to him through clenched teeth.

"We can work it out after we cut the head off the beast. Deal?" Gabriel asks.

A smile twitches at the corner of Jericho's mouth, and Bennie sighs, then lifts a shoulder in acquiescence.

"Follow me," he says before heading out the door.

A piece of rotting flesh peeks over his shirt collar, the wound crawling up the back of his neck. My stomach turns watching it, the blackened skin a gash that disappears into his shirt. I can only imagine what he looks like underneath it. How much the rot has spread.

Gabriel doesn't bother looking down the hall toward the rebel post, but the rest of us do. One by one we exit and look at our comrades. With Armand tucked safety in an MRAP parked at the curb, the rebels look relaxed. They smile and laugh. Only the sound their voices make carries, not their words. They shouldn't be so relieved just yet. There's more work to do. One more piece of this murderous puzzle to take out before any of us can breathe easy. Even then, there will likely be others hiding in plain sight or those driven underground who will support the general even in capture. His cause is their cause until the end. Dangerous thinking.

It means we'll have to end them all.

We're in the basement of The Compound headquarters building, each door Gabriel leads us through and each dingy hallway to make our way down vaguely familiar. A water stain might trigger a memory, or a door with scratches on it. Or even a flickering light as we quietly, but quickly, hustle our way down the hall toward our real destination. Images flash through my mind with each bulb flicker. Shoving needles under a man's nails. Slicing flesh bit by bit until they give in. Fucking with their minds until they break.

Those images will haunt me until I die. Maybe I could have stopped. Maybe I could have said no. I don't think I'd be standing here if I did. Everything I was put through while in The Compound was a loyalty test with the general pushing my limits a little bit further each time. I will make him feel every bit of pain I inflicted on helpless captives, members of Harvest and Service, and even his own folks from The Compound. I will repay him those tests slice by slice.

We approach a corner, and Gabriel looks over his shoulder and holds up a hand to stop us. We're about to make a turn into another hallway, and we have to breach a door to do it. We've been lucky so far, but with the way my heart races, I have a feeling our luck is about to run out.

It wouldn't behoove the general to assume everything went according to his plans down here. His confidence is as high as the sky, but he's not stupid. No. He'll have Hounds stationed at entry points all along the way to him. Human shields to take any bullets meant for him. He's worked too hard for this, planned too much. He's not going to walk away now and just assume everything is okay.

It would be better if we had shields, but we don't. We have Defect capabilities. We're just going to have to hope we don't take a bullet to the head or the heart. That's the best we can manage.

Gabriel's hand hovers just above the door's release bar, a quiver the only sign he's feeling anything other than determination. Bennie and Jericho stand on Gabriel's far side, giving him room to breach and themselves to act should they need it. I ready myself at his right side, my gun aimed and my finger on the trigger. Gabriel perches in front of me, but I'm just as exposed to the doorway as he is, ready to shoot the second I see something that looks even vaguely human.

It happens all at once. Gabriel shoves the door open and gunfire explodes in the hallway. My ears scream as guns go off. I wrap my free hand into the collar of Gabriel's shirt, no care for the wounds underneath, and yank him back as he holds his finger on the trigger and keeps firing. The gun is a boom in my hand, tiny explosion after tiny explosion as I keep shooting and dragging Gabriel back behind the wall. Jericho and Bennie swallow us as they flank around us and fire their own shots, giving us cover as they help clear the path.

We clear each other's bodies, running our hands over each other looking for bullet wounds. Nothing.

Gabriel leans into my ear, his nose brushing along the shell. "We need to assume they've had Project Titan. Take the shots, and we can grab their guns. I counted four."

I nod, confirming his number. I drop the magazine to check what I'm working with. Three bullets. Of course. My hand rests at waist height, and I motion for him to hand his gun to me. Bennie falls back just as he hands it over, and I shuffle to take her place next to Jericho.

We look at each other, a quick confirmation, before we both know exactly what we need to do. Just like on the rooftop, Jericho draws the attention while I pick them off. Different angles. Different circumstances. But I have to adapt. Adapt or we all die, pinned here by the general's mutated Hounds in a dirty Compound basement.

He's got to be running low on bullets, but he keeps firing as I locate my first hit. Their head is sticking a little too far beyond the edge of a wall. The pale flesh of their neck is a beacon under their helmet. I ready my gun, take a deep breath, lean out, and take my shot. Blood sprays in my periphery as I duck back behind the wall.

Hit.

Three more to go.

The dark skin of my next mark makes finding that sweet spot harder. The shadows of their kit sit more heavily on their skin. Something sparkles near their ear. A piercing. Bingo.

Stop. Breathe. Lean. Fire. Disappear.

The barrage of bullets lessens as another body slumps to the floor, my bullet embedded in their skull. If they are Defects, they're not getting up from those hits.

"Their ammo isn't infinite," Bennie whispers when a gun firea.

"She's right. They'll be running low," Gabriel says, leaning over Bennie's shoulder, looking for all the world like they're friends in a jovial embrace.

I nod and place my hand on Jericho's shoulder before gently pulling him back behind the wall. We don't have long. They'll have comms. They'll be calling for backup, assuming there's anyone backing them up. We have to act fast.

Jericho leans against the wall and turns to face us. "We have to move. Staying here and throwing bullets at each other all day isn't an option."

Gabriel pulls himself to his feet and crouches next to Jericho. "I'll lead. Cover me. They don't have much left, but it'll be enough to take me down if they get spooked. Which they will."

I wrap my fingers around his arm, and he winces, curling his body away from me. As if burned, I yank my hand back. I grabbed a wound. When Gabriel turns around, there isn't anger in his eyes. Impatience, maybe. But not anger.

"I'll lead. I'm smaller. I make a smaller target." I take one step around him only to hit his hand square on my chest.

It's barely a press, but it makes me stumble backward. He doesn't even respond as he moves forward, leaving the three of us at the corner. I swear under my breath as he slowly advances. Any one of us would have been a better option than an injured Gabriel, but he's insisting on martyring himself, apparently.

I fall in line behind him, motioning to Jericho and Bennie to stay behind as we creep up on the likely twitchy Hounds behind the wall. The bullets have stopped flying for the moment. My ears ring with the silence of the hallway. We step lightly, and I listen as intently as I can. It's hard to tell whether the rustling I hear is the Hounds or me and Gabriel. Something clicks, the subtle seating of a magazine into a gun.

Gabriel doesn't wait. In two long strides he turns the corner and fires his gun at the remaining Hounds. Bullets fly back. He grunts as his shoulder jerks back, blood spewing from a fresh wound. I close the distance between us and round the corner, taking shots as fast as I can. One goes down, then the other. Lifeless lumps on the hallway floor.

As the bullet reports die down and silence settles back over us, Gabriel's strained grunts hit my ears. I keep my attention on the cluster of bodies ahead of us. We slowly approach, our steps delicate. I know for a fact two of them are dead, but we dead-check each body just in case. A not-so-delicate kick to the crotch is an effective way to ruin someone's surprise. Not a single one of them responds.

I step back into the hallway while Gabriel crouches and rifles through their things. The tip of Jericho's nose and a flutter of eyelashes peek just beyond the wall before the rest of his face pops into view. I motion him forward with my head before rejoining Gabriel in his search for more weapons.

There are magazines enough for us to restock, and Gabriel and I shoulder a couple of their rifles while pocketing the remaining magazines. Jericho and Bennie stick to the extra sidearms and fill their pockets with bullets. Who knows what's left between us and the general? We'll need all the firepower we can get.

I rack the slide on my sidearm and hold it at the ready. "Do you think he's in his office?"

"Either there or in the intelligence room watching cameras," Gabriel mutters and motions away from the bodies.

Bennie shoulders a rifle by its strap. "Well, if he's watching cameras he'll be seeing the rebels surround the building and slowly make their way up each floor. Does he have an escape route we should know about?"

Gabriel shakes his head. "Believe it or not, no. He was convinced it wouldn't get this far. That we would stomp out whatever rebel rebellion was fomenting, especially when we captured the three of you."

"Only now he's realizing the rebellion runs a lot deeper than he expected," Jericho adds.

"He never thought highly of Harvest or Service. But I honestly thought he'd be smarter than that," I say. Who would have thought hubris would be the general's downfall?

In hindsight, it's actually kind of obvious. The way he always acted, the way he treated people, they were all obvious signs. That doesn't mean this is going to be easy.

"Do you know what we're looking at from here on up to him?" I ask Gabriel.

His brow furrows and he stares into the middle distance for a moment before his eyes refocus.

"That would have been the first line of defense," he says with a motion of his head toward a foot sticking out into the hallway. "The Compound has thinned, and the Hounds even more so once your attacks started. Some people bolted when they learned what the general was doing. When your hits started getting personal, even more people got cold feet. Turns out the pool of people willing to die for someone else's cause is a shallow one."

"I don't think we need to expect anyone surprising us from behind," Jericho says.

"No. We might run into one to two more groups about this size, including one posted right outside his office. I'd be surprised if it's more than that, but we only have one way of finding out." Gabriel sighs and motions with his head for us to follow him.

As he leads us through empty hallways and up stairs, making our way to General Courts's office, voices, yells, and the occasional gun firing echo through the walls. I can't make out what they're saying, but the voices sound light. Jovial, even. The rebels are making their way up the building, taking it floor by floor. Because we do have enough people to comb through The Compound headquarters, unlike the general. Well, we have more people than the general, anyway.

We hit resistance halfway up the building, a small group like Gabriel expected. Instead of emptying our magazines, we let them waste their bullets firing at us, drawing them toward us as much as we can so I can take the shots. One after another, clean, no muss. By the time it comes to the last person, they throw down their weapon and run in the opposite direction. I guess when death is an inevitability, they weren't willing to face it for the general. Can't say I blame them.

The intelligence room is a handful of floors down from the general's office. Innocuous. Unassuming. The hallway is quiet when we enter it. I can't help but wonder if everyone got to leave work early. A laughable thought. Then I wonder if the general put guns in everyone's hands and threw them into the line of fire. A member of The Compound is still a member of The Compound. They should know how to fire a gun. Emphasis on *should*.

We move in our agreed-upon formation down the hallway, Gabriel at the head, Jericho at the tail, and me and Bennie at the sides. She faces forward while we move, and I shuffle backward, keeping my eyes behind us. All is quiet. Too quiet.

When we reach the control room door, Gabriel turns and motions for us to stop before placing himself on the wall side of the door jamb. The tapping of flesh on metal hits my ears as he tests the knob, then wraps his fingers around it and turns. The door swings open quietly. Gabriel waits to the count of three, then enters with his gun drawn.

Quiet.

The rest of us file in after him, and Jericho shuts the door behind him. It takes us hardly any time to clear the room, checking under desks, in Jaxon's old office, and in shadowed corners for anyone who may be hiding. No one.

One by one we say "clear," telling our comrades that our quadrant of the room is empty. As soon as the fourth voice rings, Jericho holsters his gun and marches to his station. It hardly seems like any time has passed since I was first in this room at this very bank of screens as Jericho walked me through his job. This almost feels like an alien place, some far off planet people talk about in stories. Like the memory itself is a dream.

Jericho wakes up the computers and pulls up CCTV feeds, clicking and tabbing his way through until he finds the one he's looking for. Rebels cluster around the entrance to the very building we occupy, looking relaxed, laughing, motioning with their hands at something. They don't look on edge. They don't look like they're at war. He clicks to another feed, what looks like farther down the block. More rebels patrolling with their guns, but no resistance. Low flames lick from a building in the corner of the frame, smoke swirling around their ankles. Other than that, no one would ever know we were just in a battle for our lives.

More clicking and hallways within the building materialize. Jericho moves through them floor by floor, confirming what we already know. The rebels have taken the building. Mismatched outfits, a variety of guns, and haggard albeit smiling faces litter the screens. All rebels. No one from The Compound anywhere.

"He didn't set up much of a guard for himself, did he?" I ask anyone who wants to answer.

It's Gabriel who does. "Whoever was left was sent to Harvest if they weren't stationed here. We took out most of them. Others ran.

He not only underestimated the will of Harvest to survive, he underestimated the people of The Compound's desire to follow."

"Not enough boot lickers to go around," Jericho says with a huff.

Bennie and I chuckle, but it sounds empty. This doesn't feel triumphant. It feels unnecessary. None of this had to happen. This whole debacle was unnecessary, and it backfired on the general spectacularly.

"Let's go," Bennie says, a rasp to her voice. "No sense in lingering here."

Jericho clicks through a few more screens, taking us through views of the hallway that holds the general's office. A team of two sits stationed at his door, telling us he's inside. He looks up at us and nods before pushing himself away from the desk and standing.

Time to finish this.

26

THERE'S NO WAY TO OPEN THE DOOR AND NOT DRAW attention to us. Instead of sticking together, Jericho and Bennie take one stairwell and Gabriel and I take the other, setting ourselves up to draw fire from both guards simultaneously. Gabriel throws open our door in order to draw attention, and sure enough, bullets start flying.

At first, it's both of the guards firing at us. Until the door swings open at the other end of the hall, and Bennie gets a shot at the guard's knee. Blood bursts from the joint before he collapses to the ground, but he keeps hold of his gun and fires back at them.

We have to be careful because we're effectively firing at each other. Once Bennie and Jericho's guard throws his head back in a spray of blood on the back of our guard, the hallway grows a little less raucous. Still, our guard doesn't stop firing, swinging the barrel of his gun down each side of the hallway like a pendulum, trying to hit whatever he can.

In the second I have when he's shooting away from us, I peek out from around the door jamb and take my shot. The bullet goes in the back of his head near his ear. Judging by the explosion of his face, bits of cheek and teeth flying from his head, that's where the bullet exits.

We sit in the ringing silence left behind by the firefight, but no one else comes. If anyone heard the bullets, they're staying far away. Nothing echoes in the stairwell, and nothing but the squeal of damaged eardrums screams in my head. Jericho moves his flat-palmed hand forward, the signal to move toward the door.

We crouch as we scuttle to the door and listen for any movement inside. The door could be tripped. The general could be wearing a bomb vest. He might not even be in there at all, and all of this is an elaborate rouse to help him escape. Until his voice sounds through the door.

"I know you're not waiting for an invitation." It's a drawl, snob-bish and indignant even in the face of defeat.

With Bennie and Jericho on one side of the door and Gabriel and I on the other, Jericho motions to the door handle. I tap the metal a few times to make sure it's not hot, then pull down to open it. Jericho's eyes scan down the door jamb, likely looking for traps, before he raises his gun and steps into the general's office. Bennie follows and moves around the door, clearing the corner. Gabriel and I slide in behind them, guns up, gazes traveling around the room looking for anything that could jump out at us.

It's not a massive office, maybe a little bigger than Gabriel's. Unless he has secret doors behind the screens and bookcases at his back, the only place we can't confirm is under his desk, which he's pulled himself tight against. If there is someone there, they're cramped in an uncomfortable position.

"Hands on your head and stand," Gabriel says, his gun pointed at his former boss.

The general stares at him, a smile playing at the corners of his lips. He takes Gabriel in, the general's gaze roving down Gabriel's body before he meets his eyes again.

"I have to say, this is a surprise," General Courts says, his mouth open in a wider smile.

An unnerving smile.

It ticks up a little higher before he continues, "You had me fooled."

"I learned from the best," Gabriel retorts.

Bennie, Gabriel, and I keep our guns trained on the general while Jericho walks around to his back, yanks one hand down, then the other, and secures them behind his back. All the while the general keeps staring at us, that sinister smile scrawled across his face.

"You think you've won." His gaze flicks to me. "You think you've beaten me. Beaten us."

"We're not the ones in handcuffs," I remind him, but his smile only creaks higher. The hairs on the back of my neck stand on end.

Something is going to happen. I can feel it. But what? A hidden bomb? A poison capsule? I glance around the room looking for any kind of disruptions, like a book out of place or a shadow that doesn't make sense, but nothing jumps out at me. I blink my lie detector on and the general is the cool glow of a brilliant blue. Whatever the hell he's talking about, he's not lying about it.

He smirks. "Do you really think I'd let the rabble take hold of this city?"

"There's no 'let.'" Jericho grunts as he holds the zip ties in one hand and fists the fabric on the general's shoulder with the other and walks him out of the office. "You never should have had it to begin with."

A chuckle rumbles out of the general as he passes us, and Jericho steers him out the door. As Bennie passes me, her gun still at the ready but her shoulders softened, she eyes me and frowns before following Jericho and the general. Gabriel and I keep to her heels.

"What the hell is he talking about?" I mumble, keeping my voice as low as possible while trying to reach Gabriel's ears.

"No idea," he mutters back, the words barely discernible.

We stand at the elevator doors waiting for the car to arrive as if it's just another work day. As if Bennie, Jericho, and I haven't been in hiding. As if Gabriel isn't dying as we stand here. The ding it makes as it arrives and the *shush* of the doors sliding open are discordant against our current situation. The sounds far too normal as we take the general into custody. This is likely the last time he'll be seeing the building.

A few rebels stand scattered around the headquarters lobby, rifles relaxed and conversations casual. As if we didn't just take over a building by force. An MRAP rumbles at the curb waiting for its prisoner.

Just as Jericho hands the general over to the waiting rebel, Courts swings around, jerking against his restraints. He finds my eyes and holds my stare, his gaze hard and eyes narrowed.

"This isn't over," he hisses, spittle flying off his lips. "Don't get comfortable."

The last words are snarls, his lips curling around the letters as if they're bitter. I blink my lie detector back on and find him blue as a summer sky. Fuck. We've clearly missed something. The general's head whips around as he is yanked away from us and stuffed into the back of the MRAP. The door slams closed, and I flinch at the noise.

As the vehicle drives away, the general secure in its cage, my shoulders deflate and a knot of tears forms in my throat. Emotions, a tangled mess of intensity, well up within me, and I have to take a deep breath to stuff them back down.

Jericho and Bennie embrace, the relief of what we've just finished clear in the slouch of their shoulders and how they lean into each other. They had so much more on the line than I did, and everything, and everyone, came through okay.

Gabriel walks over to me and wraps an arm around my shoulder.

"It's over," he says, as he pulls me to him. He rests his chin on my head, and I gently wrap my arms around his body.

I hold him tight, afraid that maybe he'll float away. Or we'll be overrun by Hounds who will capture us all over again. I'm not nearly as optimistic as he is. My nerves still sing with the fear of getting caught. Being out in the open so brazenly like this. It didn't take me long to adjust to staying hidden, and it's going to take me a lot longer to unlearn the responses I've developed.

It's not only that. We've taken down Seven Hills's government. Or at least its acting heads. If what the general said is anything to go by, there are other brains waiting in the wings to crawl back out and claw back power.

One problem at a time. General Courts and Armand need to be dealt with, and I have a feeling I know how Evan wants to deal with them. Not that I blame him. I imagine he's been planning for this moment for months. Fantasizing about it. I'm just happy he actually gets to play it out, and his ire is pointed at someone other than me for once.

A warm hand that isn't Gabriel's slides across my shoulders, and Jericho comes into view in my periphery. Gabriel moves his arm, and I open mine to bring him in. He and Bennie wrap around us like a blanket, Gabriel dropping his arm across Bennie's shoulders as if they're old friends. As we stand in our exhausted, albeit relieved huddle, this is not a sight I would have expected to see in my time at The Compound. Anyone looking on could be convinced we're actually friends.

Bennie pulls up first and looks over her shoulder in the direction the MRAP with the general drove off. "I'm going to move the fuck back into my flat and get my family some nicer accommodations too. I'm sure there are empty units scattered around the Upper Hills," she says with a wink before she slides out of our huddle and heads down the street without a worry.

There's plenty to still worry about, but for the moment at least, I think we're in the clear. It's a dark thing to say, but I don't begrudge her the sentiment. Bennie has always been the most upbeat of us all. I'm not surprised she's that way now. The general and Armand nearly killed her family. Nearly killed Jericho's family. Made all of us go into hiding because we were against them killing a fucking district to feed the wealthy. She can move her family into Armand's mansion for all I care. She might have to share it with Evan. I'm guessing he's going to try and grab that for himself.

"Why doesn't this feel like the end?" I ask the two men wrapped around me, my voice hoarse.

My body aches as it stitches itself back together, muscles creaking and cramping in the process.

"Because it's not," Jericho says. He places his hand on my back and releases himself from Gabriel's grip. "We may have taken the general and Armand down, but you heard him. There's some kind of underground movement out there."

"Assuming we should believe him," Gabriel adds, as his thumb rubs against my shoulder. "We shouldn't brush him off. That would be unwise."

"No," Jericho adds. "Can't say I'm not concerned about what Evan would do."

"Clamp his fist around the city, you mean?" My eyebrow rises.

I've seen the hints in his personality. I'm not stupid. Evan is going to try to remake Seven Hills in his own image. That's going to piss plenty of people off, and I have a feeling he'll deal with them in some of the same ways Armand used to.

Which puts us right back where we started.

"Exactly." Jericho shakes his head. "Jaxon and Kai weren't his only ass kissers. Neither were the enforcers we met going up the building. Don't forget the folks on Olympia. Not everyone is ready to bend over for a new regime."

I wince at the word. "That makes it sound dirty. A regime."

"It just is," Jericho says with a sigh.

"What's our place in this new regime?" I ask while thinking over my own.

"Unknown. I'm sure I'll have one, whether I want it or not." His voice is consigned to our new reality.

I frown at the tone, not sure what he's getting at. "We always have a choice."

Jericho huffs and looks at me from the corner of his eye. "Do we? With what we've done? Evan won't let us get too far from him."

The reality of it sinks in as we watch the rebel bustle on the street. A truck drives by with a number of rebels in the bed laughing and hooting.

"Did we just swap one dictator for another?" I ask.

"Time will tell. Who knows? Maybe this will be better," Jericho mutters, his voice lacking conviction.

"Or it could be a whole hell of a lot worse," Gabriel mumbles, breaking his silence.

The general and Armand will die. Evan will smother any lingering insurgencies among the Hounds or the Olympians. The rebel leader is not in it for equality. Maybe at one point he was, but not now. Not now that he's standing atop a victorious mountain. Now, he wants revenge. I don't need to hear him say it. He radiates it, and with the way Harvest and Service have been treated, it won't be a hard sell to get.

Which makes me all the more concerned about what's to come. I guess I don't have a choice but to let that play out. Jericho wraps an arm around my shoulder and presses his lips to the side of my head as Gabriel keeps hold of my other side while staring down the street, lost in his own mind. I welcome their touches, their nearness, and wend my arms around their waists to pull them closer as we stand on the sidewalk in front of Compound headquarters. It feels like a million years since the last time I was here. It feels like a million more before Seven Hills will finally be settled, if we ever were to begin with.

Time is laid out before us. Now we just need to walk the path.

27

EVAN INSISTED IT BE IN THE COURTYARD OF HIS NEW home. Armand's old home, like I guessed he would take. The ropes sway gently in the breeze off the bay, the view expansive from up here. The gallows stand stark against the glaring cleanliness of the mansion, a relic of the past we had to dig into the archives to find. These even have lever-controlled trap doors for the drop, which makes me wonder if Evan plans on using them again. He grumbled as the gallows were put together, complaining they were taking too long. It took days to find the plans, and then another week to erect them. All the while the general and Armand rotted in cells, waiting for their inevitable ends.

A shudder ripples across my skin at the thought. Evan has proven himself efficient, if not dictatorial in his clean-up of the city, and of Olympia and The Compound specifically. He still sees me as a tool to be used and doesn't care much for my opinion on things, but he listens to Jericho and Bennie well enough. Even then, their words only go so far. The general and Armand will be the first hanged, but judging by the cells filled with their sympathizers, I doubt they'll be the last. Armand and General Courts are examples. A public display of the ending of an old regime and the start of another. Those aren't Evan's words, but they're certainly mine.

Movement near the roofline draws my eye. The barrel of a rifle disappears behind the mansard roof line. Another reason Evan wanted it here. It's tightly controlled. We've been able to round up a good chunk of potential insurgents, but there are still some out there. There was a concern they would try to sabotage the execution and save the general and Armand. There are only two ways in and two ways out of this courtyard, and only a limited number of people pack into the space. The rest are watching on screens across the city as lenses point directly at the gallows. It makes it seem like we have everything under tight control, but it's not nearly as tight as Evan wanted it.

The general was right. There's a movement out there somewhere in Seven Hills itching to get the general's power back, even if he won't be around to take it. Their numbers are greater than any of us thought, which makes our new-found position at the top of the heap tenuous at best.

Jericho stands at my right shoulder, Gabriel at my left, leaving me sandwiched between two men who loom over me. Bennie stands on the other side of Jericho, and a handful of Evan's henchpeople stand scattered in front of us. It would be an intimate affair if it weren't for the thousands of digital eyes on us now.

We all stand facing forward like the good soldiers we pretend to be. Our hands rest clasped in front of us, as if someone posed us and we're merely waiting for more orders. We've seen enough death in these last weeks to last a lifetime, but the sinking feeling in my gut tells me there will be so much more. Evan and whatever coalition he cobbles together will try to bring this city to heel. The fight we made only replaced one insurgency with another, a vicious cycle that will swirl around us until the end of time.

A door bangs open. I jolt with the noise as Evan marches out, followed by Armand and General Courts escorted on short leashes by Evan's people. The collars the two men are wearing look like the ones they put on us. Judging by their shuffling gait and bobbing heads, they're being injected with similar stuff.

They're fifty yards off, but I can still see the gray tinge to their skin and their sunken cheeks and eyes. They were barely fed and watered while in holding. *Why?* Evan would ask. *We just need to get them to the gallows.* A fair enough point. Words like *cruel* and *unusual* danced on the tip of my tongue then, but I knew better than to speak them out loud. Instead, I swallowed them down and kept my opinions to myself. With my record, I'm fucking lucky I'm not being marched up to my death along with them. Same deal with Gabriel, Jericho, Bennie, and the rest of the Hounds who defected to our side. We all got in on the right side early enough. Now, it's a matter of staying on the right side, and I'm pretty sure I'm skating on thin ice by default.

Stomping feet echo heavily around the courtyard as they walk across the wooden decking, Evan to a small podium and the prisoners to their ropes. Two people step forward and wrangle the nooses around Armand and the general's heads. The general jerks and fights as much as his bound hands and poison collar can manage, but it's for naught. His executioner makes sure to secure it extra tight, and the general visibly chokes as the knot slides down the rope.

Evan holds up his handheld, staring at the screen for a moment, before he looks at the small crowd, then the camera. "For the crimes of murder, torture, and genocide—"

"You're all dead without me!" the general screeches, his voice cracking against the rope. "I am your only hope for survival!"

"For conspiracy, theft, and imposed slavery—"

"Dead!" the general screams just as one of the executioners comes up behind him and smashes him on the back of his head with the butt of their rifle.

Armand stands mute, eyes unfocused and staring into the middle distance. His previously pristine suit is soiled and ripped, his face battered and bloodied. Gray streaks through his previously jet-black hair, the stress of the last number of months and his time in holding visibly taking its toll.

"You are sentenced to death." Evan doesn't allow them last words as he nods to the executioners.

The general's ravings are enough. Someone who was so seemingly put together just weeks ago now is nothing more than a limp sack of flesh on a gallows, his legs barely holding him up under the weight of the beating he just took.

The Sisters tried to convince Evan of a more humane method of execution. University has serums enough to help there, but he brushed them off. There was no humanity in what the general and Armand did, and he would afford them none in return. The Sisters didn't fight him. They didn't have a leg to stand on in that argument if they did. There's no arguing with that.

While the general's head hangs limp, his chin bobbing against his chest, Armand's eyes come into focus, watery and filled with fear as he blinks moisture into them for the last time. He scans the small crowd before his gaze lands on me. As the executioners move into place, Armand continues to stare at me, tears pooling on his lashes. He doesn't lash out like the general did. Doesn't try to fight. There's no use, and he knows it.

Tears knot in my throat for everything he was to me and for the life he gave me, whatever the fuck that turned out to be. On the surface I had everything, but a simple scratch of the facade revealed the nothingness underneath. Tools don't have feelings. They don't have cares. They don't have lives beyond what their wielder demands. I needed distance to be able to see that. I needed a wake-up call.

My throat twists as I choke back my feelings, forcing everything down like I've always done, except now I'm sober. My head is clearer than it's ever been. My vision is unmarred by crosshairs. I'm finally able to be myself, whoever she is.

Except I can't help but glance at Evan as he moves to the side of the stage, well away from any carnage that may happen. The fear that we're simply replacing one dictator with another knots in my stomach. I return my gaze to Armand, pushing back the thoughts of what Evan might think he can use me for.

Armand never takes his gaze from me. His breathing grows frantic, his chest heaving in short, shallow waves as the executioners wrap their hands around the levers. Evan raises his hand. I half expect Armand to mouth something to me, a final message. A final curse. But his lips remain tight as a tear trails down his cheek.

Evan drops his arm, the trap doors drop out from under the general's and Armand's feet, and they disappear under the platform. Evan didn't want their heads covered. They weren't deserving of modesty like that, he said. I reminded him that it was done in the past not for the dying, but for the viewers. He didn't care. He wanted people to see the end of the madmen, but he also wanted this to be a warning.

For the good of one is never for the good of all.

I don't think he sees the irony in that statement.

From where we stand, we can't see their heads, which is a small blessing as far as I'm concerned. I can't see their faces as they turn purple. Their protruding tongues and bulging eyes are all things I don't want tattooed in my mind for the rest of my life. Their kicking legs and grasping hands are enough.

The knots weren't placed properly, and their struggle goes on for minutes. As people start to turn away, the sight too gruesome to bear even if it is for genocidal maniacs. A couple of nearby soldiers pull out their sidearms and finish the job. The reports ripple shoulders across the courtyard, including mine.

Before Evan makes his way off the gallows, he scans the crowd and finds me. I can guess what I look like, blank and slightly sick, but the sight of me curls the corner of his mouth. Ice sluices through my veins at the sight. On one side, Jericho weaves his fingers through mine and on the other Gabriel takes my hand in his. We stand there against the blooming monster in our midst.

Not even my prophetic dreams can tell me what's coming for us when everything is all settled, assuming it ever is. What I do know is I'll never be someone's tool again. We have a new breed of insurgents to root out, and a new, power-hungry person in power willing to do whatever it takes to do that. Our way forward isn't going to be easy. Whatever path ends up in front of me, I won't be alone on it.

EPILOGUE

THE SUBTLE LAPPING OF WATER AGAINST JAGGED PILINGS is the first thing that greets my ears as I walk up on what's left of of the dock area near Exodus. Rather, what's left of Exodus. The sun sits low in the sky to the west of the broken fingers of the old golden bridge sticking out of the bay. Brine and gunpowder hang heavy in the air, a gentle mixing of life before and after the Seven Hills revolt.

The broad white walls of a couple of nearby mansions are pockmarked from recent explosions, scarred but not beaten. I wonder if there's anyone still in the house who originally owned it, or if it's been taken over by a Harvest family or two who needed to relocate after the bombardment the Lower Hills suffered.

I've been mostly keeping to myself, or Jericho, Gabriel, and Bennie as we move people around the city, us included. The flat I got in The Compound was an upgrade from the one I had in University, so I gladly handed the University flat access over to someone who needed it. Lots of property exchanged hands over these last number of weeks as we settled Armand's and General Courts's affairs for them. Lots of movement across the Hills. Lots of processing.

Funerals are a regular occurrence. The backlog is more than what the city's lone mortician can handle, but they're working through it. In the wake of the general's and Armand's deaths, Evan put together a coalition of willing volunteers from each of the districts to try and come together to rebuild the city into something fair and decent.

Jericho is on that coalition, and the number of fights he's had to break up among the Harvest and Compound delegates tells me things aren't going so hot.

Especially as Evan still holds many members of The Compound and Olympia in cells awaiting trial for crimes against humanity. Doubly especially as no one seems to be innocent of said crimes, and evidence is thin. Walking out into the Wastes and exploring the unknown is looking better and better by the day.

Bennie reminds me these things take time. Seven Hills wasn't rebuilt in a day when it originally crashed. Even she looks at Evan with narrowed eyes as he speaks, his vision for the future looking far too similar to Armand's for either of our liking.

Gabriel's back comes into view as I climb to the top of the hill, the sun slicing a blanket of afternoon sunshine across the world, washing him in thick orange under a bright blue sky. The rot from the general's serum continues to spread. He's been moving slower lately, sleeping more. Our time together is limited to merely being in each other's presence. I'll take what I can get. On the rare day when he can be touched and not wince in pain, I try to hold him. To feel the warmth of him pushing through my clothes, but it doesn't last long. The pain eventually seeps in, and I must pull away.

He must be feeling a little better because he asked me to meet him here instead of coming to mine or me going to his, or perhaps the cafeteria in Compound headquarters. Movement this far is a luxury for him, and I leave him to operate at his own pace, however he needs it.

Jericho has been supportive through it all, but I see the pity in his eyes. The apprehension. I'm not stupid. I have eyes. I know what's happening to Gabriel, but not dwelling on the inevitability keeps me lifting my head from the pillow each morning. Even if it looks like delusion from the outside. I imagine as long as Gabriel remains upright of his own volition, I can continue to have my daydream, and I'll take it.

I'm not quiet when I walk up behind him, so I know he hears me approach. It's taken me a while to get used to walking at street level without trying to hide myself. But even now I can't be at ease. The general's lackeys are plotting and sneaky, and we can never let our guard down completely.

I slide my hand along Gabriel's shoulder when I get close enough. His flinch has me yanking my hand back. I know it's not me he's wincing away from. He wants my touch, but the sores spreading over his body make touch painful for him. At times excruciating. It's not personal, but what was done to him is. For him and for me.

It's the general's wedge left between us, one we can't remove.

I lower myself next to him and hang my legs over the edge of the dock. Ocean spray speckles my boots as the water laps at the pilings a handful of feet below us. His hand rests on my thigh, his palms one of the few places unmarred by his progressing disease. At least for now.

Gabriel is wearing his usual black, only a little less form-fitting to help alleviate the brush of fabric against his skin. I slide my hand over his, careful to avoid the sores spanning his knuckles, and wrap my fingers around his. He, in turn, grips me back, a firm grasp for only a second before he relaxes, yet his fingers remain curled around mine.

Hardly any of his tan skin is left on his arms, the short sleeves exposing weeping, angry sores disappearing under the sleeves as the general's serum eats its way through him. Sores crawl up his neck and have etched their way across his beautiful face. He turns to me and smiles, something genuine sparkling in his eyes as a sliver of white teeth show through pale lips. The left side of his face is almost completely consumed by lesions, the white of his eye a dull red, his pupil blown out.

Yet I find I can't look away. All I see is Gabriel unscathed, as I was reintroduced to him months ago. A man grappling with the choices he's made in life seeing himself in the woman who was going through the same thing. Time demanded we stay apart until it forced us together again. I'm grateful for what we've had. What we've been reintroduced to. What we've built from scratch.

"Thanks for coming out here," he rasps, his voice haggard,

sounding like it scrapes over jagged glass before flowing out of his mouth.

"It's a haul, you know. What with my days being *so* busy and all," I say with a smile.

I want to brush his shoulder with mine. Lean into him. The less pain I cause him, the better.

His shoulders rise and fall with subtle laughter before he lifts his thumb to my cheek and runs the pad over my skin. The touch sends thrills throughout my body, lighting my skin on fire.

"Evan keeping you busy?" he asks, his voice a whisper that gets washed away with the crashing waves.

I huff a laugh and shake my head. "Yeah, with me trying to dodge him as much as I can. Jericho or Bennie act as a buffer most of the time. It helps."

"You're in good hands with them," he says with a nod as he looks back out at the bay.

Sun glints across the waves, making it shimmer in bright oranges and yellows. It matches the paint left on the old bridge, making it look like it actually fits in with the landscape instead of what it really is. A scar from Before.

"My hands are good enough," I say with a jovial edge of irritation. I know what he's getting at, but the reminder flows out of me all the same. "They're good when mine get tired."

"That's what matters," he says, as he rubs my knee and squeezes it before moving his hand away.

He shifts, the movement jostling into my shoulder, before he settles again. Wafts of brine hit my nose as the water laps below our feet. The moment is serene, pleasant even. It's nice to stop every once in a while and just *be*.

Gabriel sighs, then says, "It's time for me to go, Lots."

I smile, my eyes on the lump of land on the other side of the bay. "Got a hot date?"

When he doesn't respond and the silence between us grows thick, I turn to find him staring at me, a sad smile struggling to lift his lips. Something glints in his lap as he shifts, drawing my eyes down. His hand sits atop his sidearm, safety finger resting along the barrel.

Waiting.

What I'm seeing doesn't compute, and I frown at the tableau. Gabriel's hand. A gun. He has to go. Go where? Hunting?

"I wanted you to be the last person I see," he says calmly before he breathes another hearty sigh.

I shake my head, his words still not making sense. "I don't understand. Where do you have to go?"

He turns to face me, a knowing look in his fading eyes, the rot of him on full display. "You saw the University lab, Lots." He shakes his head before looking back out at the bay. "That's not how I want it to end."

I scoff, indignation bubbling up in vicious torrents. "What? You think Evan will pick up where the general left off? Besides, the lab needs to be rebuilt anyway. It's useless."

Denial leans its heavy weight on my shoulders, but just underneath it the truth scratches through. Brutal and miserable and entirely unwanted. I can feel it, but I don't want to.

He wraps his arm around my shoulder, bringing me in close to him, no sign of wincing or gasping even though I know this must hurt him. He pushes his lips to the side of my head, and I can't help but close my eyes against the feeling. The power of it. The intensity of this moment. A knot builds in my throat as tears gather on my lashes.

"I want to go on my terms," he whispers into my hair.

A choking sob wracks my body as my desire to throw myself at him and knowing that my touch hurts him war with each other. I sniff and choke back tears as I pull myself to my knees and grab his face. He flinches, but that's the only indication he gives me that I've hurt him. It's clear he's trying not to show the pain, not to flinch under my touch. But I know. I don't need him to tell me this hurts.

"Please," I choke, spit thick in my mouth as tears streak down my cheeks. "There has to be a cure, right? Buried in a file somewhere. We'll find something. You can't—you can't just give up."

His bottom lip quivers as tears brim in his eyes. When he inhales, it's a jagged mess of a breath, his chest hitching. "The general didn't care about a cure. You know that."

"Then we'll find one." My lips, my face, feel swollen, my cheeks flaming as my knees dig into the splintering wood. "There's always a cure, right?"

His thumb trails down my jaw as he gives me a watery smile. "I won't last that long, and you know it." He presses his lips to mine, tear-soaked and painful. I grasp him behind the neck and hold him to me, afraid of letting him go.

I know, buried deep down inside of me, there is nothing to help him. Caring about curing the people he fucked up wasn't on the general's to-do list. Finding a better serum that didn't dissolve its receivers was where his efforts went. If things didn't go in our favor, no doubt about it Gabriel would have ended up on a slab in the University basement lab, the general picking him apart to figure out where he went wrong. Gabriel's body would be just another thing on a table to General Courts.

I gasp as our mouths part and we lean our foreheads against each other. Chills wrack my body, my teeth chattering even though I don't feel the cold, yet it settles in my marrow all the same.

"Please don't go," I whisper into his mouth, my eyes clenched shut as I hold him.

Hold him.

Hold him.

"You have work to do, Lots. It's time you do it," he mutters.

Tears trail down his cheeks, but his gaze is fierce. Knowing. The thing is, I don't want to do it without him. I don't know if I can. He was gone for so long. It's cruel that he's being ripped away again so soon, and with no chance of ever getting him back.

"What I need you to do now," he says, as he strokes his thumb down my cheek, "is get up and walk away, and don't look back. Will you promise me you won't look back?"

A sob gasps and heaves its way out, like hands around my lungs, choking the air out of me. The world is a blur of tears, my body full of them, the well never-ending.

"I can't—" I choke, as I fist his shirt.

"You can," he replies, his look stern. Almost scolding.

"I love you." It's barely a gasp, my lips moving but my voice getting buried under the waves. He hears me. I know he does as he presses his lips to mine one last time. The finality of it is a weight bearing down on my soul.

"I love you," he whispers back, the catch in his voice choking me even more.

My legs don't want to move, but eventually my wobbly knees bear my weight, and I pull myself to my feet. I hardly feel the skin on my body. My existence in this world seems thin, like I'm barely tethered to the ground. One step after another, I move farther and farther away from Gabriel, my hand sliding from within his fingers one final time.

I walk for years only moving inches, the far side of the street an infinity away. Nothing but a ringing in my ears keeps me company as I move toward the buildings, fighting the urge to look over my shoulder. I want to see him one last time. One last moment. One last breath. I fight the urge to turn, to peek from my periphery.

I want to.

So, so bad.

Until the report of gunfire pierces the quiet. I jerk to a stop. The crumpling thump of weight on the dock answers the gunshot, before the splash of water consumes everything that is left.

A scream, loud and piercing and shrill, rips from my throat as I drop to the ground, my knees smashing into the pavement as I crumple into a knot of flesh and bone. Great heaving sobs roll out of my body in a tsunami, my wails echoing off the buildings. I fall to my side, curl my knees into my chest, and let the well run dry. My noise will draw people to me. Let them come. Those who aren't still afraid of me or afraid of Defects will have an easy target.

I don't know how long I stay here, but I'm jolted out of my stupor by a subtle buzz in my pocket. Through it all, I don't turn around. I promised, and I'm nothing if not true to my word. I swallow the thick saliva pooling in my mouth and smash the heel of my hand against my swollen eyes, trying to rub the emotions away.

Yet I don't want to let go of it. This feeling. Of anger. Of pain. Of love. I went so long without feeling anything, and now I've felt everything. I would give anything to get Gabriel back, but he left me with this, and I will not let it go.

With a catastrophic amount of effort, I push myself to my knees, my body the weight of a building, my head twice that. I pull my handheld from my pocket and try to focus on the screen with half-closed, tear-blurred eyes.

It appears Evan has a job for me. Utilizing my particular skillset.

Does he now?

I slide my handheld back into my pocket and pull myself to my feet. My Defect powers are already churning, the ache and the pain being knit into something sharper. I take a deep breath and walk through the alleys of Olympia, making my way to Evan's new home.

He and I are going to have a little talk. And if he doesn't want to listen to what I have to say? Well, I'll cross that bridge when I get to it.

And blow it up if I have to.

SUBSCRIBE TO MY NEWSLETTER_

If you liked what you read, then you definitely belong on my side of the book world! Sign up for my newsletter at rianadarabooks.com to stay up to date on my writing, book releases, and everything in between!

ACKNOWLEDGMENTS_

The Project Titan series has been a whirlwind, Revolt especially. Thank you to Suzi and Traci for being my second eyes and helping me make this book what it needed to be. Thank you to Molly for another amazing cover. Thank you to the best imaginary friend, Laura, Cass, and Sabrina for being early cheerleaders. To my husband for helping me figure out the best way to body flip and break a fool's arm (appropriate research is essential). My parents, as always. To the Fantasy Author Legion for helping me army-crawl this book into the light among like-minded sci fi and fantasy folks.

Most importantly, thank you to the people who keep fighting. The world needs you, now more than ever.

ABOUT THE AUTHOR_

Rian Adara is a multi-genre author who has a deep love of morally gray (or black) characters, writing with a hint (or a lot) of darkness, and varying levels of spice. She enjoys destroying her readers with her words and riling them up at the same time. And may or may not derive joy from creeping them out too. When she's not writing she's reading, papercrafting, taking moody photos, wrangling her cats, and spending time with her husband. The gothic aesthetic of New England will always be considered home, no matter where she lives.

You can find her on her website, www.rianadarabooks.com, or at @rianadarabooks at Instagram, Threads, and Pinterest.

www.ingramcontent.com/pod-product-compliance
Lightning Source LLC
LaVergne TN
LVHW041800060526
838201LV00046B/1074
* 9 7 8 1 9 7 1 5 4 1 0 0 6 *